Geminknot

by

Alexander Francis

Geminknot

by

Alexander Francis

Arcus Verba Publishing
P.O Box 210
De Forest, Wisconsin
53532
www.arcusverba.com

Cover design by Alexander Francis

Publication 2014

Printed in the United States of America

ISBN:978-1-942420-07-1 print edition

ISBN: 978-1-942420-06-4 e-book

Table of Contents

A note of appreciation

On a visit to see my elderly parents, I was struck by the affection they had maintained for each other over a lifetime, a marriage lasting nearly seventy-five years. They never quite made it that far, my father dying only months before their anniversary.

I began to realize that some people are uniquely mated, even if by accident, fulfilling the Ancient Greek philosophy of two halves, separated at birth, joined again in happiness forever. A story was nagging at me and then I read of a theft of a twin shortly after birth, the story instantly created in my mind. What followed was a natural and rewarding novel which seemed to me as real as if it had happened. I chose to tell the story from several perspectives, like seeing a photograph from various positions, each illuminating some otherwise hidden fact.

Of course, we humans, and even other animals, have a natural revulsion for physical attraction to our siblings, undoubtedly the work of evolution to protect the species. Here, in this little tale, the natural attraction for their missing half overcomes their avoidance of each other, and in the end, their love is proven pure and natural after all.

I dedicate this book to the memory of my parents, David and Willa. May their love last long after death.

Alexander Francis

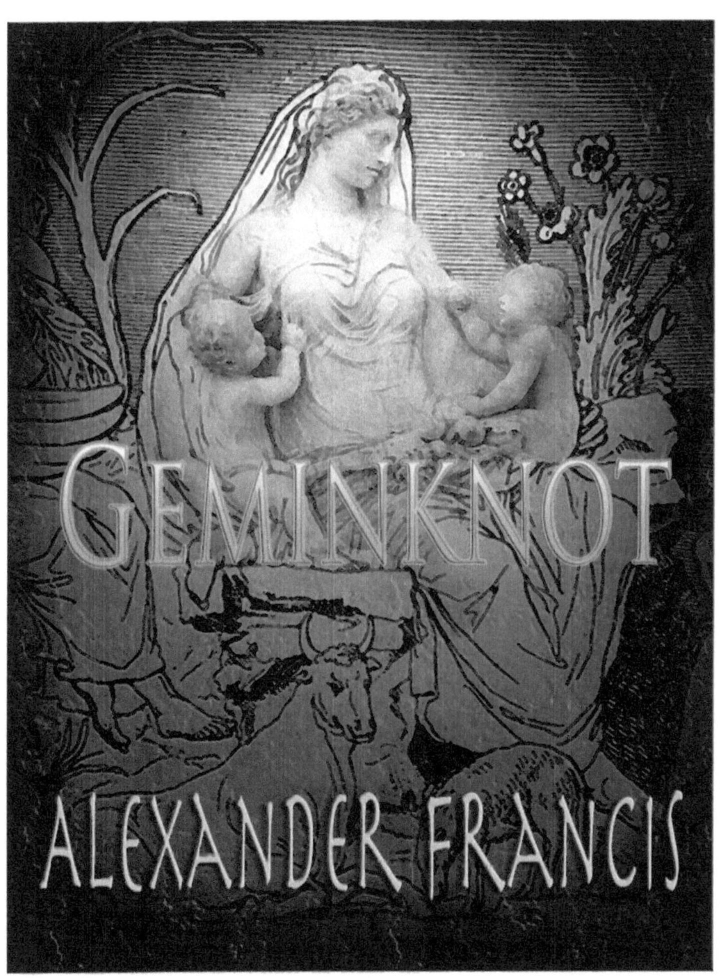
GEMINKNOT
ALEXANDER FRANCIS

Chapter 1

A SIMPLE ASSIGNMENT

Jill knocked briefly at the door and then hesitantly opened it. Mr. Burns was seated behind a desk with a large stack of papers seemingly in permanent disarray. He was approaching sixty, overweight, with a big head full of grey hair, and he was looking over the top of his heavy glasses at her.

"What?" His gruff voice was impatient. Jill was used to it, and she knew that Jules Burns wasn't a tough guy like his first impression would imply. He would soften his attitude toward her almost immediately, as he always did.

"Mr. Burns, sir. I have a question about this assignment. May I have a moment?" she asked sweetly.

He took his glasses off and leaned back in his chair and beckoned her to come in. "It's pretty simple, Jill. All you have to do is go and talk to these people and write a story about what they tell you. Isn't that the stock and trade of a reporter?"

"Well, Mr. Burns, after six months of doing the obituary columns and reports on hot topics like the garden club meetings and the stray dog reports, I was hoping for an assignment with more meat in it. Don't we have to track down corrupt government officials who take bribes or perhaps an unexplained murder or two?"

"Do you know of any graft or corruption in this small town, Jill?"

"No, sir, but I'll bet that you do."

"Well, I don't. Go do the story. Think of it as pushups to make you fit for later. Who knows, you might just find something interesting for our readers. Now go away, because I have work to do."

"Yes, sir," she said meekly and closed the door behind her.

"Rats, rats, rats," she thought as she went back to her desk to collect her purse and coat. She let out a big sigh, which was heard by Tommy in the nearby cubicle.

"Problems, Gorgeous?" he asked over the short wall, with his usual flippancy.

Jill came around to his side as she put on her coat. "I am asked to go interview an ancient couple in a nursing home. Their claim to fame is a long marriage, I'm told. Nothing new for me. Perhaps I will witness a crime on the way over there, and Burns will be forced to let me write the story." She had a pout which she displayed for his comment and sympathy.

Tommy glanced up briefly from his keyboard and gave her a quick smile. "Don't count on it. Remember, I did your job for four long years. You'll get used to being a small cog in a large machine. You could always quit."

Jill found her small car in the crowded parking lot and looked at the map one last time. The nursing home was on the edge of town, thirty minutes or so from here. She sighed again and headed that way. No violence or any other interesting thing occurred on the trip, and she found the place without any problems. The Memorial Retirement Center sprawled in front of her like a spider. The three-story structure in the center had a large two-story porch wrapping around three sides supported by large white columns. The wings shot out at angles and were decidedly more modern. Jill remembered that the old structure had been in use since the Civil War and was something of a museum on its own. She sighed again. Old warehouse of old people. It was always depressing for her to go into these places, because it reminded her not only of her failing grandparents, visits she had made to one of these places when she was young, but, increasingly, awareness of her own fate. Just walking in, the history of the place was apparent. Yellowing photographs on two walls were of a time when people wore dark clothes and hats, the men long beards. The floor creaked as she walked toward the highly carved and ornamented reception station. Muffled voices accompanied by the occasional clink of metal echoed from a distance.

"Can I help you, Miss?" the older lady behind the counter asked. She looked up from her work, quickly sized Jill up with her glances, and impatiently waited for an answer.

Jill took out her notebook and after flipping a couple of pages said, "I am here to interview Mr. and Mrs. Condor." She looked up from her notes and gave an unappreciated smile to the lady behind the counter.

"You are not a relative, I see. Do you have a card with your name on it?" the receptionist asked.

Jill dug into her purse and presented a card which read: Jill Longly, Reporter, Newtown News and Commentary.

The lady silently took the card and inspected it. "Are you expected?" she asked.

"Yes, my paper arranged it. The Condors were told that I would come this morning," Jill assured her.

The lady picked up the telephone and punched a button. "Hi, Ruth. I am sending a Jill Longly in your direction. She is here to talk to the Condors. Yes, right away." After hanging up the phone, she leaned over the top of the desk and pointed. "Take that corridor on your right, down all the way to the nursing station, and don't stop until you get there. They will be expecting you."

Jill walked down the long hallway, discovering that the facility was larger than it looked from the outside. Some of the doors she passed were closed, but some were open and revealed the sight of an older bedridden patient lying in a narrow bed and looking at the ceiling or sleeping. There was a short pleasant-looking woman standing in front of the nursing station waiting for her.

"Hello, I am Vivian Folger, one of the nurses on duty. You are here to see the Condors, is that right?" she asked.

"Yes," Jill answered.

"You are in for a treat, my dear. These are very interesting people, and I'm glad someone took notice of them before it's too late. Poor Mary is not well, and I don't know how much time she has left, so my advice to you is to invest some moments with them while you can. Mr. Condor is doing well, but when Mary goes, things may change. They are in separate rooms, and I think you should start with Mr. Condor. Come with me, and I'll introduce you." They walked a short distance, and Vivian knocked on a closed door. "Mr. Condor, I have a visitor for you. May we enter?"

"Yes, come," the voice responded.

The door was opened, and Jill walked into a surprisingly large room. A neat bed was in the corner and on the opposite wall was an antique wood desk. A small computer was open on the drop-lid, and it was on. Mr. Condor was seated in a comfortable leather lounge chair, and he slowly got up to meet his visitor.

"Good morning, I am Michael Condor." He extended a gnarled hand for her to shake. Jill looked him over as she smiled and extended her hand. Mr. Condor was a large-boned man, now somewhat stooped. A sagging, weatherworn face surrounded bright clear eyes. His heavy dark red robe contrasted with his waist tie and leather slippers in a dapper sort of way.

"Good to meet you, sir. I am Jill Longly, reporter from the Newtown News and Commentary. You agreed to an interview, I am told?"

"Agreed, hell. I asked for one. Good to meet you also. May I call you Jill?" he asked.

"Of course, Mr. Condor."

"Alrighty then, you are required to call me Mike. Will that be OK?" Without waiting for her response, he took the small chair from the desk and pulled it out for her. The nurse silently withdrew and closed the door.

They looked at each other after Mike carefully sat back down. "You need to know, Jill, that an older person doesn't feel old in their mind, just the body. We all feel young at heart or so it's said. I was ninety on my last birthday, so I have been around feeling young for a long time. It doesn't feel so long, though, and I remember back to events in my childhood like it was yesterday. And, in many ways, it was just yesterday."

Jill looked relieved that this would be a two-way conversation. Mike was full of life, she could tell, and after a few moments with him, she could almost see him as he was when he was young.

"My dear Jill. Could I ask you to fetch that large scrapbook from the shelf? You can look at the things inside as we talk," pointing to a scruffy thick black book on the top shelf beside the window. She got up and pulled it off. Very heavy, she thought, but expected for a book holding a lifetime of memories between its covers. She sat back down and put it on her lap.

"Sir, I mean, Mike. Why did you want to talk to a reporter?" she inquired.

"You are very direct, young lady. I like that. Don't ever be shy with me. There are going to be questions that you want to ask but will be hesitant. I'm telling you right now that there is no cause for you acting polite with me. You remember that I just said that I am ninety years old? I want to start out by telling you that I have been in love with the same woman for ninety years, and you are going to want to know how that is possible. Aren't you?" He smiled at her and waited for her response.

Jill blinked and her mind processed his words. She could envision no explanations which seemed possible. Mike was right. This was going to be interesting.

Chapter 2

MEETING MARY

Jill opened the cover of the large scrapbook, and on the inside of the front cover was a black and white photograph taken of a bride and groom at a wedding. The couple stood facing the camera but with entwined arms. She recognized the groom as Mike in his youth. He beamed with a big smile, and his eyes sparkled right off the page. Both were markedly attractive people and handsomely attired. She glanced at the opposing page which was a full-face professional studio portrait of Mary. Long blonde hair and an incredibly beautiful face jumped off the page at her. Just looking at Mary's photograph made Jill feel somewhat inferior, even though most men have told her that she is very attractive. Not like this, she thought. The next page was a similar one of Mike in his prime. Wow! Jill wished she could meet a man like that. She looked up as Mike started to speak.

"Now that I have your interest, I would like to give you a synopsis of my life with Mary and then you can decide if it would be worth telling you the whole story." Jill closed the scrapbook and smiled at Mike to continue. "First, you might wonder why I am in a nursing home when I look like I might be able to get by out in the world just yet. I am here because Mary is here. We have never been apart except during the War, and I missed her every moment when I was away from her. We were born on the same day, at the same hospital, and were raised by the same mother and father. They considered us twins and raised us as such. As far as our parents were concerned, we were in the womb together and were brother and sister. My first memories in life are of Mary." He paused to let Jill consider what he had just said.

"You married your sister?" she asked incredulously. "How could that have happened? Isn't that illegal, immoral and unwise?" She felt suddenly soiled and felt the weight of the book in her lap.

"Calm down, young lady. No, this isn't a case of incest. It is a case of love from birth and the struggle that it caused us. That is the story here. We have told very few people other than family the story of our lives, because they would all have the feeling of revulsion that you are just now experiencing. Let me make one fact clear before you hear any more. We were switched at birth. Someone wanted a girl child and left the boy in the nest as exchange. No one knew. We didn't find out for many years, and it caused the most wonderful suffering that anyone has ever known. Mary and I are not related at all, in any way, and our love for each other is as pure as the snow. Another thing that you will come to know. We never had any sexual contact before marriage, in spite of the draw toward each other while we were growing up. Think about it. No sex before marriage. How many couples can say that?" He laughed and waited for her response.

Jill took it in and realized that this was indeed an interesting story. "Wow, Mike. You are right. At first I was repelled, and now I want to know more about it. About the other thing, from what I hear, virgin brides are as rare as a snowstorm in Havana."

"Well, I didn't say that Mary was a virgin bride, but I believe in my heart that she was. She used to tease me about her exploits while I was away at war. I never believed any of it. She delighted in seeing my jealousy. It made her feel wanted, as if I ever wanted anything else in life but her."

In a pause, Mike poured himself a glass of water. Jill took that time to flip through the big book. There were hundreds of old photographs tucked away of the two children and odd objects from their youth. The majority of photos were of them together, smiling at the camera as they would later do at their wedding. They seemed so healthy, happy and beautiful that Jill could feel her tears forming just under the surface, and she opened her eyes for the fluid to be absorbed, then had to wipe her nose. There was a light tapping on the door before it opened. Nurse Folger leaned in and caught Mike's eye.

"She's awake now, Mike," she informed him.

Mike slowly rose from the chair and put his arm out for Jill. "Want to go see the love of my life?" he asked, putting his arm gently over her shoulder. They went around the corner into Mary's room together and found Mary sitting up in bed, smiling. She had a pleasant grandmother's face and a warm inviting smile. Mike went to her, kissed her on both cheeks and patted her arm. He held her hand in his and said, "Mary, this is Jill. She has come from the newspaper to get our story. We just got past the scary part, and I thought that you could talk to her a little, if you're up to it."

"Well, I think so. Pleasure to meet you, Jill. I'm afraid that there is only a common story of true love, but thanks to a baby thief, it took a long difficult time of trying to deal with our feelings without understanding why we felt that way."

"Nice meeting you too, Mary. I snuck a look at your scrapbook a few minutes ago and was bowled over by your beauty. In your youth, you must have been the most stunning woman in the world," Jill said, patting her other arm.

"I believe that Mike thought so. There were a few others who said similar things at the time. Only...look what the years have done to me!"

"Now, now Mary. You are still the most lovely thing alive. I am as enchanted with you as when you poured soup on my head at the dinner table."

Mary put her hands to her mouth and giggled like the girl she was when it happened. "Anyone else had done that to him, it would have resulted in their swollen lip. Not me. He didn't say a word about it."

Jill smiled at both of them and said, "This is a wonderful and interesting story. Did you ever find out who switched the babies and why?"

Mary said, "No, we never could find that out. The hospitals in those days were a little careless compared to today, especially the smaller ones. We tried for a while but gave up. It didn't matter, because things worked out, and we were happy."

"It mattered most to me," Mike said. "I never got a look at where I came from or found out who I am. Getting to be with Mary for ninety years made it worth it. I came out ahead, I am sure."

"To be confidant I have this straight, let me repeat to you on what I just heard. You, Mike, were switched with Mary's twin sometime just after your birth, and no one ever knew until you grew up. All that time, everyone, including both of you, thought that you were brother and sister. You realized while you were growing up that the love you felt for each other was beyond the normal sibling affection, and you felt a physical attraction as well. You both resisted becoming physically connected until you married as adults. Did I get that about right?" Jill said.

Mike patted Mary's arm and said, "Jill, you make it seem so simple. A lifetime in a sentence. Well, we can tell you that it wasn't simple at all. If we would have only known...well, that might not have been good either. Speaking for myself, I can say that I loved Mary with all my heart from the first day of birth. There was never a moment I didn't love her, but it caused heartache and anger and frustration inside of me that I didn't deal with very well at times. It was an itch that I could never find or scratch or understand. I felt dirty and low for having the feelings that I had, and there was never anyone I could talk to about it, except Mary, who was going through the same thing. There are words that you can't give voice to even when you are speaking to the most important person in your life, especially at that time."

Mary smiled up at Mike and caressed his arm. "Things happened inside me also during those years, but I never felt the need for violence that Mike did. There were times I wanted to say something to him about the way I felt, but I aways thought that he somehow knew. He seemed to know me better than I knew myself, so I held my tongue when I should have been more open to him. I tried to hide my feelings, even from him. He cracked up frequently, at least others thought so. I knew what he was going through and why, but I was afraid of what we would do if we admitted our affection openly. There are reasons why brothers and sisters hold each other at some distance, and that was acting on us also."

"You have me completely hooked on this story," Jill said. "Before we all put the time in that it needs to get it right, I have to ask how far you both will go in telling me the details, and what will you allow me to do with the story when we get finished?"

Mike said, "We will tell you every detail, nothing held back, if you wish. As far as the written story goes, we aren't going to live forever, so you can do whatever you wish with it. We would like to tell what we went through so perhaps it can help someone, or lead to a better understanding of what human attraction is all about."

Jill thought about it all for a moment, then said, "Tell you what, I need to speak to my boss at the paper, since he assigned me to come out here. I'll tell him what this story is about, and if he feels that it is not what the paper would be able to use, then I'll take it on myself to write a book about it. Either way, we will get this story to the public. I'm excited about it, and I want to thank you for letting me get involved."

"Oh, yes, my dear. That's what we wanted to hear," Mike said, sounding relieved. "There is someone else you need to talk to, and she will be here near about four in the afternoon tomorrow. Her name is Lilith, and she is our granddaughter. She has a great passion for our story and has done a lot of digging around, and I'm sure she will add something interesting. By the way, she is an attorney and something of a little firebrand. She can be impolite if the mood strikes her so try to get past it, and I'm sure you will become good friends in the long run."

"Well, start thinking your story out, and I'll be back tomorrow to meet Lilith, and we'll figure out what to do then," Jill said.

Mary gently touched his arm, smiling up at him. "Mike, don't you think it would be a good idea to let Lilith know beforehand so that she can come prepared? You know how she likes to be ready for things."

"Yes, my dear, I'll call her this afternoon and let her know. You are right, of course," Mike agreed.

On the way back to the newspaper office, Jill thought about what she had heard. On the surface of it, there wasn't much to the story. There was no action, no murder and little or no sex. How could she tell the story of these two people in a way which could capture the public's attention? She pondered about it while she drove the car in robotic fashion. "There isn't any news to this story. There was a crime, but it happened ninety years ago, and the person who did it is long since dead and forgotten. Forget it," Jill said out loud to herself. Yeah, that is what Burns is going to say. She had a big sigh. There was no choice except to tell him and get shot down. None. No matter what Burns said, she thought, she would return tomorrow and see what Lilith has to say. What is there to lose?

Chapter 3

LILITH ROBERTS -ATTORNEY AT LAW

Jill settled down in the spartanly upholstered chair in the lobby of the Memorial Retirement Center, checking her watch once again. Four o'clock, she noted. Just twelve minutes since she checked the last time. She was determined to catch Lilith before she went back to her grandparents' rooms. She assumed that Mike had called Lilith as Mary suggested and that she was informed that Jill was also going to be there. Reflected light from a car skipped across the room, and she got up to view the parking lot. A woman emerged from a small luxury car and took a box out of the trunk. She was smartly dressed in a dark blue suit and was about the same age group as Jill. Jill moved to open the door for the woman who was carrying a rather large cardboard box. As the woman came in, she and Jill smiled at each other.

"Thanks for the help," Lilith said. "You must be Jill."

"Yes, I came early hoping to catch you as you came in. I am looking forward to talking with you." Lilith put her box on a nearby table and shook Jill's hand.

"You were called in to see about writing a story about my grandparents, right?"

"Yes, we met for the first time yesterday, and Mike, your grandfather, gave me a synopsis. Enough to get a glimpse of their story and enough to make me want to know more about them."

"Then you know that the real story is what they went through living together before Mike left for the War?"

"Yes, that's what I surmised yesterday," Jill said. "Isn't this just a wonderful story about two people who fall in love and are miserable for it, then find out that their love wasn't evil after all? Such an appealing love story."

"My great-grandmother was a dedicated diary keeper. She wrote in her diary each day and filled one per year. I selected the ones which start the year my grandparents were born, and I am sure you will find them fascinating. If you get the story from each of my grandparents and then are able to get their mother's view of them as they grow up, it will fill in a lot of blanks. The interesting thing is that Mike and Mary have never seen these. Long ago, they stopped asking questions and just lived their lives. They had one child, my mother, and I am the only grandchild. It is up to me, I guess, to find out how and why this whole thing started, but I'm having a lot of difficulty doing it."

"What problems? I would assume that all the key people are long ago gone, but aren't there hospital records?"

"As a lawyer, I am embarrassed to tell you what a legal hornet's nest you can get into digging into old medical records. That, and as you said, there is no one left to talk to. You just have to have some cooperation to get access to old records. There are hospital records and three physician records that I would like to see, but their legal guardians have put up roadblocks. In addition, just tracing who actually has the records is beyond my ability," Lilith summarized.

Jill thought about it for a moment and then asked, "Do you know if any of the records actually still exist?"

"Here is the problem, Jill. In some states, malpractice has a statute of limitations, but the catch is that the time is not started until someone recognizes a problem or that a delayed injury has occurred. The record holders won't just give out old medical records out of the goodness of their heart. You have to get a court order for them to open up. Mary and Mike have never wanted to pursue this, because they are happy as they are. Also, you never know what devils will creep out when you start opening those old containers."

"Well," Jill said, "we know that there would never be any legal action as a result of knowing what happened, but I see what your problem has been. What you need is a private investigator who knows some tricks."

"Got one?" Lilith asked with her eyebrows raised.

"I have an old boyfriend who would qualify," Jill admitted.

"Old boyfriend? Does that imply some problem?" Lilith guessed.

"Old because he is just too tricky for a relationship but tricky enough for a problem like this."

"Maybe later," Lilith said. "I want you to take these diaries, but, please, take good care of them, and I want them back when you get finished."

"I came today to see you, Lilith, but I haven't gotten the go ahead from my editor yet. This will give me a small advantage in helping to persuade him to let me go ahead with this. I'll call you as soon as I know something, and thanks for this treasure you brought today. I promise to treat them with care." The two women briefly embraced, and Jill headed out to her car with her head swimming in the story she now wanted so badly to write.

Jill checked her watch and noted that it was just after eight. The glass door with the gold lettering, "Jules Burns, Editor," was open, and she could see the scattered wads of paper on the floor. He was there. "Good morning, Mr. Burns," she said as she cautiously entered the lion's den.

"Don't you have anything better to do, Jill, than to annoy me? Tell me what you want, then leave as soon as possible." He tossed a stack of papers onto his desk, glowering at her, looking past his bushy eyebrows and over his glasses.

"I need to discuss my assignment with you, if it's all right," she said.

"If you mean the short report about the couple out in the nursing home, then just write down what they told you and get on with it. What else could you do?"

"Well, it's more complicated than that. May I discuss it with you?"

"If you weren't so pretty, I would say no. However, close the door and pull up a chair, and tell daddy your little problem." She did as he asked and took out a small notebook.

Jill looked at Mr. Burns to be sure he was paying attention before beginning. "The story, in a nutshell, is this, Mr. Burns. The two elderly people over there were born at the same time and raised by their mother as twins. They weren't, twins I mean, and eventually found out the truth and married. Mike said that he was in love with his wife for ninety years, and she says the same. I think it's pretty neat as a story, but I don't know what you want me to do with it. What I mean is that telling the story will be a lengthy process and will take a lot of my time spent in interviews with them and reading their mother's diaries." She looked up to see what his face showed.

"Why do you find this interesting, Jill?" Mr. Burns asked.

"Don't you see," she asked. "They were always in love. Normal siblings never do that. They usually repel each other. Even more unusual is the physical attraction to each other that they were able to resist until adulthood. It is this attraction and how they dealt with it that makes the story."

"How did they find out that they weren't related?" he asked. This time he was stroking his chin, and Jill could tell that he had some interest.

"I don't know. It will take a lot of time with them to get the full story and then there are the diaries of their mother. A huge stack of them."

"So, my dear Jill, are you advocating writing this story as a series of columns or as a Sunday supplement, or just what do you have in mind?" Mr. Burns asked.

"Isn't this for you to decide, Mr. Burns? That is why I am here. What do I do with it?" He leaned back in his swivel chair and looked at the ceiling, rocking back and forth.

"Look, Jill, this isn't our usual content for this newspaper. You have two choices here. You could write a short piece of a couple of paragraphs telling about what you have told me, or you could write a book. As I see it, it might take that many words to do justice to the story. On the other hand, perhaps we could do a series. This is a different direction for us, and I will need to get permission from above first. Tell you what. You get started and write as you go, and let me see what you do with it. We will make a final decision later."

"How much time can I devote to it?" Jill asked.

"No more than three hours a day until we see where this is going. Is that satisfactory?"

"Sure. But I think it will take a lot more than that to write this story, but that will cover the interview time, at least. One more thing, Mr. Burns?" She added the last part, because he had already picked up his papers and was flipping through them. He looked up with a frown.

"I have a question about style. There are three perspectives here. The boy, the girl and the mother. There may be others, but we can only guess their views and experiences. There is a fourth, also. The reader's view. The question is…should I make the story a changing first person account or tell it in the third person. You know, a bird's eye view versus one seen through the eyes and mind of the person at ground level?"

"Ground level? Where did you get that stuff, some distinguished lecturer in college?" Mr. Burns laughed.

"No, sir. That one is from you," Jill remembered.

"Am I that full of crap? No, don't dare answer that one. Just go start putting it down on paper. The story will tell itself. You will figure it out as you write it. Now, are we done here?" he asked.

Chapter 4

MIKE'S STORY

L ike I said," Mike repeated, "my first memory is of Mary. I was probably looking into her eyes on my original birth day, and judging from Mother's photographs, we were kept in the same bassinet and in the same bed for years. We did everything together and learned to walk and talk at the same time. Since we were the only children in our family, there were no other distractions for us, except each other. Mary was my playmate and partner in childhood, and I was hers. Everything I know and remember was learned shoulder to shoulder with her. We bathed together, slept together and got sick at the same time together. I can't give you a chronologic report, because my memories jump around, kind of like links. One memory leads to another, but sometimes they are years apart. If you are patient with me, I will try to remember the past as well as an old man can."

I wish I could remember seeing Mary on our zero birthday, but I'm not sure that I can. On the other hand, I sometimes have a blurry flash of memory of her face that I can't place and which goes way back. Perhaps we do remember everything we see. What I do remember well is our first celebrated birthday. You know, the one with the cake and the cameras? On that one, she was dressed in something pink with little frills. We had a single cake with two candles spaced widely apart. She reached out and put her hand deeply into the cake and icing and applied a fistful to the vicinity of my mouth. I remember being snatched upward followed by a quick bath. Mother was so meticulous with us. We could sort of stagger walk by then, and I remember following Mary around a room full of legs.

When we were very young, we had various infections with chickenpox, measles, mumps and many colds. We usually stayed in bed together, keeping each other company. I remember the tents we made with the bed sheets and fencing with our oral thermometers. There was nothing made of our differing sex, and we interchanged clothing and took baths at the same time. At an early age, there is no sense of sex, just acceptance of things as they are. We went to the physician together, got shots together, and cried together.

At some point, I started to see the differences between us. I don't know when that happened, but it was before we went to school. We were about the same size for a long time, but we started to develop differing ways of dealing with life and different interests. Our mother started to dress Mary in little dresses, and of course, she had long hair. We were still inseparable, and if she played with dolls, then so did I. If I wanted to throw a ball, she was always there to catch it for me. At dinner, we were expected to eat everything on our plates, no exceptions. Mary was, and still is, picky about food. I was always right beside her and what she didn't like, she put on my plate, and I ate it even if I didn't want it. When I had something that she wanted, she just helped herself from my plate. I was always physically gifted and sure of myself, but Mary had a slight clumsiness and would easily trip or drop things so I always made sure that I was around to pick her up and straighten her clothes and brush her off. She never had to thank me, because it was just what we did. I was just meant to be there for her, and there was no thanks expected or given. When she dropped something, I was the one who admitted breaking it, and I was the one who got punished. Our father was fond of spankings, and I got a lot of them. Mary was always there, holding her clenched fists to cover her mouth and with her sorrowful big eyes tearing in my behalf as I took my lickings. Afterwards, especially if I was taking punishment for her, she would tenderly touch my cheek with her hand, tears streaming down her face. I always felt more sorry for her grief than my own stinging rear end.

Our world was so small. The little house and the little yard and Mother and Father. Not much there, you understand, but, oh, the memories. Dressing up for church on Sunday, we stayed dressed up for extended family gatherings in the afternoons. We had a set of coloring crayons that we passed back and forth while we studiously drew and colored the day's cartoon strips from the morning paper. Hanging on Mother's skirt while she ironed, we listened to her radio shows while waiting for our clothing to come at us hot from the iron. We had a set of wooden blocks that somehow got scattered around the house like they had lives of their own to attend to. Mother made us find all of them before Father got home and tripped over them. These little scraps of memory are like the old yellow photographs in the box. Just little glimpses and fragments. The visual images, like the photographs, are incomplete without the feeling associated with them, and I remember the feelings best. One thing I remember clearly is that I felt love for Mary long before I knew what it meant. She and I were the right and left arms of a single being, and no matter what happened, we had each other.

Things started to change as we came closer to school age. There were other children our age who appear in my memory. Often when we were with other kids, we would keep eye contact with each other to be sure our sibling was near. There was one really obnoxious boy who seemed to know how important Mary was to me. He probably noticed the connection we had, even if separated by yards. "You ever play show me yours, and I'll show you mine?" he asked one day.

"What do you mean," I innocently asked. He pulled his pants away from his waist and pointed down. I got what he meant.

"No," I said. "I don't play that game."

"I'm going to see if your sister will play that with me," he said, grinning. It was the first time I had ever hit anyone with my fist, and it was a good solid one. The boy ran screaming, holding his nose, blood seeping past his hand. I knew that I was going to be in trouble, but I also knew from experience that I could take a beating and live through it. Anyway, I sort of enjoyed the sight of that boy receding rapidly in the distance. I saw Mary looking at me from across the yard, and she cocked her head ever so slightly as if to ask, "What just happened?" By the time we went into the house, Mother was waiting for me. The boy's mother had already called.

"Mike, did you hit little Franklin in the nose?"

"Yes, Mother." That was not what she wanted to hear, and I could see the anger in her eyes. I was going to get another whipping and this time before Father got home.

"Franky hit me first, Mama. Mike was just the one who hit him back, that's all," said my wonderful lying sister.

"You mean that Franklin hit Mary, and you, Mike, came to protect her?" Mother asked me.

I didn't answer, but Mary did. "I told you, Mama. Franky hit me first. After Mike hit him, he ran away, but I was going to hit him too."

I could see that Mother wasn't buying it, but she looked back and forth between us and knew that she was licked. She just dropped the whole thing and walked away.

One winter day, and I can't recall the year or our age, Mary wanted to build a snowman. I enthusiastically helped, and together we rolled the snowballs and hefted them up as we had seen others do. Mary disappeared inside and emerged with Father's hat and some vegetables for the eyes, nose and mouth. We stood proudly in front of the snowman looking over our work, when Mary suddenly had another idea. "Let's get married. The snowman'll do it!" I am sure that I didn't understand the concept of marriage at that time, and I just stood there helpless in front of the minister made of ice. Mary did, though, and hustled us back inside to dress in more formal attire, alerting our mother in the process. Mother was delighted with the whole cute idea and went looking for her camera and film. Even though the temperature was below freezing, and we were dressed in our Sunday, not very warm, best, we had several photographs taken of poses in front of our snowman preacher. When it was happening, Mary and I exchanged kisses as is necessary at a wedding. Her cold nose pressed into my face, and I remember the faint odor of her hair. I think that I was mesmerized, and my brain shut out most everything else about that day. The photos are still in our old scrapbook, and the two little, red-cheeked faces stare out in utter happiness at the camera. It's really marvelous when you compare the photos to our actual wedding many years later.

When school started, we always attempted to sit together when possible. This happened not only in class but at assembly, class singing, and in the lunchroom. Because we were so close and shared our work, and at times our tests, the teachers frequently made attempts to separate us in the classroom. It was, by necessity, when we learned about silent communication. A brief eye contact can exchange an enormous quantity of information, and believe me, we used it. At that early level of primary school, boys and girls didn't seem to mix well in those days. Boys had their friends, which were other boys, and girls did the same with girls. It was like they were afraid of the opposite sex, and the result was that the two almost never mixed. But not us. I made sure to take her into any group that I was in, and I mixed easily with her cluster of girls. For this reason, I received more than my share of kidding, occasionally hostility, from other boys. After being called a "sissy" one too many times, I learned to fight. I discovered that if I struck first and hit hard, concentrating on the face, the fight was over before it started. Unfortunately, I spent a lot of time sitting on a hard chair beside the teacher or the principal. The good side was that I was not only known to not be a sissy but someone not to tangle with. I quickly became the most feared boy on the playground, a fact not unnoticed by my sister. She and I walked home after school, a respectable three blocks, and she usually took my arm in hers during the walk. Safe from all harm. I was so proud to be there for her.

Once, we were standing in a group watching some of the larger boys engaging in little contests of strength or speed. Mary was watching one boy in particular who seemed to have a physical edge on the others. "Look at Charlie! He can beat anybody!" she said with obvious admiration of Charlie in her voice. It stung me deeply that she noticed him. Looking him over critically, I wondered what she saw in him, like other males have done for endless time. I was jealous of Charlie, and he probably didn't even know that Mary was alive. Something clicked in me that moment, and I resolved to always be the best in Mary's eyes, both in things physical and in the classroom. I wanted to have her look at me like she did Charlie. Mary will tell you that she would have loved me as much if I had a deformity and was retarded. It was always there, the caring and affection that Mary had for me. At times, she had a certain soft look about her that was meant just for me. I knew it then as I still know it now, but at that time, I was determined to be the best that I could be so that I could never lose her love or admiration.

Even our teachers noticed a change in me. I was no longer content to be a quiet boy forced to sit in the back of the class, dutifully doing my work. My homework came back on time, and the effort I put into it was noticed. I asked questions in class and always was first with my hand up, either answering questions or volunteering for something the teacher wanted done. Shortly, I was placed back on the front row where Mary could keep me in view. That is what I really wanted. What I discovered is something most young people should be told. Once you're on top, it's pretty easy to stay there. The impression that you make on people stays with you, for good or for bad. I always tried to be the smartest, the strongest, and the one who struck first in a fight. Mary was noticed too but in a different way. Mostly, she was quiet and shy and preferred to be near me so that my glow would keep her in shadow. Her problem, and mine, was that she became a young beauty, her loveliness growing year by year until just about everybody commented on it. We were known as Mike and his beautiful sister, Mary. The boys started to notice long before middle and high school, and many of them came down with bloody noses. I realized that the flood was happening and that a few whacks in the face wouldn't make much of a dent or prevent the attention toward her, which was growing by the month. We continued to walk back home together, arm in arm, until our after school interests and commitments started to keep us away from each other. Back home, we usually would huddle with our heads touching and tell each other about the day's events.

We continued to sleep in the same room until we were nearly ten. By that time, we had individual single beds, separated by about two feet. There just weren't any other arrangements possible in our small house of two bedrooms. The day that we moved to a slightly larger house made me realize that Mary and I would be separated by a wall. I can't speak for Mary, but I cried myself to sleep that first night apart from her. Before going to bed, I frequently would sneak into her room to lay beside her and talk with her until she went to sleep, then return to my lonely corner without her.

Our parents thought that our close relationship was just wonderful until they suddenly decided that it might be something needing close supervision. I saw the looks and felt the unspoken alarm in them at times, but I didn't understand at all. Mary came first in my life, and I would have to say that I came first with her. We didn't confide in our parents like most children do, but in each other. One day, without warning, we were taken to a new doctor's office for a visit. We had been to the doctor before for shots and exams, and I recall that, for the most part, medical offices had a certain familiar smell about them which were threatening or assuring, depending if you were sick or not. The new one had no familiar smells, and the only interesting thing in the waiting room was a large moose head high above a door. When our turn came, we went in as a group of four and met the physician. He was dressed in a dark suit and had thick glasses and the faint odor of tobacco about him. He perched on a small stool and looked us up and down while giving a stiff and unassuring smile.

"Hi, children. I am Doctor Beck, and we are going to have a little talk."

I don't remember much about the questions he asked or our responses, but after a while, we were escorted out of the room, leaving our parents alone with Dr. Beck. After they emerged, we all drove home silently. Mary and I looked at each other with puzzlement. Had we done something wrong? We never found out what was said behind closed doors, but nothing changed, and we forgot about it quickly.

Mary and I were sleeping apart in our separate rooms and had gotten used to it. It didn't change how close we were when awake, and we still sat together at dinner, often with our shoulders touching, on purpose. At the sixth grade level, we started to drift apart in our interests. Mary started taking dance lessons, and her gracefulness and femininity came into full bloom. I would put anything I was doing aside to watch her practice and stretch. She made me feel like the stiff monster from the old Frankenstein movie. I started to be aware of her body's curves, and as her breasts developed, I noted that her waist grew tighter, the woman in her emerging. It's embarrassing to admit, but we had no instruction at home or in school about sex. There was no written information lying about that I could study, and no one to discuss it with except Mary. Many times I wanted to talk about that subject with my best friend in life, but I couldn't bring myself to do it, realizing that the reason was that it was all about her. I couldn't look at her physical beauty any longer without it impacting me, but I didn't let myself fantasize about her, because she was too precious to me to debase in that way. All the effects I was experiencing were subconscious, but certainly were there. Did she have any similar feelings toward me? I don't know if she did, but she never spoke of it to me.

One day, my mind changed forever about Mary. It was a school day, and we were expected to do our homework and take a bath before going to bed. Routine. On that day we, as usual, did our work together on the kitchen table after supper. Mary got up to bathe first, also as usual. I knew her time in the single bathroom down to the second, and I was waiting patiently outside the door for her to finish. The door opened, and the steam in the air poured out behind her like a dramatic movie. She was wrapped in a big fluffy towel, and she maintained steady eye contact with me. I knew instinctively that something was up and waited for her to say what she was thinking when she dropped the towel and stood there for a brief moment in full view. The power of the moment hit me like a concrete block had been dropped on my head. I couldn't understand what was happening and without my wanting to, my eyes had time to search her entire body. She walked past me toward her bedroom, dragging her towel and my eyes, which were fixed on her receding and perfect figure. Since our young childhood, this was the first and last time I saw Mary unclothed until our marriage many years later, but it was an image which made it back into my head thousands of times afterwards. Even now, I can summon that image, and it will cause arousal in me. I dealt poorly with it then, and I think that it made me finally realize what I felt toward Mary. There was no doubt. I loved her body and soul, completely and fully, and there was no going back to innocence. It nearly drove me crazy to really say what probably was always in me, that I loved her. The thought made me feel ashamed and unworthy to be her brother. It was that Mary was so perfect, and I had defiled her in thought, if not in deed. My unwilling thoughts made me feel worthless, and that night I was torn between her image and the knowledge that I shouldn't be thinking of my sister in a sexual way. My mind went back and forth all night. Submission to desire and denial of desire. Surely this was not the way to love your sister. It was like her shape was imprinted into my brain, and it surely was.

The next morning at breakfast I felt like I had just swam the English Channel as I dragged myself to my chair. Mary was already up, and her long blonde hair swung down from the band behind her head. I had seen her hair all my life, but this time I saw it differently. She looked up and caught my eye, and I could see the sparkle there that backed up her little smile. We shared our secret with that glance, and she was letting me know that what I saw was a gift from her to me. As always, in her presence, I relaxed as if I had just returned home from a long arduous trip. Things would be all right. Mary was there for me.

As we entered the ninth grade, we entered the world of unabated male and female interest and pairings. I was never comfortable with seeing any boy getting friendly with Mary, and when I considered that he was going too far, I would usually pay him a visit out of her view. My reputation for violence grew on its own but was enhanced when I formally entered training for boxing after school. Most boys aspired to the football or the basketball teams, but I traveled a different direction. I still had enviable grades and could compete with anyone on campus in an intellectual way. Pushing hard in everything I did, I grew thick with muscle and confidence. If you could ask our contemporaries, they would likely say that Mary and I were the most attractive students at school, and the most pursued. They would also tell you that for some strange reason, we never dated anyone.

One day, in those years, Mary asked me an uncomfortable question. "Mike, have you been keeping boys away from me?" It was a simple direct question, and the simple answer was, or should have been, "Yes." Because I surely was. I did it behind her back, and the male victim was always warned that if he ratted me out, I would make him regret it. Obviously, someone ratted me out, in spite of the warning.

"Why do you ask me that, Mary. Did someone say that I was doing that?" I answered a question with a question. Brilliant.

"No, they didn't. They are probably afraid enough of you to not say anything. I know, as everybody else does, that you would take anyone apart who touches me. You are just trying to protect me as you have always done, Mike, but you don't even let anyone talk to me. I am beginning to feel like I have a disease. Can't you let up a little for me?"

She and I were standing only two feet apart and were alone, face-to-face. There was that glance of communication again streaming back and forth from our eyes into our brain. I didn't have to tell her that I loved her, because I could see in her eyes that she not only knew but also felt that way toward me. When we were little, we could have hugged and kissed, as we so often did, but not any longer. If I were to really hug her, she would set my flesh on fire. I had to keep a distance. It was an awful moment of truth. She was asking me to set her free, and I knew that I had to, but I knew that it would nearly kill me to think that some boy was pawing her, and it would kill me to imagine that she would respond back to him with lust. It was a question I couldn't answer so I just stood there looking at her like I would never see her again. It was, for me, the moment that she would start to slide out of my life. Clearly, it was obvious to Mary that we couldn't be together as our bodies and minds wanted to. Nevertheless, life would have to go on. Me? I would have been happy just being able to look at her and have her near me forever. Yes, that was condemning both of us to a half-life. I had to do as she asked and let her go, and we both knew it.

I went for a hard distance-run after that encounter with Mary, and that night I tore up my boxing partner in anger and was nearly thrown off of the boxing team. The emotions were welling up in me like vomitus, and the brief moments of quiet were broken with the return of what only could be panic attacks. We had three more years of high school. Mary, with her looks, could be anything she wanted and have anything or anyone she desired. I had the grades and the drive to conquer any subject or any hill, and my inner frustration would make me push ever harder. I saw other young couples with their heads together, occasionally exchanging kisses in public. I knew what was possible with a girl that was in love with you. Not for us. We loved and ached to love and were self-denied the touch that would complete our happiness.

In the ninth grade, I was seated beside another boy with whom I eventually developed a friendship. For me, friendships were hard, because I devoted so much of my efforts toward looking out for Mary and pursuing my strategy of excellence. Most other boys avoided me for various reasons, and I drew apart from my classmates in many ways. Phillip was different in that he didn't see any need for competition with me and didn't seem to show any outward interest in Mary. Any male in our classes or even in the hallway knew to keep his eyes off of Mary while I was near, because the word was out about me. Phillip had an unruly shock of red hair complemented by pimples, awkward teeth and a ragged smile. He was interested in cars, airplanes and dogs but never mentioned Mary. Compared to me, he was slightly built and was completely uninterested in sports or competition. Phillip was a good student and very bright, and his grades were nearly as good as mine. Due to his continuing efforts to build a bridge of friendship with me, I gradually talked to him and grew to like him. It was like being drawn into a different world than mine, where small things matter, and no epic struggles were ongoing. A simple world of balsawood models and musical instruments. Phillip was taking lessons in guitar and could play really well. Mother had started picking up Mary with the car for her dance lessons after school, and during those interludes I walked home alone or with Phillip. His house was on the way to mine, and occasionally, I accepted his invitation in. Phillip's room was decorated with his model airplanes and posters of fast cars. He was an only child, and his mother was a pleasant, short and plump, woman who adored him. She was always quick to offer fresh cookies, making me feel at home and welcome. I would sit there listening to Phillip play his guitar, while looking around his room filled with his interests and feeling transported to a different planet than my own. Seeing Phillip's world caused me to remember that what I had in life was Mary. Wonderful, magical Mary. When her image returned into my head, my existence came sharply back into focus. There was no hope of ever being happy. I was destined to lust after and pine over my own blood sister. What a hopeless moral degenerate I was. Occasionally when this happened, I had no choice but to say my goodbyes and leave, because my mood would change, and I had to get out into the fresh air to breathe again. In due course, it became apparent that

Phillip was perceptive enough to understand at least a little of what I was going through. He was a kind and patient friend and, later, to Mary as well.

Mary and I told each other every detail of our lives except our feelings for each other. That subject was off-limits, especially in my case, because I was willfully trying to suppress it. I knew how much Mary cared for me because of her daily, hourly, actions toward me, and ever since our birth, I could see her soul through her eyes. She knew about Phillip and was most interested that I had formed a friendship for the first time which didn't include her. She encouraged the relationship, I think, partly for me and partly so that she could do the same thing. We tried going to each other's lessons a few times, but when she showed up to watch my sparring matches, it was like a brilliant light was turned on in the shadows of the room, and all eyes were on her. The same for me when I tried to watch her all-girls dancing lessons. All the girls paid me so much attention that the desperate instructor asked me to leave and not come back. One day, Mary was free to walk home with us, and the three of us walked together for the first time ever. I was in the middle so that there would be minimal contact, because I didn't want to be angry at Phillip, and the two of them carried on their conversation by looking around me, both in front and behind me. It got to be funny and awkward, and after that, I allowed Mary to be in the middle. One day, we decided to stop by the pharmacy and sit at the fountain bar drinking cherry cokes. Mary was in the middle and seemed to really enjoy another dimension to our relationship. The conversation was animated, and in an unthinking and innocent moment, Phillip had Mary's graceful hand placed on his forearm. The vision of it shot through me like a bullet. My eyes probably bulged, and when they saw my reaction, her hand and his forearm quickly were retracted. I was not angry at them, because I could see no danger in what happened…I was angry at myself for allowing my jealousy about Mary to be so destructive.

At the beginning of our sophomore year, Phillip and I were walking home one day when he stopped and turned toward me. I could tell that he was having problems voicing what he was thinking, and I patiently waited.

"Mike, you know how much I like being around you, so I don't want to say or do anything that would get between us, but I want to talk frankly with you, and when I finish, if you want to split my lip, then go ahead."

I didn't answer him, and my eyes searched his face, waiting for the shoe to drop.

"Look, Mike, everyone knows that you protect Mary, and the poor thing is going to be shut out of things important to her this year because of it. The guys I know would be afraid to pick up her handkerchief if she dropped it, because they know what would happen to them after school. I know it's because you love her and want to protect her, but you are crushing her. She is a wonderful girl, funny and fun to be with. Yes, she is the best looking girl any of us have ever seen, but there is more to her than that. You know me and, I hope, trust me. Could I beg you, and I mean on my knees if that will help, to let me accompany her to a couple of dances? No other boy will dare ask her and all her friends will be there. If you don't let her go, she will die from embarrassment. I know that she won't ask you, because she would never hurt your feelings, so I am asking you for her. I promise with my whole heart to treat her with the same respect that I do when you are right there watching me. Please, Mike. Now if you want to hit me, I am ready." Phillip closed his eyes tight and stuck out his chin and waited.

Phillip chose the perfect moment and had the perfect presentation. What could I say? If she went out with anyone else but Phillip, I would get angry and mean, but Phillip was easily the least of evils. I reached out and playfully cuffed him gently on his waiting face. "Yes, Phillip. I won't object. Go ahead and ask her." It was one of the hardest things I had ever done. I didn't need to warn him to behave, because I knew that he would treat her exactly like he said.

He opened his eyes and started jumping in one spot like a Masai tribesman. "Thank you, thank you, thank you!" he bellowed.

"Calm down, Phillip, or I'll change my mind," I said. We continued to walk in silence while I thought about what this meant. Phillip was going to be the first boy that Mary had in her life other than me. She was bound to be grateful and appreciative to him and get closer to him in the process. Was I making a big mistake? If I thought of Mary instead of myself, I should be grateful to Phillip for breaking the ice. It had to happen. I had to let Mary live, and this was part of it. Since I loved her as much as I did, I had to see that she was happy, even if I wasn't. If I was willing to die instead of her, why couldn't I let her be happy? Okay then, it was done. She will start to go out with Phillip, but I knew some guys who had better not ask her if they valued their faces. There was only so far I was willing to go. I get to pick her dates, even if I am doing it from the shadows. What about me and my happiness? Do

I get any? The only thing in the world that would make me happy is off-limits forever. I had to let it go, had to shake that feeling for Mary out of my system. But each time I saw Mary, all the feeling came flooding back inside me, and I was helpless to stop it. I simply loved her.

Phillip wasted no time in asking Mary out, and she rapidly accepted. It was done out of my earshot, so I could only imagine what took place. I never thought about it before, but it dawned on me that Mary had been doing the same thing with girls interested in me. She didn't threaten them with death or injury but displeasure, and it was enough to keep them away from me. Word quickly got out about Mary seeing someone, and it seemed that Phillip's reputation with girls became the talk of the school. Finally, someone got to be with the fabulous Mary and live to tell about it. The other end of it was that I was now supposed to be fair game, and I soon discovered how aggressive females can be. It took only two days before the first girl approached me with a suggestive and alluring smile. No doubt about it, I had really never looked at another girl before. I sort of knew that they were alive, but I never thought about their various attributes. Now, I had female attributes that I had overlooked thrust into my face. At first, I was really shy with them because I was taken by storm, you might say. I quickly got used to the flirtation and the gentle caresses and the close distance they would assume. Me! I was the school's genuine bad boy in every way. The unusual part is that I consistently achieved the best grades in school. I had my choice of stunning girls. Pretty much any or all of them. Then there was Mary. She had not considered what would happen when she went out with Phillip. The other guys were still afraid to talk to her, but the girls had nothing to fear and came out of the woodwork to talk to me. Mary was jealous, and it showed. I caught it in her face when she was in sight of one of them talking to me and standing really close. It was a flash of lightning from her eyes. So far, I hadn't taken the bait and gone out with any of them, but it wasn't because of Mary's disapproval. It was because all my life I had been near the most wonderful female in the universe and no one else measured up.

I knew something was coming because Mary was a little distant late one night when we were doing our homework on the kitchen table. There was scant chitchat, and we had our heads down, working on problems or reports.

"Mike, I saw you with Janice the other day. Does she interest you?" she said calmly without looking up.

"She's pretty," I admitted without looking at her.

"You know, she is developing sort of a reputation." I could feel her glance in my direction.

"Easy conquest, huh?" I answered, pretending to concentrate on my homework.

There was a long silence and then her pencil made a strike against my book and went tumbling onto the floor. I looked up at her and could see the pout. My God, she was gorgeous when she pouted.

"What does that mean? Do you mean to take her out and have a little conquest then?" she said loudly.

I gave the signal with my hands to hold down the voice level. Our parents were in the next room listening to the radio. "No, Mary, I am just teasing you. I have no intention of exploring that opportunity with her." She started to stream tears and sniff, but she wouldn't break her gaze at me. I realized that Mary felt as possessive of me as I felt for her. There were a lot of things unsaid that night, but we both understood each other better. It made me feel like soaring like a bird, and I would have done it if I was able. This is why Mary never really complained about me keeping the guys away from her. She felt the same about me.

"Can I make a suggestion?" Mary sniffed.

"I will obey like a slave like I always do. Just command me and see," I answered.

Mary smiled a little at my joke and then said, "Since you picked out a harmless date for me so that I could get back into the world, I want to do the same for you. Will you do this for me?"

"Does this let Janice out?" I asked.

"Don't be stupid. I'll work on it and let you know."

"Can I date someone who won't make me cough or gag all evening?" I asked.

Mary got up and came around the table and wrapped her arms around me from the side. She hugged me and gave me a long kiss on my ear and said into it, "We both know what this is all about, Mike, and I am dealing with it as best I can without going crazy. Thanks for being so understanding with me." I didn't wash that ear for over a week.

It took Mary about two weeks, but one day I saw her in the distance heading down the hall toward me. She had some girl in tow and even from this distance, I could see the sparkle in Mary's eyes. The girl was obviously destined to be my new date, and I resolved to accept her with a smile and without questions. As they got closer, I could see that she was plain, but attractive and also shy. Next to the spectacular Mary, almost any girl would look plain or ordinary. I was pleased, and when I smiled, it was mostly from relief.

"Mike, this is Frieda. Frieda, this is my brother, Mike," she said. We both smiled at each other, and I stuck out my hand for a shake. Frieda put her limp wet hand in mine and gave a slight little bow. I looked at Mary for answers.

"Frieda was born in Austria, Mike, and she has a wonderful accent to go with her manners."

"Everyone knows about you, Mike. I am so pleasured to meet you," Frieda said and smiled her wan smile at me.

"What are they saying about me, Frieda? I have a right to know, don't I?"

Frieda looked at Mary for support, and Mary said, "Go ahead and tell him."

"Well, some say you are dangerous and unstable, some say that you are uppity, and some say that you are in love with your sister." She smiled again at me and made a little bow.

"What do you think, Frieda?" I asked politely.

Frieda hesitated, her hand to her lips, then said, "They all are probably right." Then she giggled.

"And so they are, Frieda. Will you go out with me to find out?"

"Are you asking me to the dance this weekend?" Frieda asked.

I shrugged at Mary and she understood. "Yes, Mike, there is a school dance this weekend, and I think it would be nice of you to ask Frieda." Then she spoke the magic words, "Phillip and I will be there also."

Standing at the curb, I patiently waited for Frieda's parents to drop her off in front of school that Saturday evening, and finally a car pulled up and out came all three of them, Frieda, her father, and mother.

"I am Herr Lubisch; you must be Mike. We have heard so much about you from Frieda," he said rather loudly and extended his hand for a shake.

"I am honored to meet you, sir. You have a fine daughter, and I am so pleased that she could accompany me this evening. I promise to do my utmost to entertain and take care of her." It was right out of a novel, and I acted it to the hilt, even meaning a lot of it, but I was looking most forward to keeping a watchful eye on my beautiful sister. This would be the first dance for both of us, but since Mary had already taken four years of dance classes, it was something which would come easily for her. Boxing footwork is not a substitute for dancing instruction. Mr. Lubisch, I mean Herr Lubisch, said his goodbyes, and they both kissed Frieda on both cheeks, as if telling her farewell forever, and then left us standing there looking at each other.

Music drifted out the doors of the auditorium, and I was much relieved to hear jazz instead of a waltz. We came through the double doors into the crowd, and I searched the heads for a crown of bright red hair, spotting Phillip quickly, and right beside him was my sister. There was a ring of boys around them two deep, and we headed that way to rescue her.

They looked relieved to see help arriving, and the small crowd of boys parted for us. Mary was lovely as always, and she turned on the radiance like a switch when she caught my eye. Three large boys who were on the football team stood together, watching us with interest. To me, they always seemed to be loud and pushy, and tonight was no exception. One of them, a fellow named S. Peter Gibbons was called "The Monster" by his football buddies. All of them seemed to have pet names, much like the gangsters we read about in the papers. I never liked any of them and up to this point had little contact with them. "The Monster" had dark full hair that he kept wet with lotion and swept back toward his neck. He obviously felt that he was attractive to the girls and, for all I knew, he was. I led Mary and Frieda away from the little crowd, and Phillip followed. We sat down as a group on the chairs lined up against the wall and waited for the music and dancing to start back up. I could sense fingers pointing and heads bobbing across the room at us from clustered groups of boys and girls. We were receiving a lot of unwanted attention. The music did resume from the live band, and they were very professional. The four of us tentatively got up and went a few feet onto the floor. I took Frieda's wet hand in mine, and we started slowly moving to the music while being sure that I could see Mary and Phillip. It was a mismatch, that much was obvious. Mary was graceful and fluid, and Phillip balanced precariously on two stiff sticks. She made sure to frequently find my eyes, sending me a faint twinkle of gratitude. We had a steady stream of silent communication going between us. She was smiling and obviously enjoying herself, and I didn't resent Phillip's hand holding hers, so we were doing all right so far. A large shadow was moving in her direction, and I took a longer look. Monster was grinning and walking through the other dancers like they weren't there, fixated on Mary. Trouble coming, I knew. I stopped dancing and quietly asked Frieda to wait for me by our chairs, and I turned toward Mary and the advancing predator just in time to watch him roughly tap Phillip on his underdeveloped shoulder. In the distance, his two buddies were laughing it up and slapping their thighs.

"I'm cutting in, buddy," Monster loudly said to Phillip. Poor Phillip looked stunned and moved slightly away from Mary who was watching me come toward them.

"No, you aren't," I said, closing the distance. Monster turned to face me. He was a fair amount larger than me and a lot heavier, with a big head and thick course hands.

"Don't bother me, man. I know about you, and I'm not afraid of you and neither are my teammates over there. You can't stop me from cutting in, them is the rules," Monster sneered. I could hear the slaps from his buddies across the room.

"You are not going to touch my sister...ever. Got that?" I said calmly. The other dancers stopped and started falling back, spreading out like a drop of oil on water.

"And why not? Why am I not good enough for your sister? Are you in love with her like everybody thinks?" He took a step toward Mary who shrunk away from him.

"I am giving you the choice to walk away or be humiliated and carried away from here. You will regret forcing me to hurt you," I said calmly, while changing my foot position for balance.

"You? You're no match for me or my guys over there. Back off before I nail you." He reached out and pushed my shoulder, and my fist shot up, striking his chin with a powerful uppercut. Monster's head flipped back, and he fell backward into the floor with a crash. At first he was moaning but started to flail as he lost consciousness, then was still. My peripheral vision saw his two large friends heading my way as they pushed past the crowd. I sprinted to meet them, striking the first one full in the nose with a very hard solid hit before he realized what I was going to do. The second fellow froze, looking at his fallen comrades and then back at me before starting to back up. I moved toward him aggressively, and he turned, fleeing for his life out the double doors, to the laughter of the watching crowd. The band stopped playing, and the crowd formed a large circle around the three of us, the two large football players sprawled out on the floor like fallen prey. We could hear the screech of tires as the surviving football hero fled the scene in his car.

Principal Thornbush was there, of course, and he ambled toward the scene as fast as his stubby legs could. He came up right after Frieda had come back from the wall. I stood, one arm around each girl, waiting for him. A couple of adults were bending over the fallen, trying to revive them with little success. Principal Thornbush was red with anger, and you could almost see drool from his lips. He looked me up and down with hostility and then back to the large boys, who were finally showing some sign of returning consciousness.

"Mike Condor, this is a fine mess. You have ruined the dance and the reputation of this school tonight. I am considering calling the police and having you charged. To think, the finest student I ever saw could do this kind of thing. Well, it's unimaginable."

Two classmates of ours, whom I really only knew by sight, stepped forward out of the crowd. "Wait a minute, Principal. You have the wrong idea," one of them offered. "Mike was defending himself. They hit him first. What do you expect him to do, just turn the other cheek for this big gorilla?" This was welcome news for the principal and fitted his plans better. Now he didn't have to damage his star pupil after all. The big dumb and crummy football players would have to take the blame and lick their own wounds. Much better. Principal Thornbush wiped his face and added a smile.

"Well, my apologies, Condor. Seems that you did the right thing after all. Any problem arising from this...well, I'll back you up fully. Now all of you resume your dancing and enjoy the evening!" He signaled to the band to resume playing, just as the feet of the barely conscious bodies being dragged disappeared out the double doors.

Dancing resumed, but it became uncomfortable for the four of us to remain at the dance because of the wide berth we were given, and the stares. I suggested that we leave early, but Frieda's parents were not due back for another hour, and she lived too far away to walk. Instead, we sat, talked and tried our best to ignore the other students. I started thinking about the boys that I had to hit. Their egos likely wouldn't permit them to let this matter go. The entire football team was embarrassed tonight, and the more I thought about it, the more I realized that there was more to come...there just had to be. Tonight was not the time for a long walk back in the dark. I felt that I could handle myself, but Mary would have to take the walk with me. Gambling that my grades and class standing would help me out, I excused myself and went looking for the principal. He was easy to find, standing with two other teacher-chaperones along the opposite wall, guarding the punch bowl. When he saw me coming he smiled and stepped forward. The other teachers were also smiling. My reputation was secured that night, and I could tell that they all were on my side.

"Principal Thornbush," I said. "I need a favor."

He patted me on the shoulder and said, "Anything I can do for you, son, it's yours for the asking."

"About tonight," I began. "There may be an attempt to get even. Some on the football team have cars, and I expect trouble on the way home. Mary and I have to walk, you see."

It didn't take but a blink of his eyes, and he understood. "I understand what you mean. Would you permit me to take you and your sister home?"

"I would be grateful, sir. I feel bad about having to ask you, and I wouldn't except for Mary. There is Phillip also, and he only lives a couple of blocks from here."

"Mike, there isn't a single person at this school who is unaware of how you feel about your sister. It's so refreshing. Most brothers and sisters try hard to avoid each other during the high school years. I admire the way you always look after her. Never apologize for it, son. When did you have in mind leaving?"

I looked up at the large clock on the high wall and said, "My date, Frieda, expects her parents to pick her up in about forty-five minutes. Will that work?"

"Well, that's perfect. That is when this dance is supposed to be over. I'll meet you streetside then." He patted me again, and they all waved to me as I went back across the gym to my companions.

The crowd thinned as couples drifted away, and finally the band played their last number. Trash covered the floor, and the containers were filled to overflowing, the life of the place evaporating as the last note faded from our ears. Tony, the janitor, was attempting to clean up and was moving very slowly.

I got up and summoned Phillip to rise also. "Let's give Tony a hand until we have to leave. It's the least we can do for a ride home." Phillip agreed, and grabbing long brooms we started moving litter off of the floor. The teachers noticed, and I could feel the amazed looks. I didn't care what they were thinking, because I only wanted to help poor old Tony, and it was better than sitting and waiting. In only fifteen minutes, we had the place looking good, and Tony smiling, because he could go home early that night.

A car horn sounded, and I noticed that Frieda was getting up. I accompanied her, holding the double door open. Her father's car was idling at the curb, and both her parents were patiently waiting. The driver's door window was lowered, and I leaned down smiling, "Sir, thank you for letting your daughter come with me. I am sorry that it didn't turn out better, and I'm sure that she will tell you the whole story. If I can have another chance to have her with me someday, I will appreciate it." Herr Lubisch looked confused, but he smiled and gave a little wave. I helped Frieda into the rear seat and politely wished her goodnight. Tears glinted in her eyes, but I wasn't sure why.

Shortly, as he promised, the principal was waiting by the curb, and we three gratefully piled into the back seat. He seemed to know where we lived without being told, and dropped Phillip off first.

Phillip hesitated before he got out, looking for a long moment at Mary before speaking. "I will remember this night my whole life. Thanks to you both, it was my dream come true." Phillip could seem so sincere. I didn't say anything, because I was tense, waiting for him to try and sneak a quick kiss, but he made no such move. Mary gave a little laugh and reminded Phillip that she would see him in school the next day. The car rolled away leaving Phillip standing on the sidewalk watching us until we were out of sight. As we approached our house, an old car rattled by, moving menacingly along the street. When the two cars passed, our headlights lit up the interior of the other car and its complement of large boys. They were, indeed, looking for us.

Principal Thornbush twisted to look directly at me, "Looks like you were right, Mike. I would say that you have a big problem. Better tell your dad about it, and from now on, be very careful, especially at night." He dropped us off in front of our house and waited until we got safely inside. Father was waiting up, smoking his pipe. He had begun to slow down a lot as he aged, and it was easy to see the years creeping up on him. Father had served in the World War and been in combat. He never talked about it, but he had some ugly scars on his back and at times limped noticeably. His closet contained a loaded gun, and I always assumed that he knew what to do with it. Anyone could see that he was no match for these large ruffians patrolling our street, and I didn't want to burden him with any such bad news. I would handle it tomorrow.

He got up from the couch and stretched. "Have a good time tonight, kids?" he asked.

Both of us smiled and said that we did. Even without talking it over, Mary and I saw it the same way. We went into the kitchen to get some milk before calling it a night.

"What are you planning, Mike?" Mary asked me in nearly a whisper.

"Not sure yet, but I will come up with something. From now until I get this settled, don't go anywhere alone. Okay?" She didn't say anything and looked sad, as if everything was her fault. I knew what she was thinking, and I had to put a stop to it.

"I have never said it out loud before, Mary, but I have thought it nearly forever." I turned to face her across the small table. "You are the most beautiful girl that could be found. It makes my head spin to look at you. That's my problem. Your problem is that almost every male out there will feel the same. They will seek you out and turn on every little charm to be near you. Some may even try force. It will be the price you pay for looking like you do. If you don't get careless, I will be there to watch out for you like I always have been. You have to understand that you carry a treasure with you, and the treasure is you." She was near tears anyway, but my little speech brought on a flood. I moved around to embrace her and let her cry on my shoulder until the sobbing stopped.

"I wish a lot of things could be different, Mike." She said haltingly. After blotting at her nose, she resumed laying her head against my shoulder. "One thing in my life that I value the most is you. Please don't let them hurt you. Promise?"

Something really bad was bound to happen to someone because of tonight's events. A possible solution twirled in my head like a moth caught in a bright light, but I didn't realize how much it was going to cost all of us until later.

The next night was my regular boxing training session at the Seventh Street Fight Club. My father had taken me over there three years ago for a couple of lessons, and afterward, I kept going back. We usually sweated out an hour of hard calisthenics or bag work and then were allowed an hour sparring in the ring. The gym was dirty, old, and dark but also rough in many other ways. Quite a few older, tough-looking men hung around. Some had been fighters in their better days and would show up to watch or pretend to work out. There also were several young boxers who were currently professionally fighting and had their own trainers and crew. The paint-chipped walls were lined with signed photos of boxers who had come and gone through the years. A pug-nosed, cauliflower-ear ex-pro named Mickey managed the gym, and he was nearly always around. I never heard who actually owned the place, if anyone did. There were others who came and went and seemed to know everybody but were given a wide berth by the regulars. The two who had become most familiar to me dressed in very shiny dark blue suits over clean sparkling shoes. They sat in the corners, watching everything with hard, dark, little eyes. We were told by Mickey to stay away, far away, from them. The rumor circulated that they were mob-connected. One of them always seemed to watch my work in the ring and occasionally gave me a thumbs-up or a clap or two. His name was Mr. Cohen to us...Shark to the older fellows.

When I stepped off of the bus, I saw the Cadillac parked at the curb. Shark was there that night. I pushed the creaky wooden door open to the slaps of the skip rope and grunts of the speed bags being worked. Somewhere, a trainer was yelling at his charge to "keep your gloves up, stupid." I made my way to the lockers and quickly changed. On the way past, I noticed Shark in the corner, and when he saw me he acknowledged with a nod in my direction. One of the young pros was huddled in the corner with Shark, and I saw a thick yellow envelope exchange hands. The fighter stuffed it in his loose boxing shorts and left. I made my move toward the corner with Shark following me closely with narrowed eyes.

"Hi, kid," he said. "Your name is Mike Condor, isn't it?" I nodded yes, and he continued. "You know, I've been watching you closely. You have the moves, kid, to turn pro later on. Ever think about it?"

"Well, Mr. Cohen, thanks for the complement, but I am only in the tenth grade right now. It'll be a while before I can decide that," I said.

"Then, what do you want, kid? Need some money?"

"No, Mr. Cohen, not today. I need some advice, that's all." Shark smiled a half-smile, showing a couple of partially gold front teeth, and motioned for me to sit down beside him. He pulled out a smoke even though he was sitting right under a "No Smoking" sign above him. He arched his eyebrows and indicated for me to tell him the story.

"It's like this, Mr. Cohen. Last night at the school dance, I got into a fight with a couple of guys and had to knock them out in front of everybody. They are on the football team, and on the way home, we spotted six of them cruising around in a car probably looking to get even with me. Got any ideas?"

"Sure, kid. You shoot a couple of them, and the rest will beat it. Want a gun?"

I gave a nervous laugh. "No, Mr. Cohen, I was hoping to avoid that sort of extreme."

"Football team, huh? Probably large guys and you took two of them out just like that. I love it, kid. You sure got it." He pulled on his cigarette and studied me before speaking. "Gimme some names, kid."

"The one called Monster and the other called Butch are the ones I flattened. There was one who ran away, but I'm not sure who it was," I said. Shark nodded and jotted something down on a small piece of paper.

"I'll send someone to discuss this with them. Don't worry about it again, kid; it's taken care of," Shark said and showed his gold teeth again. I began to worry what I had started.

"You aren't going to have them killed are you, Mr. Cohen?"

"No, no, kid. Nuttin like that. We'll just explain to them why it will be a bad idea to bother you again. You got nuttin to worry bout. Relax."

"Thanks, Mr. Cohen, I owe you," I said.

"Yes, you do, kid," he said and blew a smoke ring high into the air.

When I walked away, I saw Mickey watching me, and he motioned for me to come over. "What the hell was that about, Mike? Didn't I tell you to stay away from that bunch?"

"Nothing to it, Mickey. We just had a chat. Seems like an OK guy to me," I said confidently, but inside I thought that I had just made a big mistake. It was the, "yes, you do," part that had me worried. Mickey swatted me with his towel and kicked me in the butt on my way past him.

Nothing changed during the next two days at school. In the halls, I got frowns and glowers from the football types, and I ignored them. One on one, they were no match for me, and they knew it, and besides, I had the principal backing me up. What worried me was trying to take on several of them at a time, which is how I expected they would come at me when they had an opportunity. My biggest fear is that they would harm Mary to get at me. I made sure to walk her home every afternoon, even if I missed track practice. I loved that this put us back together, and we made sure to touch our shoulders together often as we walked. She asked me if I had any problems with any of them, and I answered that I had not. She was reassured and happy that it was over. I knew that it wasn't.

The third day things changed. I noticed that the football team was avoiding me. No more glares, in fact, no eye contact at all. I couldn't have found them if I tried. Something had happened, making the entire team go into hiding. From a distance I saw Monster and Butch walking together with their heads down. I could see the white nose splint on Butch even from a distance. At least they weren't dead. The last class ended, and I got hit with a small spitball from the rear. It was Phillip signaling me to wait for him.

When everyone else had left but us, he moved close and said quietly, "Did you hear what happened yesterday?"

"I haven't heard anything. Most of the guys are afraid of me, and all the girls want to go out with me. What happened?"

"After football practice, the bunch who always leave together in Frog's car were cornered by two slick-looking guys who had switchblades. They were told that they had a friend who was being bothered, and they wanted it to stop. After they were let go, they found Monster's dog in the back seat of Frog's car. It had been cut in half the long way! Blood was everywhere! I heard that they all got sick and had to have their parents come and get them. Is this connected to the dance? Are you the friend?" Phillip was breathless but couldn't help smiling about his story.

"I had nothing to do with it, Phillip. They all act so badly that one of them probably pissed off the wrong person. It could have been worse, you know."

Phillip's eyes rolled at the idea. "Yeah, it could have been one of them in the backseat split open from head to end. How do you guess they could have done that?"

"I don't know, and I don't want to know. It's got nothing to do with me," I said, but I knew better. It was lucky that it wasn't one of the high school kids cut open. The mob plays for keeps. What had I done?

Whatever was in store for me from my mob connection was unknown, but at least, any other worries were over for a while. Mary and I were as close as ever, and after the display at the dance, I didn't have to worry about boys moving in on her. The stories told about it pushed my reputation through the roof, and girls sought me out incessantly. About a week after the event with the dog, we were walking home and noticed a squad car slowly following us. When I turned around, they signaled us to stop. When we did, a patrolman and a man with a suit got out and walked up to us.

"Your name Mike Condor?" the man in the suit asked.

"Yes, sir," I said.

"Did you have anything to do with the butchered dog in the car last week?"

"No, sir. I was at school all day, walked home with my sister and spent the evening at home," I said truthfully.

"We were told that you had a run in with those same boys only three days earlier. Is that correct?"

"Yes, sir."

"Do you have any explanation for this connection?" the plainclothes man asked.

"I don't know anything about the dog. I had nothing to do with it."

"Do you know a man called Shark Cohen?"

"He hangs around the boxing club where I train."

"Look, son, we know what happened and why. I want to tell you that this is real bad company you are keeping. In case you don't know it yet, they do you a favor and then expect you to do them one. Only it won't be one. They will try to suck you into the organization and then you'll know too much about them to ever be allowed to quit the mob. You'll end up either dead or just like them. We checked you out. You are a fine young man, and when you took those two knuckleheads down, you had good reason. The follow-up by the mob was over the top. I'm warning you, son, to get away from them while you can."

"Here is how it happened, sir. They came looking for us that night. A whole carful of them. The principal saw them too…ask him. The next day I asked Mr. Cohen if he had any ideas of what I should do. I know that that was a mistake now, but I didn't ask for any harm to come to those boys, and I didn't ask Mr. Cohen to do anything. I just wanted advice."

"What the hell did you think he was going to do, go to church and pray for you? Don't be stupid here. Surely you suspected that he was going to get rough. You are lucky that they didn't kill those two or even the whole team. If they had, I would be arresting you now instead of talking to you."

I felt the blood draining from my face. Mary noticed and reached under my arm to give me some support. After a moment of recovery and reflection, I said, "Sir, given what you just said, I promise that I'll quit boxing and stay away from that place. Thanks for the advice."

"That's good, son, but keep your fingers crossed that it will be that simple. If they want you, they will come and find you. Here is my card. If you need us, just give me a call, and I'll see what can be done. Looking at your sister, here, I would bet that they will use her to get you to do anything in the world they want you to do. Good luck, son, and I really mean it."

We were both shaken by that conversation, and we wanted to run away. I had made a terrible mistake, and I was sure that more was to come. We helped each other home, and I went to bed early, missing supper that night.

I did quit going to the club, as I said I would, and it worked out as it had to anyway. Father was missing work because of chronic illness, first one thing then another, and our family income was slipping. He always wanted us to have every possible opportunity and never required either of us to work. Times change, and now it was time for me to step up and help. I told Mother in confidence that I would work, and the money I made would pay for Mary's dance lessons. She agreed not to tell Mary or Father. It was to be our secret.

I started with afternoon deliveries of groceries, carried in my bicycle basket. It was hard work, and the pay was so low that I couldn't pay for new tires for the bicycle. After a couple of months, I got a part-time job as a grease monkey at a service station. The pay was a little better, but grease gets embedded into your skin, under your nails, and of course, ruins any clothing.

We parted company with the tenth grade for summer, and I was able to work full-time during the day. Father got a little better and resumed going to his job, and Mary continued her dancing and got more beautiful by the day. I looked forward to getting up in the mornings just so I could see her at breakfast. Father occupied the newspaper, and the only thing that had my attention was Mary. I think it was at these morning gatherings that I fully took in femininity. It's a whole package, that thing called a woman. They are graceful, compassionate, intelligent and so beautiful. The most wonderful package ever created was having breakfast right beside me every morning with her shiny gold hair swaying slightly, like a hypnotic charm.

Mary started to work part-time in a dress shop. She did some modeling for them and was also being taught the art of making clothing. In some ways, it was like I had grown up and had my own family. I worked hard, coming home to let the women repair me for the next day. I didn't think about school or boxing, having put all that behind me. One day, late that summer, I rode my bicycle back home from the service station job, taking my time about it, when, just ahead, I recognized an unpleasant and unexpected sight. Shark was standing outside his Cadillac, leaning on the hood, watching me come toward him. There was a beefy younger man with him, wearing an untucked dark shiny shirt and long slick black hair. I braked, stopping just short of them.

"Hi, kid. Long time no see," Shark said, blowing a smoke ball into the air. He smiled the familiar gold-tooth smile. "How ya doing, kid?"

"Hi, Mr. Cohen," I said.

"Working hard, kid? I mean, covered with grease like you are, I expect so," Shark chuckled. The tough standing nearby laughed.

"Thanks for the help that time, Mr. Cohen. They never bothered us again," I said.

"No problem, kid. It's what friends do. Glad to help you out." I didn't respond to the last remark and sort of stood there waiting to see what he actually wanted.

"Say, kid. What's the pay like for what you do?" Shark asked. The other fellow laughed again.

"Well, I get three dollars for the full-time work."

"You mean three dollars an hour, don't you, kid?

"No, sir. I mean three dollars a day." He showed mock surprise, and they both had a good laugh. Shark took a long drag and blew another smoke ball.

"Look, kid, I'd sure like to help you out a little bit with money. How would you like to make a clean fifty bucks tonight for not much work?" Shark asked. They were both silent and serious now.

"That's a lot of money, Mr. Cohen. What do you want me to do?" I asked.

"Nuttin to it, kid. All you have to do is pick up a package and deliver it across town. You can use your bike if you want. Easy and no danger," Shark said and smiled.

"I have to tell you, Mr. Cohen, that I encountered Detective Smith after our last talk. He seemed to know all about the whole thing and told me to stay away from you. That's partly why I haven't been back to the club since."

"Oh, the crummy coppers always say that sort of bull. You and me, kid, are friends. I do something for you, and you do something in return. This is the return. I want you to do this for your friend." He looked serious and his young tough stood up and put his hands in his pockets.

"If I do this for you..are we square then?" I asked.

"Sure, kid. We'll be square, and you'll have fifty to spend. No sweat." He grinned at me.

I knew that I had no options. They didn't say it, but the threat was there, plain enough. It didn't seem so bad to just transport his package to get out of my bondage. Then the fifty bucks sounded good also. "Okay, Mr. Cohen."

"Good choice, kid," he said, then wiggled his finger at the tough punk standing at the ready. "Spiny, tell the kid what he needs to know."

Spiny came around the hood to my bike and leaned real close. There were no other people around so I assumed that his body language was serving as an additional threat.

"Here's da plan. Ya pick up a package behind Twelfth Street Liquors...know where dat is?...and be dere xactly at ten tonight. Dey will be expecting ya. Don't open da package, got it? Then deliver it to the Memorial Park cross town. Be fast. Someone will be there and pay ya off. Got dat?"

I had no idea what I was going to tell the folks about going out that late on a bicycle. This was obviously something either dangerous or illegal or both. The distance across town was in miles so this whole event would keep me out most of the night. Well, for once and for all, I would be rid of Shark and his hoodlums. I resolved to do it. "Yes, I got it. Don't open the package, right?"

"Do dis, kid, and ya in good standin. Another ting. Watch out for da cops, and don't get caught. If ya see dem coming, toss the package. Got it?" They both slapped me on the back on the way past, and I rode home with a stomach ache.

Mary saw me come in, and her expression changed. She knew me inside and out and always knew when something was up. "Want to tell me about it, Mike?" she asked.

"After supper, if I can eat supper," I said and went to my room and closed the door, flopping on the bed. I lay there looking at the ceiling in my soiled clothes trying to think this out. Should I call Detective Smith and tell him? I figured that there was no evidence of any wrongdoing, and Shark and Spiny would get me for ratting on them. Dangerous. It could be just a test to see if I would actually work for them, or it could be a trap to get me arrested and beholden to the mob who would probably get me out of jail. I resolved to do what they asked but not get caught. This would be the last time, however. I sprang to my feet and headed for the shower.

During the meal, Mary sought out my eyes without much success. She reached under the table and held my hand in hers for a short time. The touch of her skin felt better than anything I could imagine, and it struck me what powerful emotions can be transmitted by touch alone. I couldn't even contemplate life without Mary. After dinner, we sat alone in the kitchen and talked. I told her the story, sparing no detail, and she was horrified.

"Oh, Mike, I am so scared. It's all about me. If I didn't go to the dance this whole thing wouldn't have happened. Look what I have done to you. You ended up being the school bully just to protect me. Now crime. I'm not worth that." She began to cry and couldn't look at me.

I reached across the table and took her wrists in my hands. "I would do anything for you, Mary. To me, you are the most important person in the world. It is my privilege to be around you and keep you safe. I don't regret a moment of it, and I believe that I was put on earth just for you, and I am grateful for it."

That was too much for her, and she collapsed onto the table weeping. I came around and knelt beside her. "Don't Mary. I need you to help give me an alibi for tonight. First, we need to keep this secret. I plan to leave after Father and Mother go to bed, and I don't know when I will get back so don't wait up for me. You have my promise that I'll come into your room when I return and tell you what happened. It will be up to you to concoct a cover story if our parents find out I was out all night. Next, if any policemen investigate this, you have to swear that I was here all night. Will you do that?"

"Of course," she said.

At nine, I went to my room and closed my door. Our parents routinely retired before ten, and around nine thirty, I left by the window. It was an unusually dark night, and I had problems finding my bicycle without making any noise. I was smart enough to wear a dark pullover sweatshirt, and in the dark I made my way carefully across town toward Twelfth Street. There were scattered street lights functioning which helped, and when I got two blocks from Twelfth Street Liquors, I got off the bike and ventured into the alley. I didn't own a watch, at least a reliable one, but I knew I was close to being on time. Ahead, I saw something move in the shadows, and I stopped abruptly. The shadow came toward me in a threatening way, and I froze.

"Hi, bub," the large man said, continuing to advance toward me. "Your name Mike?" he asked.

"Yeah," I answered.

"Been expecting you," the raspy voice said. "You are gonna pick-up and drop-off, ain't you?"

"That was what I was told."

He dropped something heavy in my bicycle basket, "There it is. Now get over to the park and drop it off."

"Who am I supposed to meet?" I asked.

"I got no idea. You'll figure it out when you get there. Now take off and make it snappy."

Pushing off, I made my way clumsily down the dark alley. A quick look behind assured me that the large shadow was still standing there watching me. I took a couple of quick turns, settling on a street going north in the general direction of the park. It was necessary to stop and get off to look closely at a sign to be sure where I was headed. Each time I saw headlights in the distance, I left the road and became obscure until they passed. One such time, I picked up the package. It was rectangular and about the shape you would expect of a large stack of paper money, five inches tall wrapped in paper and tied with a string. This whole business was illegal, and I knew it. Just touching the package I was probably breaking the law, but wasn't sure exactly how. I continued to make progress until one episode when I was a little slow getting off the road. That was the moment the policemen probably caught a glimpse of me, and when their car reached my position, the searchlight came on. Before their spotlight lit me up, I tossed the package into a big bush and then just stood there, innocently waiting.

"You! Come out into the open," a deep voice commanded, and I readily complied, walking my bike toward the patrol car. The one in the passenger seat got out and looked me over with his flashlight. "You look like a high school boy. What are you doing out this late, and why were you hiding?"

"I made some enemies at school, and I didn't want to caught out alone. It was better to hide," I answered, somewhat truthfully.

"Where do you live?" the one with the flashlight in my face demanded.

"22 North Elm."

"Well, boy, that is the other way. You lost or something?"

"No, sir, I was taking the long way so they couldn't find me." While the close one kept his light in my face, the other one was searching the area I came out of with his light. Luckily, he missed the package.

"Nothing here, Bill," the searcher said.

"What's your name, boy?" the first one asked.

"Mike Condor." He wrote it down in his notebook.

"Okay, Mike. Now go home, and it's that way," he said, pointing in the other direction.

I told them thanks and headed back the way I had come. They watched me for a while, and then slowly drove away. I turned around and raced back to pick up the package. This time I was more alert and got off that street at the next block. The rest of the trip was tiring but uneventful. I had no idea what time it was, but the town was nearly deserted and most of the house lights were off.

The park was just ahead and dead dark. I got off the bike and walked with it into the park, trying to make no sound. After a few hundred yards, the road turned, and I had to feel the edge with my feet, because I couldn't see it. Suddenly, I was captured by bright headlights from a parked car just ahead of me. My blood suddenly ran cold, and I figured the cops had caught me right out in the open with the package. I was done for. The car started up, moving toward me, and I just stood in place helplessly watching the lights get closer.

When the big car got alongside, the window rolled down, and I could see the glowing end of a cigarette. "Well, kid, have the package?" Shark asked. I handed it to him through the window. "You did good, kid. Any problems?"

"I was stopped by the cops about a mile from here, but I did like you said and tossed the package. They didn't find it and let me go."

Shark was quiet for a moment and then asked, "They get your name?"

"Yes, and my address."

"You are still pretty dumb, kid. Never give them your real name, understand?" Shark said sharply.

"What happens if they catch me lying?" I asked.

"The thing is to not get caught, kid. Here's your fifty." He handed a folded wad of bills to me and then drove off leaving me in the darkness. I put the money in my shoe and then started making my way home, being careful to avoid anyone seeing me. By the time I got there, the edge of dawn was creeping up to the edge of night off to the east. Easing back through my window, I sprawled on the bed, dead tired and smelly from nerves. I felt unable to move and then my door slowly opened. It was Mary.

"I heard you come in. Thank goodness you are finally back," she whispered. She put her hand on my forehead and quickly pulled it back. "You are soaking wet. Why don't you go shower before Father gets up."

"Was I missed?" I asked.

"I didn't hear anything, so I don't think so. Everything go all right?"

I reached into my shoe on the floor and pulled out the wad of cash and handed it to her, then laid back down. She counted the cash.

"There is fifty dollars here. How did you get it?"

"They paid me for tonight. All I did was ride my bike for miles and miles and give Shark a package. I have no idea what was in it, and now I am done with them. I want you to keep the money. I don't want it."

"It takes Father a week to bring home this much money. You keep it because you earned it," Mary said and offered the money back to me.

"No, Mary. The only way I'll feel good about this is to see you use it for something that will make you happy. Buy clothes, shoes or anything you want with it. If I were to use it, I would just be reminded of the whole dirty business, but it will give me pleasure if it will buy something you want. Don't argue with me, I'm too tired for it." She silently slid the cash into her robe and briefly stroked my hair, leaving without another word.

Starting school in the fall, I soon forgot the whole affair. No one at school had forgotten us, the school beauty and the school bully. We could tell by the looks. I determined once again to best everybody, at least at grades. Father was holding his own so I stopped working at the garage, usually staying at school in the afternoons to practice with the track and field team. I had gotten behind because of working at the garage while the rest continued to train together all summer. There was also another dance coming up, and while Mary didn't mention it, Phillip did.

He caught me in the hall one day, "Mike, do you remember that you agreed to let me take Mary out on occasion?" He grinned at me and waited for my answer as others passed us on both sides.

"What occasion, Phillip," I asked, knowing the answer in advance.

"There is a dance in two weeks, Mike. Are you going?"

"Hadn't thought much about it. Have you asked Mary?"

"No, Mike. I thought I would first clear it with you."

"Yes, Phillip, you can ask her but only on the condition that I go also. You remember what happened last time? Want to be there without me?" I asked, also knowing the answer.

"Are you asking Frieda?" he inquired, ignoring my second question.

"I haven't talked with Frieda since that night. She might not want to go out with the likes of me again.

"Sure she will, Mike, and if she doesn't, I hear that you could probably take your pick of any girl in school." He grinned at me, and I cuffed him on the ear.

He was right that I had lots of choices, but if Mary had to get clearance from me to go out, I had to let her do the same thing for me. While I was walking to my class, I noticed several of the girls giving me a little wave as we passed. Sure, I found some them attractive, but something was broken inside of me that caused me not to pursue any of them. I was aware that I was actively trying to suppress my desire for girls. Frieda had been wisely chosen by Mary, because I didn't have to suppress any desire for her. I felt that life was passing me by in some ways. There was an emotional part of me which was not developing, and it worried me. All that energy that the other boys put into developing a relationship with a girl, I put into my studies or into my muscles. I was pulling ahead of them in those fields, but they seemed happy, and I was not. I missed boxing, because I found that I could trade hitting someone for passion. So far, the only time I was ever kissed on the lips by a girl was when we were eight and had our snowman wedding. I needed to hug and be hugged, kiss and be kissed, but I would feel that there was a betrayal of sorts if I found someone who would do it. I imagined, and frankly hoped, that Mary had the same feelings. The other part of me refused to think the unthinkable, that I wanted to kiss Mary and not anyone else. My mind was thinking it without my permission, and my subconscious was churning with it, but I steadfastly refused to allow such images into my awake mind.

You shouldn't be blamed for your dreams, however. What goes on after you are asleep, you can't control and are not responsible for, and no one knows but you what happens when you dream. I would be embarrassed to tell you what mine consisted of, but they were recurrent and had the same theme, and I frequently and uncomfortably remembered them the next day. I think, looking back, it was how I got through the days. I lived for my dreams.

We were standing outside the gymnasium, waiting for my date to show. Mary had used some of the money I gave her to purchase a stunning gown from the dress shop that employed her the previous summer. She was standing next to Phillip, showcasing the vast difference between a young woman and a little boy. Phillip was dressed nicely, but his eyes projected immaturity where hers were steady and confident. Once again, Mary had chosen my date, and this time, she was someone whom I had never seen. She was a newcomer to school and had quickly made friends with Mary. Her name was Janel Cicero, and in Mary's eyes, she was attractive and well-bred. Armed with that information, I still didn't know what to expect when she arrived. Several members of the football team with their dates passed right in front of us without a glance or comment. I was poison as far at they were concerned, and what had happened last year was history recorded in blood and stone.

A long black car smoothly pulled to the curb, and the driver emerged dressed in a grey suit with brass buttons. A chauffeur! He came around, opened the door and extended his hand for the occupant. As the girl emerged, I heard Mary catch her breath. Some of the students stopped to watch this spectacle as a gorgeous young woman in a shimmering dress got out. The dress emphasized her full bosom, small waist and her long, strawberry hair. She wore a small white corsage already pinned to her strap while the piece of jewelry in her hair caught the light, reflecting a dazzling rainbow of color.

"That's Janel," Mary said in a low voice. She gave me a push on my shoulder in Janel's direction and reluctantly, I stumbled toward her.

"You must be Janel," I said extending my arm. "I'm Mike Condor."

Janel gave me a slight sideways nod of her head and smiled a brilliant smile as she turned fully to face me. "I've heard a lot about you, Mike. This will be my pleasure, I assure you." Her voice was melodious, graceful, just like the rest of her. I couldn't understand why Mary chose this girl for me, but like everyone in sight, I was captivated. I felt too young, naive and underdressed to be with her, clearly out of my element.

"At this moment, Janel, I feel like the luckiest kid in the world. You look wonderful." She smiled and then acknowledged Mary and Phillip with a nod, taking my offered arm. We walked into the gymnasium like royalty, followed by my sister and her date. The crowd seemed to part for us, and the murmurs were like summer locusts in the forest. The live band had started, and we walked to the center of the floor, which opened like magic. I glanced over my shoulder at Mary and saw the furrow between her eyes. Whatever was happening was something she didn't expect. I put my hand at the small of Janel's back, holding her right hand, as we started swaying to the music. She looked up at me with her perpetual smile and never looked away. As we danced, she moved closer and closer to me until we were touching at the chest and hips. The lights played in her shiny perfumed hair. I couldn't help it. I became aroused. I'm very sure that Janel could tell, and she pushed against me even harder.

"Janel, could we sit this next one out and just talk?" I asked.

"Of course, Mike. Would you like me to walk in front of you?" she asked with devil in her eyes.

"If you wouldn't mind," I thankfully said. She didn't mind at all, skilfully blocked any view of my pant's front as we made our way to the chairs against the wall. I felt burning in the back of my head as all eyes followed us across the dance floor. After we sat down, I could see Mary looking in our direction as poor Phillip made an effort to dance with her.

I searched for something to say to Janel to change the obvious subject. "Janel, are you from around here?"

"Yes, but I just changed schools, that's all."

"Why did you leave the other school?" I asked.

"Personal reasons, Mike," Janel answered. I decided to let the issue drop.

"I feel immature around you, Janel."

"You feel like a man to me," she said and grinned. I could see Mary leading Phillip, as they headed our way.

"You are incredibly beautiful, Janel. I hope I don't disappoint you tonight."

"So far, you are full of surprises. Just keep it up," she giggled and flicked her eyes below my waist. I was returning to normal and just in time, because Mary was standing just in front of us. I could tell that she would like to know why we sat down and was waiting for some kind of response.

"Mary, you two should be out there dancing. We'll join you in a little while. I just didn't like the number they were playing, so I asked Mike to sit down a moment," Janel said with a calm voice and smiled innocently up at them. Phillip gave us a thumbs up and gently put his arm around Mary as they walked away. He gave me a backward look to be sure I wasn't getting angry with him.

"Ready to try again, Mike?" Janel whispered in my ear. Even that minimal contact almost did me in, and I shook my head no. She just sat there looking at me and then asked, "What's the deal with you and Mary? Everyone talks about you two, and nobody appears to be able to figure it out. Want to tell me?"

"There isn't any story there. We are twins, and we have always looked out for each other. Call it mutual admiration or brotherly love or something. I feel protective of her as she does for me."

Janel raised her eyebrows, "I've seen brothers and sisters before, and they tolerate each other. They sure don't have that kind of feeling for their sibling, and I don't think I have ever seen the affection you two have before now."

"Are you saying there is something wrong with the way I feel about Mary?"

"It's worrisome and the subject of gossip. I'm sorry, but I have to ask you. Have you two ever been, you know, physical?"

"If you were male, I'd take a swing at you. No, no, no. There has never been any physical contact between us, and there never will be. I love Mary, but not that way. Does that answer your question?"

"Yes, it does. Now I have to tell you something," Janel whispered into my ear.

"Okay," I whispered back toward the floor.

"I plan to make you mine, completely mine. That idea excite you?"

"Honestly, Janel, any more excitement, and they will have to carry me away on a stretcher. Face down. Why in the world do you want me?"

"Well, let's see. You are handsome, smart, tough, and, oh yes, you are the most talked about and sought after boy in school. Yes, that covers it." She smiled again at me, imprinting her beautiful face into my mind. She let what she said soak in for a moment then put her hand softly on my shoulder. "Feeling conquested yet?"

"Now, I want to ask you a question. Can I get a truthful straight answer?" I asked.

She puckered her lips and laughed. Was this a yes or no? I decided to ask and see what she said. "What did you do to get Mary to agree to us going out together?"

"Mary has to agree? I didn't know that," and laughed again.

I could see that I was just getting in deeper, so I let it drop. They were playing a jazzy number which didn't involve hugging or touching, and I got up and nodded toward the dance floor, extending my hand to her. She sprang to her feet and pulled me into the crowd. She was very good, probably as good as Mary, and others started watching her dance. I swung her around, and she spun in place and just as quickly came back into perfect form. When she extended her neck and looked up, her long hair flowed in a mesmerizing stream behind her. She was really too good for me to enable her to show off her best dancing. The band suddenly switched to a slow number, and she slowly pulled me in close to her, keeping steady eye contact. If you could get drunk by proximity with a girl like Janel, I was plastered. There was no other way to describe it but mountains of sex appeal. I was being drawn in like a nail to a magnet. This girl was aware of every possible allure that women possess and understood how to use them all. I glanced again at Mary, and sure enough, she was alertly watching. Phillip was concentrating on his own dancing and didn't know anything beyond his feet at the moment. Janel moved into tight contact with me and put both arms around my waist so that she could press her pelvis against me while we danced. It was too much, and I started sweating.

"Do you think Mary would approve?" Janel asked and winked. I felt a tendency toward recurrence of my previous problem and moved away from her.

"What about a glass of punch?" I asked, leading her toward the crowd gathered at the punch bowl.

"Didn't you enjoy dancing with me, Mike?" she asked. She knew the answer and insisted on teasing me as we made our way past the dancers to the refreshment area. The group parted silently for us, and I heard a few giggles. Surely, they couldn't have seen my problem, I hoped.

One of the guys came up to us as I poured our drinks and asked, "Having a problem, Mike? I would be glad to take her off your hands." I turned to see Jimmy Hays, the school's top basketball player, gawking at Janel who was returning his look.

Before I could come up with an answer, Janel did, "I'm not changing partners. Find someone else." She wasn't smiling, and the curt response was enough for Jimmy, who spun around without another word. Janel put her arm under mine and smiled at me to demonstrate the exclusion of others nearby. We all got the message. I was hers. Mary, what have you done?

Could it be that I was the only boy in the nation who would be distressed by having a stunning girl aggressively pursue him? I was torn between running away or taking her in my arms. Doubtless, I was a novice at all things concerning women, because after all, I had been only kissed once previously and that was when I was eight and in front of our mother. I didn't know what Janel wanted or how far she was willing to go, but clearly, she was not a novice at anything. She was like a twenty something, and I was closer to a ten something. I was profoundly physically attracted to her, and it sure seemed that she was attracted to me. It struck me that I could look at Janel and admire her in a physical way without feeling any guilt about it. Here was God's gift to mankind right in front of me, and I could touch her and hug her, and there was no wrong in it. All the yearning for Mary that I wouldn't face or admit had built up inside of me like an explosive force. It suddenly seemed that I could see the world more clearly, and this girl was helping to bring my repressed feelings out into the open. I took her arm and led her back onto the dance floor. This time I felt my fear drain away, and when I touched her hand and waist, things were different. I pulled her close, pressing her face against my chest as we danced, and for a moment, time stood still.

I admit to having a marvelous time that night. Dancing every number, I was able to hold and touch a Venus without any hesitations. We were able to maneuver to the other side of the room, avoiding reproving looks from Mary. I could see her in my side vision at times, watching every move we made. In my view, she had set this date up, wanting me to have a good time, so that is exactly what I was doing. Janel never once looked away from me, and I relaxed as we moved to the music, sparkles from the overhead globe playing on our faces. The band played the last number to loud applause from the crowd, and then the principal announced the dance to be officially over.

Janel gave me a powerful hug and said, "If you come with me, I can have the driver take the long way home. There is a glass behind him, and we can do anything we desire in the back seat."

For a young innocent like me, this was the offer of a lifetime. No matter how long you live, an opportunity like this will only come once. I was taken aback by her forward manner, and I looked away from her just in time to see Mary and Phillip headed our way. Lovely, graceful Mary. One look at her face, and I knew again how much I loved her. Those eyes and mine locked for only a split second, but it was enough. I wouldn't trade a frolic in the backseat with Janel for a single quiet moment shoulder to shoulder with Mary.

"I can't do it, Janel. Tonight has been the single best night in my life, and it was all about you. It would be better if we don't go too far the first time we meet and ruin the rest of what could turn out to be a great friendship."

For a moment, I thought she was going to cry, but she recovered quickly. "I'll make things happen to you in that backseat that you will remember the rest of eternity."

The way she said it, I had no doubt that what she said would be true. Again, I felt like a little boy, not a man around her. I just wasn't ready for that yet.

"Let's go out and wait for your ride," I suggested, changing the subject. I almost felt that I had let her down. She had offered me paradise, and I rejected her. After all her efforts that night, she had failed to completely reel me in. She looked away from me for the first time, and we headed out the double doors toward the curb. I glanced at her and saw a tear running down her cheek, ripping a pink slot through her makeup. She turned back to me and gave me a quick smile and a hug around the waist.

"Mike, you are the real thing. You are honorable. So far, I have never met anyone as pure as you are. I want to tell you that meeting you tonight makes me realize what I never had and probably never will have. If only I had met you years ago, and you could love me like you love Mary. I would give anything for that." The long black car purred nearly silently to the entrance, and the driver came out again. I hardly noticed him and concentrated on Janel's mesmerizing face as she prepared to leave. After the door closed, hiding her from my view, I glanced at the driver and saw the grinning face of Spiny, otherwise known as Gerald Spinnazzo, the Shark's boy. He gave me a quick semi-salute and a tug on his hat brim, and the car floated away.

The three of us walked back home through the darkness. Mary in the middle, flanked by me and Phillip. I was in no mood to see Phillip's arm around Mary, and fortunately, Phillip seemed to know it and didn't try. We walked in silence the four blocks to Phillip's home. When we arrived, I could tell that Phillip wanted to steal a kiss from Mary. He stammered and appeared agitated. We just stood calmly and waited for him to get something out of his system.

"Gee, guys, I had a good time tonight. Thanks, Mary, for being such a good dancer. Someday, I'll keep up with you." There was a long agonizing pause, but his courage failed him. "Well, goodnight then. I expect I'll see you tomorrow, and thanks again." He headed up the porch stairs with slumped shoulders, and we turned to walk the remaining three blocks back home. I noticed that Mary's shoulder occasionally brushed mine, seemingly intentionally.

"Have a good time tonight, Mary?" I asked.

"No. What about you?" she said quickly.

"I'm sorry that you didn't have a good time. Was it something I did?"

"It was something that I did and regretted it all night," she said.

She didn't need to say more, because I knew that it was because she set up the date with Janel for me. I didn't want to rub it in by telling her that I had a good time until the last moment. Seeing Spiny at the end crushed me and removed all the good feeling that I had about the evening. I was left with the hollow feeling of sexual lust after the act. We walked in silence for a while with just the sound of our shoes on the pavement.

"Mary, how did you meet Janel?"

"She seemed to find me. Sought me out after starting school. She is new there and needed someone to show her around. It didn't take her long to find out about my brother. She seemed nice and didn't wear any makeup. She looked so innocent. She said that she spent much of her time on the farm. I thought that you would like her, and you sure seemed to."

"I guess that she looked different tonight, huh?" I asked.

"She sure did. I had no idea that she had any money. Even a limousine with chauffeur. Did you find out any more about her?" Mary asked.

"Not much other than she seems to know her way around the block. I need to find out more about her, in case our paths cross again."

"It would make me happy if I didn't see her again. I feel that I was used," Mary said.

"We both were, Mary. This probably is not over. I have a bad feeling about it."

In the darkness and without any words, we put our arms around each other's waist and walked home with our shoulders touching.

Things came back to normal quickly in the coming days, and we were back into our routine. Mary went to her dance classes, and I ran with a pack of sweaty boys every afternoon. After practice, I usually rode my bicycle home or walked. There was one day that seemed brooding and threatening. The sky was darker than usual, and there was a puffing cold wind as I made my way on my bicycle past parked cars. Ahead, I saw the flare of a match and the glow of a cigarette from someone standing beside his car waiting...on me. I had the sinking feeling that I knew who it was before I could see his face. The Shark. He was intently watching me. I pulled up and stopped.

"Hi, kid," he said and blew a puff a smoke at me. "Long time no see." I didn't respond at all, because whatever he wanted it wasn't good. "Say, kid, did you have a good time with Janel the other night? Have you thought of what you missed not riding in the car with her?"

"Sure, Mr. Cohen. I thought about it a lot. In fact, it is about all I have thought about since then. Is she your girl or something?"

"Mine, personally? No," he laughed and blew some more smoke. "The little dish started working at The Farm part-time a couple of years ago, and now she has become one of the main attractions. You really messed up, kid.

They say that she will really light you up if she likes you, and believe me, she really liked you."

"I felt the same way about her, Mr. Cohen. Was she working for you that night?" I asked.

"It was my way of sending a little pleasure your way, kid. You remember the fifty you got last time you worked? Well, there is a lot more of that action you can get if you want it. Plus, you can have Janel any time you desire. She'll do anything you ask, kid, and you can get it any time of day or night and as often as you want. Free. That interest you?"

"I'd be lying if I said no, Mr. Cohen, but I don't think that is what I should do at the moment."

"You are a strange kid, Mike. Might be that you need your nuts tightened a bit, if you pardon the expression. By the way, you did good that night with the delivery. Find it thrilling?"

"Mostly tiring and scary, Mr. Cohen."

"Let you in on a secret, kid. You were only carrying a brick. We couldn't trust you with anything valuable until we saw that you would follow through. Next time is for real, though."

"Next time? I thought you said that would even us out. Debt paid and all that."

"Yeah, I said that. Problem is that you were only being tested, and it didn't count. Plus, there is Janel, and even if you didn't taste the merchandise, you still bought it. You owe me another one, kid."

"I didn't ask for Janel, Mr. Cohen. And I didn't know it was only a brick. In fact, I don't know that it was a brick. I don't want to do any more runs."

"Here is where I need to set you straight, kid. Perception is fact. The cops spotted you and have your name. All I need to do is let them know that you were delivering for me, and they will make a folder. Ever heard of a rap sheet? You will have one even if it was a brick you were carrying. As for Janel, word will get around that you brought a pro to a high school dance. No girl in town will date you after they hear that. You might as well go have your fun with Janel, because that will be all you will ever get in this town and, by the way, you are working for us whether you want to or not."

"What are you going to do if I refuse?" I asked.

"Are you kidding me? Think about it, kid. You are not the only person I can have my way with. You have family, right? Come to think about it, I hear you have a real bombshell sister. Want them involved? No, you don't. Come in with us, kid, and we'll have you swimming in cash and women. What more could you want? Think of this as a career move."

"I'll think about it," I said.

"You be at the boxing club tomorrow night at six. If you don't show, I'll send Spiny to fetch you. You hear me?" There was a lot of malice in the way he said that, and it gave me a shiver.

"I hear you."

"Fine. And I'll tell Janel to get ready to give you a good time. See ya, kid."

There was no choice, and I was at the boxing club at six the next night as ordered. I walked into the familiar sounds and sights, catching Mickey's eye from across the room. He stood erect and gave the palms up sign for "what's up?" I scanned the large room and sure enough, Shark and Spiny were huddled in the corner with a muscular fighter dressed in his shiny boxing trunks. Shark spotted me and waved me over.

"Well, kid, good thing you showed up," Shark said and showed his gold teeth to me. "This is King, one of our young prize fighters. King, meet Mike."

King stuck out his gloved hand and whacked me on the back and smiled through his mouthguard. I said, "Good to meet you too, King."

Shark stood up and put his hands on both our shoulders. "Kids, I want you two to get in the ring and go a couple of rounds for us to see what you got."

I said, "Mr. Cohen, I haven't been in training for several months. I'm sort of out of shape for boxing right now."

"Ain't no matter, kid," he said. "I ain't expecting you to win. Go a few rounds with my boy here, just for fun."

I looked more carefully at King this time. He was lean and fit and about three or four inches taller than me. He had a nose that was pushed to one side and thick ears, all signs of a professional who had a lot of fights behind him. The other thing that I saw was in his eyes. He was mean and tough. I was about to get a terrible beating from King. Shark and Spiny smiled at me, because they were about to teach me a lesson in obedience. They saw this as retribution for me talking back at Shark last night. There was nowhere to run and hide from them. I was going to be a member of the mob, like it or not. Shark waved at Mickey across the room and summoned him over. Mickey threw down a towel in an angry way as he went around the ring toward us.

When Mickey got close enough, Shark said, "Mickey, fix the kid up with some gear. They are going to put on a show for us."

Mickey sputtered, "Show! You know this young lad is no match for a pro. They aren't even in the same weight class. You can't do this."

"I don't remember asking permission from my daddy, Mickey. Just do it and spare me the lip," Shark growled.

"Come on, Mike, and let's see what we have that will fit you," Mickey said, while we walked toward the dressing area. When we were out of earshot, Mickey leaned toward me, "You're going to get creamed, Mike. You remember that I told you to stay away from them? Now you are going to find out why." We continued around the corner, and Mickey picked through his supply of trunks, shoes and gloves. When he finished, he pushed them at me and said, "One thing I can tell you that might help is this. King is tough and has a long reach, but he has a weak point that I haven't been able to get him to correct. He can be taken out by an undercut, because he never protects for that. You catch him with a good one, and the fight is yours. Get in close and come up inside, connecting on his chin as hard as you can. Either fist will do. Remember that." I nodded that I understood, and I tried to calm myself down as I put on the gear. Mickey wrapped my hands with tape before tying the gloves down, then slapped me on the back. "Good luck, Mike. You're going to need it."

The lights came on, and the boxing ring was standing there like an icon or alter from a distant age. The only thing missing was drifting cigarette smoke and yelling fans. We climbed in from opposite sides. No referee. We would be on our own, especially me. Mickey rang the bell, and we started circling, gloves up to our chin, heads down. The helmet I wore was slightly too big and kept moving over my eyes. I could tell that King was fit and ready, and he shuffled and skipped, rapidly moving from side to side, partly to warm up, partly to intimidate me. I stayed planted and moved around to keep my front to him. In a blink, the first blow landed on my gloves, pushing them back into my face with a snap. It hurt but woke me up. This fight was no demonstration but for real. King was probably told to hurt me and knock me out if he could. I ducked and dodged a couple and got the feeling back of being the target in the ring. He could outreach me, but I felt that I could hit harder than he could. I slipped one of his left jabs and came in close, and let him have a volley in the abdomen. King staggered backwards, and I saw the surprise. He wasn't going to get me easily.

"Hit him, King. What are you waiting for?" came from the sidelines outside the ring, causing King to lunge back toward me with menace on his face. I learned long ago that if someone moving toward you gets hit with a stiff left, the force is doubled. My punch connected and knocked his mouthpiece to the floor, and he fell backward against the ropes for a rebound toward me. This time he connected on my exposed forehead, and I felt and saw blood seeping into my left eye. I backed up, waiting for him to follow, and he did. He caught my left ear with a hook, and the resulting pain and throbbing were hard to ignore. I was inside, though, and remembered what Mickey told me. I put everything I had in a powerful uppercut which landed with satisfying force on King's chin. He fell backward like a tree cut with a chainsaw, landing sprawled on the mat.

The yelling from outside the ring would have awakened the dead but did little to revive King. He was out.

Mickey came rushing through the ropes and grabbed me, picking me up like a feather. "You did it, Mike! You did it! King had thirty-two fights behind him, and you took him out in the first round! You did it!" He spun me around in a circle, and I could see that King was still lying there, nobody trying to revive him. The lights were bright enough that I couldn't see Shark or Spiny, but I knew they were still there. Mickey put me down, whipping out his ever-present towel and wiped the blood from my face. I held my gloves out, and he started to unlace them just as King rolled to a sitting position. He put his glove to his face for a moment and lay back down groaning.

"You might as well stay there forever, King. You are finished. Get up and get out of here and never come back. You just let a green kid take you out," Shark screamed into the ring. King continued to lay there looking blankly at the overhead light. In a way, I felt sorry for him, but I was sure if I were laying there instead, he wouldn't give it a thought. I no longer liked boxing. It is as brutal a sport as has ever been created. Climbing down, I headed for the changing rooms, ignoring the mobsters. This day I won, but they would make sure that I would still be under their control and still have to do their bidding. But after that day, I was no longer afraid of them for myself. I was always afraid of what they could to Mary if they chose to. So far, she only got honorable mention, later that could change just as Detective Smith said it might.

After I showered, dressed and came out, they were still there, but King was gone. He must have left with only his trunks. His gloves were still in the ring. Shark said, "Quite a show, kid. You surprised us tonight, and thanks for getting rid of the deadwood, King. Good riddance. Now, you go on over to The Farm. Tell them that Shark sent you. Janel will be there waiting to get rid of any pains you might have. Take your time with her, you've earned it."

"Yeah," I said. "If you are done with me, I'm going to take off now, all right?"

"Sure, kid. We have plans for you. We'll be in touch." Shark slapped me on the back and so did Spiny. They had new respect for me now. A kid, but one who could fight.

Time passed, and I tried to forget the unpleasant things hanging over me. About a week after the event at the boxing club, Phillip came up and tapped me on the shoulder as he usually did when he felt he had important news for me. We huddled in a corner as the other students streamed by. I had to lean forward to catch his whispers.

"Know what I just heard?" Phillip asked and smiled his conspirator smile.

"Of course I don't."

"That girl you dated at the dance. Janel?"

"Yes, that's her name. Go on and tell me," I said.

"She works at The Farm! They say that she is a prostitute and that all kinds of things go on there. My father said one time that there is gambling, drinking and drugs out there, and it should be closed down. Did you know that?" Phillip asked with big eyes.

"Never been there, Phillip. I don't know anything about The Farm. I only met Janel that night and haven't seen or talked with her since. As far as I am concerned, she is a beautiful girl, and I had a good time."

"Maybe you could get me a date with Janel? Think so?" Phillip asked.

"Maybe, but if I did, you could never speak to or look at Mary again. Ever. Still want the date?" I asked.

"No, I don't think so, but thanks anyway." Phillip turned away from me, dejected. The thought of him and Janel together was sadly funny. I passed Mary in the hall going to class, and we exchanged meaningful glances. Such an amazing link! It was nearly like touching someone's brain for a second. It turned out that Phillip wasn't the only one who had heard about Janel's night work. Two other guys asked me about her and how they could link up with her. Janel never showed up for classes again after our date so I and everyone else assumed that she had returned to The Farm. The rumor that was being passed around suggested that there were several professional girls out there, but Janel was the best looking. The Shark was right. That night with Janel had stained my reputation. I think that most of my fellow students suspected that I had some kind of ongoing contact with her. That, and the legend of the slain dog the previous year, made me appear as a junior mob member. When I returned to class sporting facial bruises from my fight with King, not one person asked how I got that way. They assumed the worst, and in fairness, it was partially true. I got the injuries from my association with the mob.

I made up for it with my grades. There was no question, I had the best grades in school. The teachers delighted in calling on me, because I was always prepared and always gave a good response. I was making progress in track and field events and even won a few middle distance races. The counselor who worked with me was hinting that I might qualify for a scholarship to the University. I seemed to do my best work in the science fields, and I especially excelled at math. Unless I got some financial help, there was no way I would ever go on to college. We were getting by, but that kind of money was simply not going to show up. All the papers, and Father, said that another big war was coming to America. The Europeans and Asians were already at war, and there was constant talk of the draft for us young men. The future for the country and for me was bleak.

Mary focused on her dancing and was usually the star of any performance her group put on. Notice of her graceful movements and singular beauty on stage had even made it into the local newspaper. I could see that her future would be in the theater somewhere, someday. She too, needed to go on after high school for additional training and education. We spent hours together going over the various dance schools, their location and costs. Again, the financial requirements were beyond our means. For some reason, I never worried about my future, only hers. I realized that there were too many unknowns for me to plan for myself, but I was determined that Mary should see her dreams come true even if it meant that I worked some job just to pay for her education. My future would be taken one day at a time, and fortunately, I didn't know how hard that was going to be.

We made it through winter without hearing from any bad people. Shark, Spiny and Janel were sliding into the past for me, and I no longer worried about seeing Shark in the street waiting for me. That changed abruptly one day in May. Mary and I were walking home after school one warm sunny afternoon when we heard a car pulling up behind us. Turning, I recognized the black Caddy belonging to Shark. I urged Mary to walk ahead, and gave her a little push in the back to speed her away from whatever was in that car. Too late. The driver's door opened, and Spiny emerged, all slicked down as usual.

"Hey, if it isn't the fighter and his good-looking sister. Hey wait up, ya two. I wants a word wit ya." Mary hesitated, in spite of my effort to spare her this encounter, and we both turned to face this brute from the gutter.

Over the winter, I had gained a couple of inches in height and about twenty pounds since Spiny last saw me, making me a close match in size with him. I walked toward him, knowing that I could intimidate him, since he saw first hand what I did to poor King. There were no smiles from me that day, and since he chose to be that close to Mary, he would have to bear the consequences. He immediately saw the danger and gave a little Italian shrug.

"Hey, man, I jus wanted to say hello to an old friend. No risk to ya and the lady. Be calm." He looked around me and smiled his greasy smile at Mary. "Hi ya doin? My name is Gerald Spinnazzo, but my friends call me Spiny. Glad to make ya acquaintance, I'm sure." I moved to block his view of Mary.

"What do you want, Spiny," I asked.

"Shark sent me to bring ya for a conference. Ya sister can come too if ya like or just ya. Either way suits me." He gave me a big smile and opened his coat so that I could see his pistol. I was close enough to him that this was a mistake on his part, but other than kill him, there was not much I could do. I didn't want any action to be right in front of Mary, and I, for sure, didn't want her hurt.

"What's it about, Spiny?"

"Don't know, my young friend. He just said to bring ya so I'm bringing ya. Coming with?"

I half-turned to Mary and indicated with my chin that she was to walk away and then I said, "I'll go with you." We got back in the car, and I watched Mary's frightened face looking at the car as it drove away. We headed to the west side, and I suspected that I was about to visit The Farm.

"So, how ya been, kid?" Spiny said with mock friendship.

"Okay until I saw you," I answered.

"Now, kid, don't be dat way. We's been good to ya. What's ya problem? Ya one of us now, and we take care of our own. Ya'll see." After that exchange, we drove in silence. Sure enough, it was The Farm. I had been past it once or twice but never really looked at it. There was a small sign advertising "The Farm" on the first line and "Entertainment" on the second. Driving by, you could easily miss it. We turned on the gravel road beside the sign, and ahead, there were several low buildings with some connected and some freestanding. A large parking lot contained a few scattered cars, but there was no one in sight outside the complex. A large trash bin overflowed, and empty beer bottles lay sprinkled around the entire area. The heavy car's tires ground at the loose rock, and we came to a gritty stop. A sign outside the entrance said "Girls, Girls, Girls" and had an attached silhouette of a dancing girl. Everything was dirty, and as we neared the door, I noticed the stale smell of spilt beer. Spiny went in ahead of me, and I followed him into a large room with a bar along the far wall. To the left was an empty small stage elevated about a foot from the floor. Colored spotlights in the vaulted ceiling traced little rainbows of color across the wooden floor. A couple of women were seated at the bar, their bare backs to us. At the right were scattered tables, and at one was seated The Shark, playing cards with himself. He intermittently watched as we came forward but was silent.

"Boss, I got ya fighter for ya. No problems," Spiny said, turning to leave me alone with Shark.

"Kid, kid, kid. What am I going to do with you. You just won't cooperate even when I'm trying to do right by you. This is your first visit to The Farm, isn't it?"

"You know it is," I replied.

"Kid, you see that marvelous female back over there?" He pointed to a woman perched on a barstool facing the far wall. I could see the familiar strawberry blonde hair and the hourglass shape from where I was standing. It was Janel.

"Janel?" I acknowledged.

"Yeah, that's her. She is the hottest number anywhere, and I mean anywhere. Guys tear up their marriage contract just to watch her breathe. You! You could have had her for free, and you never even came to say hello. Well, I can tell you that it hurt her. Bad hurt her. She told me about you, you know. She said that you have a really hot sister, and you are madly in love with her. Pretty strange, I thought, but then I realized that you would do anything to keep your sister safe. Not that I blame you a bit, you realize, but it goes without saying that it means that I have your number."

Every fiber of my being bristled. I was out of my element, standing alone in Shark's domain, but he was talking about the only subject that was off-limits. "You ever touch my sister, I'll kill you." I meant it to the bottom of my soul, and if the situation would have been right, I might have done it right there and then.

"Pretty tough talk for a kid. Relax. No one wants to do anything to your sister. I have absolutely no intention of ever even talking to her. Put it out of your mind. The only reason I bring it up is to make it clear to you that you have to do what we want you to do. In return, you are under our protection and not only will we look after you and your family, we will shower you with things you want. Doesn't that sound like a pretty good deal?"

"I would just as well prefer to be left out of the whole thing. Don't pay me anything, just leave me alone," I said.

"Not going to happen, kid. We need new blood now and again, and a young tough like you is our bread and butter. You belong to us, and you will do what you are told or face the consequences. Understood?" I didn't answer and just stood there clenching my fists. I learned the meaning of the old word "impotence" that day. That was me in a nutshell. I had absolutely no options.

"Now that we got that clear, kid, I want you to go over there and make up with Janel. You owe it to her to make it right, and I won't have it any other way." He stopped talking abruptly, and I knew that our conversation was over for now.

I turned toward Janel's back and came silently up behind her. I didn't realize at first that she was watching me in the mirror the whole time. Before I said a word, she said, "Hi, stranger." Over her shoulder I could see her face in the mirror. She was smiling her brilliant smile at me.

"I saw that fantastic figure of yours when I came in. That and the incredible hair that you have. Hi, yourself," I said and touched her on her shoulder. She spun her seat to face me and laid her chin on my arm and just looked at me like a mellow favorite puppy.

"You can't believe how many times I thought about you, Mike. I had such a good time pushing your buttons that night, and the dancing was pretty good too. Have you missed me?"

"It took a week for me to calm down. You are pretty intense, you know. Sure, I have thought about you a lot. What male wouldn't? Dancing with you was heaven after I got control of myself. Shark just reminded me again that I didn't come out to see you, and he said that you were upset about it. Before you answer, let me tell you that it wasn't any rejection of you that made me stay away. I was trying to get away from being tied up with the mob."

"I wasn't sure what you felt after we tricked you, and you found out who I actually am. It was a nasty bit of devilry that Shark cooked up to get you hooked into this life. I'm glad you resisted, but here you are after all." She put her arm around my waist and drew me closer.

I said, "Shark told me to make up to you. Can I tell you that it is good to see you again and that I never held it against you for what you did? I know that you were ordered to do it, and I actually hoped that you had a good time with me like I did with you."

Small tears were forming in the corners of her eyes. "I am only two years older than you, Mike, but I feel a hundred older than that. I don't want them to see me cry. Can we go to my room and talk for awhile?" I answered by helping her up, and together we went through the door toward the bedrooms. I could feel eyes on us as we left the bar. She had a large room, and it was decorated mostly in pinks. There were no windows, but she had two large skylights. All the lamp shades had frill on the bottom, and there was a very large gilt mirror on one wall. We sat down on her bed, holding hands.

"I'm ashamed that you have to see me for what I am," Janel said, and the tears started in earnest. I put my arms around her and held tight. She had a good cry, and one that was obviously long overdue.

"Janel, to me you are a perfect and beautiful woman. I get a thrill just touching your hand. Don't treat yourself so badly."

"Mike, you don't understand. I am ruined, and I am the one at fault. I can never be pure again. There is no going back from where I've been."

"Quit it, Janel. Listen to me. You are beautiful! Do you hear me? Beautiful. You are intelligent and fun to be with, and you are not dead. Life is still in there. You have more right now than most of us ever get. Look at me. What am I but a poor high school student with no future. I can never go to college, because I couldn't afford to. The best job I ever had was in a gas station greasing cars for fifty cents an hour, and it is what I'll have to go back to when I finish school. Now, the worst news of all. The mob wants me to do their dirty work, and I can't get away from them." She returned to weeping and held on to me pressing her wet face into my chest. We embraced each other like that for a long time, but at last she started coming back from the depth of her grief, blowing her nose while she looked me over.

"I guess I am supposed to take off my clothes now. Would you like that? She asked.

"I don't want to be ordered to have sex with you, and I don't want you to obey them like that either," I answered. "If you take off your clothes, I won't be able to resist you, and we will do their bidding. Besides, I've never even been kissed by a girl yet. I don't think I'm ready for much more than that. It could kill me." Janel started laughing so hard that she flopped back on the bed, continuing to laugh at the ceiling.

"Are you kidding me, Mike? Never been kissed? That is so amazing!" and she started laughing again until I felt that perhaps she was ridiculing me.

"No, my dear Janel. Never been kissed. Scout's honor," I promised.

"Would you do me the favor of kissing me, Mike?" she said with sincerity. "You should know that most of the men I see would never kiss me. They consider girls like me too dirty to kiss."

"I would like to kiss you, Janel. It will be wonderful to have a woman that I really care about kiss me for the first time." When I finished speaking, she sat up, sliding off the bed and came around to face me. I stood, and we, very slowly, moved into an embrace, eyes locked on each other. I wasn't sure what to expect, but when she pressed her soft lips into mine her scent drifted into my nostrils, transporting us somewhere else as the room and its contents disappeared. The kiss was a long one, and when she slowly pulled away, I felt my lips tug away from hers as if they had been attached and were reluctant to separate. Her eyes remained so close to mine that I couldn't actually focus, and she was a heavenly blur of blue. I felt her warm breath on my face, the touch of life itself.

"Thank you, Janel. That was a wonderful experience for me. I think that I am forever changed by your touch."

"No, thank you, Mike, for letting me feel what it would be like to be in love rather than be in lust. That kiss changed me also." She embraced me again and looked up into my face. "Now I feel dirtier than ever, because I know what it could have been like for me."

"I don't know what is going to happen now, Janel, but I want to get away from these people, and I would like to see you get away also. If I could, would you let me help you?" I asked.

"Oh, my God! If there was only a way, Mike. It would take money, lots of it, to run away from them. I can't think of anything either of us could do to get that much in our pockets. We are probably doomed to be controlled by them forever or until our deaths." Her tears resumed the path down her sweet face.

"For now, I'm afraid that you are right. At least you and I have something in common and that is the affection we feel toward each other and the desire for something better in life. If you ever need me, I will come to you. I give you my promise that I will keep my ears and eyes open for a break that might set us free, and you do the same." She put her hand on my cheek, slowly sliding it away, and we just stood together, an endless embrace of two people thrown together by fate.

There was a loud knock on the door, "Mike. I gotta go. Let go of that dame, and I'll take you home. Five minutes." It was Spiny.

"I'll be there," I shouted.

Neither of us wanted to let go. She felt like she belonged in my arms, and I rested my chin on the top of the red-tinted hair and just took it all in. Without words, we just swayed slowly together, much as we had done on the dance floor.

"I should go get my ride while I have the chance. Don't think that this is goodbye, Janel, but I don't know when I will get to see you again. You remember what I said. You have value, and there will be another life for you when you get away." I could feel the nod from her, more that she heard me rather than agreed. When I pushed away, she hid her face and turned away from me. Understanding that I was her last hope, I resolved to help her escape as I had promised. I tenderly kissed the back of her neck and left the room, softly closing her door behind me. Spiny was waiting impatiently by the exit door. I waved to Shark, giving him a thumbs up, indicating success with Janel. He ignored me and continued to play at his cards. I knew that I had not seen the last of him yet. On the ride back, Spiny was anxious to know what Janel and I did together in her room.

"Hey. So how was it man? Isn't she something else?" he said, egging me on for detail.

"Yes. She is a great girl. So incredible to look at," I agreed.

"Did ya get a great ride?" Spiny asked with a grin.

"You bet. I hated to part with her," I truthfully answered.

"Ya heard Shark. Ya can have her any time ya want. Just tell her what ya want, and she'll do it. Ain't that the best?"

"Is that what you do with her?" I asked, not really wanting to hear his answer.

He hesitated and the grin left, "To tell da truth, I haven't had much luck with dat one. She don't like me. I usually use Joy. She always a lot of fun." At least his admission made me feel a little better, but I knew that Janel was always in the embrace of someone out there, if not Spiny. Some things you can change and some you can't. I let out a big sigh. There had to be some way out of this mess.

"What do you want from me, anyway?" I bluntly asked.

"Think of it as training, kid. Ya do whatever Shark wants at dat time. Ya can see that he watches out for ya, can't ya? Ya got to do something to repay him, ya know."

"Sure, Spiny. But what's next?"

"Another delivery, I expect. Soon. Can't tell ya more," he said and concentrated on driving.

The next morning found Mary and I walking to school. The end of the junior year was near, and summer was fast coming our way. I loved these morning walks with her. She smelled so fresh, her hair shone in the morning sun, and generally, she was happy and talkative. I noticed her reluctance to talk that morning and finally had to ask bluntly what it was all about.

"You never told me what happened to you last night. For our entire lives, you have always told me but last night you didn't say a word. You went to The Farm, didn't you?" she asked.

I walked for a moment thinking of how and what I was going to tell her. "Mary, I never like to tell bad things to you, and there was nothing but bad out there. Forgive me, but I always want you to enjoy the good, happy things in life, leaving out the bad."

"That won't work, Mike. I need to know everything about you and know every little thing you do. It's always been that way. Don't you trust me any longer, or are you hiding something?"

I sighed. She was right, but I hated to tell her the truth. "Synopsis version first. Detail later, if you wish. You are right, Spiny took me to The Farm. It is a run-down beer hall with every sort of illegal pleasure, including girls. Shark was there, and he told me that I was part of his team whether I liked it or not and that I would be doing jobs for them from now on or else. He gave a not-too-veiled threat against you to convince me that I had no choice."

"That's what I thought would happen. Did you see Janel out there?" Mary inquired. I realized that this was her biggest problem. She had heard the rumors also. I never told her how often Shark had insisted that I visit Janel, and the real reason I was brought to The Farm. Shark wanted me to desire Janel so badly that she would be the main reason I worked for him.

"Yes, I saw her and spoke to her. Apparently, she is there full-time."

Mary walked along silently, thinking, and then said, "Did you have any...?" She couldn't finish her sentence.

"Mary, that is not something I would ever do. You know that. I didn't and never will. That is what Shark wanted me to do out there, other than threaten me. He virtually ordered both of us, Janel and me, to do it. We didn't, I promise you that we didn't."

"I just hate that girl. So dirty," Mary said.

"No, Mary, she's really not like that. She has been trapped out there and hates herself for it. No one can think lower of her than she thinks about herself. You should feel sorry for her as I do. I wish there was some way she could get free from them, before it is too late."

"It is too late, Mike. Face it, she is a prostitute, and she will always be one. I wish you could never see her again."

"She thinks of me as her only friend, Mary. Don't you think people can change if they get the chance? I do."

"No, Mike, she can't get rid of her past, and she might drag you down with her. Stay away from her. You are attracted to her like a moth is to flame. You can't help yourself, and you are going to fall into that fire with her."

I made no response to this because I knew she was correct on every point. Wishing otherwise wouldn't help, because part of me knew it would never be made right.

Mary continued, "It's my fault. Our situation makes us yearn for something we can't have. I know it's somehow weird and wrong, but I love you as much as you love me, and it creates such tension in me. We have to be careful using the wrong people as surrogates for what can never happen between us."

"Mary, I always wondered if I was the only damaged one. Thanks for telling me that. I don't know what will happen, and I guess time will sort it out. I know one thing for sure. The day that I can't be around you will be the worst day in my life."

"Mike, don't you think that it's time you told Detective Smith what is going on? He said that he would help if you asked him."

"I've often thought about doing that, Mary. The problem is that this isn't about just Shark and Spiny. This is a mob which sticks together. They would find out and come after both of us, even if it took years. It's risky to talk to anyone because it's bound to get back to them."

"Are you just going to be part of the mob then? Aren't you going to fight or resist? I would rather be dead that watch you sink that low," she hissed, passion in her voice.

"There are worse things than death. Look at Janel. They would do that to you, if they chose to, and there isn't much we could do about it."

"Well, I don't agree, and I am going to talk to Smith without you, if that is what you want. I am not going to just do whatever the mob wants." She was right. We had to at least talk to Detective Smith, before I got in too deep to get out.

"Okay. I'll call him and set it up. Want to be there also?" I asked.

"You are not about to leave me out after telling me what could happen. Of course, I'll be there."

At lunch, I found a pay phone and called the police headquarters. There was a long delay before Detective Smith got on the phone, requiring additional nickels to keep the connection open.

"Smith here," the gruff voice finally said.

"Detective Smith, this is Mike Condor. We need to talk."

"Well, Mike! I thought that someday I might get this call. I've kept up with your activity more than you know. What do you have in mind?"

"Detective, my sister Mary and I both want to talk privately with you. I don't want this to get around, you understand. Can you pick us up in an unmarked car after school and somewhere a few blocks away so that we can't be seen?"

"Sure, Mike. Go to the grocery store not far from where you live, and I'll be waiting in the alley. Okay?"

"Thanks, Detective. We'll be there about four. See you then."

As he said, his black car was there idling in the alley when we turned the corner. He waved to us through the back glass, and after we got in the back seat, he drove away. I reached out and held Mary's hand, and we slid down in the seat so that nobody could see who was being given a ride.

"Hi, kids," Smith greeted us cheerfully. He drove inexorably toward the west, and I intuitively knew he was headed to the park where I made my first delivery for Shark. When we arrived and he shut off the motor, I calculated that we were in the very spot Shark had used. He turned around and looked us over.

"Well, I know that this is about Shark Cohen and his boys. They are trying to recruit you, aren't they? And they are threatening, obliquely for now, to do something to Mary, aren't they?"

I answered, "Yes, that's about it."

"And this is about the place that you made a delivery of a package to Shark last year, isn't it?" Smith asked.

"You knew?"

"We know a lot. Sure, we followed you. We would have busted you that night, but you were only being tested with a fake package. It would have come to no end...then. Now, it's going to be for real, isn't it?"

"Yes, Detective. They consider me one of them now."

"The girl, Janel Cicero, they fixed you up with her, didn't they?" he asked and looked at Mary to see if she knew about it.

Mary spoke up, "That was my fault. She pretended to be a new student, and I was taken in."

"That's okay, dear. She takes everyone in. We've had her in the station more than once, and the officers there make fools of themselves over her. She can look so innocent and perfect, you can't believe there could be any evil in her. All men feel that way about her, probably including Mike here." He looked at me and smiled to invite a response.

Mary stared at me, and I felt her brain telling me, "I told you so." She said, "Yes, Mike is a sucker for her. Even I admit that she is a fantastic package."

"Detective, I feel bad for Janel. She is trapped in a life that she wants to get out of. She is a very unhappy person. She needs our help, not our criticism," I said.

"I'll bet that she told you if she only had enough money she could get away from them, didn't she?" Smith asked.

"Well, yes, but it seems obviously true. She can't just walk away with the dress on her back. Anyway, they would never let her leave," I said.

Smith laughed. "Sorry, Mike, I know that you are sincere and feel bad for her, but she has told that story to almost every man. When they get a wad of money to her and expect her to leave, she just uses it all for drugs and goes to the next man for more. She can leave there anytime she wants. They can get another one to replace her tomorrow, so they don't care at all what she does. She likes it there, that's why she stays."

Smith's words clubbed me senseless. I remembered the kiss and what I felt at the time for her. For the first time, I realized that the kiss was from a female, that was all. It wasn't Janel that made my bells ring, it was a woman. My body and mind were ready to get that sensation, and my species has been developing for a million years so that I could feel that way. It was a weight being lifted off of me. Janel was not my problem, no matter how sad it was to see a beautiful creature trapped like that. What was happening to Janel was far beyond my ability to change.

Detective Smith broke into my distant thoughts, "Forget Janel. There are some things you both need to know. The first is that not all the cops in this town are honest. Some are being paid by the mob, and they can't be trusted. Even I don't know everyone in their pocket. The County Police are worse, they are all corrupt. Never trust one. The State Police so far seem to be above it, but they are not around here unless the Mayor or the Governor calls them in. That never happens. You can trust me, and I won't let you down, but I only have a few people I can absolutely trust so we have to be careful. The only way to really get out of the mob's clutches is to leave the city completely. If they don't have any reason, such as a double cross, they won't come after you, and you will be free. I know that you can't do that yet, so we have to have another way. Here is what I suggest. Mary, you just stay as far away from any of them as you can. Never go with your brother to any meeting with them, giving them an excuse to get you involved. Don't talk to any of them, don't inquire about any of their activities. If they bother you at all, come to see me, and I'll pound a few heads. Mike, you have the bigger problem. I want you to do what they expect for now. I'm sure that at first it will only be delivery of drugs or money to different places. Stay away from Janel, she will only help them trap you. If you want sex that bad, go find a fellow high school girl and get it out of your system. Keep records of whom you see, where you go and what is delivered. Open your eyes and see what they are doing.

You are smarter than any of them and should be able to get a picture pretty quickly. Write all this down and give it to Mary who will get it to me. That way, if you get caught by cops, we can get you off on the basis that you are a snitch working for us. Of course, you will be on the mob hit list and will have to flee, but at least you won't be in jail. Do anything they want you to do short of armed robbery or murder, and we'll let it pass. I will personally see to the surveillance on you, and other cops don't need to know that you and I are cooperating. They will all think that you are just an underling part of the mob. Most of the time, we never go after the small-fry like you." Smith stopped to see if we were taking it all in. We were.

I put my arm over Mary's shoulder and said, "Is this what you want to do?"

Mary answered, "It is our only option, Mike. What else is there but a life of crime?"

"Yes, Detective, I'll do it. Thanks for all the information. I had no idea that anyone knew what was going on."

"Mike, you are a good kid. I wish I had one just like you. By the way, was it you that knocked out that prizefighter, King?"

"I was supposed to get a beating from him to teach me something. I got lucky."

Smith laughed. "We found him wandering around dressed only in his boxing trunks. The arresting officer took him in as a drunk. His head didn't clear until the next day, when he told us the story that some young high school boy knocked him out causing Shark to throw him out into the street. You must be better than you think, Mike."

"You do what you have to when there are no other choices, Detective."

Smith looked at us for a long time, studying our faces. "You two are interesting. You love each other, don't you?"

We both answered that we did.

"I'm sorry for saying this, it isn't my place, but I can't get it out of my mind," he said. "Mike, you just look different than Mary. Everything about you is different. I just can't see any similarity. Are you really brother and sister?" It was the first time I ever heard that. I looked at Mary, but all I saw was the wonderful familiar face that I had always known since birth. Mary was my sister, we had the same mother and father. We had known each other since before we could see each other, floating around in Mother's womb touching shoulders and heads. Of course Mary was my sister.

"There isn't any doubt, Detective. We were born together," I said and Mary nodded to the truth of it.

"Born here in town then?" he asked. We nodded yes. "It's interesting anyway. Forgive me again, but I would like to know. Does your feeling for each other cause you some problems at times?"

Mary answered, "Since we grew up, it's been getting worse, Detective."

"Mike, you love Mary enough that you would kill for her if needed?"

"Funny you should ask. I have already had that thought. Yes, I would."

"Well, son, I hope it doesn't come to that. Let's work together and see if we can find a way to get you out of this crap." He turned around and started the car.

He dropped us where we found him, and the walk home was short. I felt better that we got on that side of the police. At least, I really didn't have to worry about the cops busting me, and maybe we could do some damage to the mob. What Smith said about Janel bothered me, though. I still believed what she had told me. She was so sincere about it, and she looked so helpless. I didn't believe that Shark would let his top girl go very easily. He probably made a lot of money from her, and she was a big draw for men to go to The Farm and get fleeced in other ways. There was no way that I was going to be drawn into a sexual relationship with Janel, no matter how desirable she looked or acted. If I could actually help her, I would, and when I went to The Farm, I would spend some time with her. Perhaps I would be able to figure her out if I knew more about her.

My mind churned over what Smith said about Mary and I not looking related. It didn't take much thought to know that he was right. Mary was more fair than me, with blue eyes and blonde hair. I had more skin pigmentation and dark hair and eyes. Our noses were different shapes and so on. I had always known these differences, but I felt that since I was male that made the difference. Now I began to think of all the brothers and sisters I knew in school. You could always see the family resemblance, even given the sex difference. They were fundamentally alike. Even kids with different fathers were more similar that we were. It was like we weren't related at all. Mary's shoulder bumped mine and that brought me back to the present. I looked at her, and she smiled back. She melted me every time she did that. I never took her for granted, she was Mary.

"Mary, did you get bothered by what Smith said about us?" I asked.

"It's been in my mind since he said it. No one has ever said that before. I'm trying to analyze it, but I'm not getting anywhere. What about you?" she asked, intentionally bumping my shoulder again.

"He's right. We don't look alike. Don't worry, though, I love you anyway," I said and bumped her shoulder.

"Thanks for that, I was worried!" she teased. "Want to ask Mother about it?" she asked in a lower voice.

"Mother raised us the same. If one of us didn't belong, I think we would have felt the difference by now. As far as I am concerned, we are blood-related, and that's what I think Mother feels too. Too bad though. It would explain a lot."

"What do you mean, too bad. Don't you want to be my brother?" she asked. I couldn't tell if she was serious.

"I don't know what I want. I am confused enough right now. All I know is that I can't imagine life separated from you, however much stress it causes. I look forward to seeing you next to me every morning at breakfast, and I always loved doing our homework together and talking over the day with you. When I see you in the hall at school, it's like finding the end of the rainbow. It's like you and I are part of each other, like the Siamese twins we hear about rather than siblings."

"I don't want you killing anybody over me, Mike, but I believed it when you told Smith that you would."

"That idea that Smith had about me finding some girl at school was a good one, don't you think?" I asked.

"Do you feel like I should do the same?" Mary asked.

"No, please, please don't," I begged.

"Nor you, please."

"Phillip ask you out to the prom yet?" I inquired.

"I can tell that he's getting up the nerve, but not yet. You going?" she asked.

"Since my last two outings were real memorable events, both damaging my already questionable reputation, I have no real desire to go. If you go with Phillip, I will go even if I just hang around the room and drink punch. I'll try not to bother you by being there, but there is too much going on to let you go without me."

"Mike, there are a lot of girls who go with another girl just to be there. If you went alone, I'm sure you would find plenty of attractive available young women who would want to dance with you."

"Not with my reputation. Who wants to dance with a mobster?" I asked.

"From what I hear, all of them. The mystery surrounding you makes you all that more attractive to women. You are all some of them talk about. One thing though, I don't want to see you go outside with any of them, and certainly not to a car. And...you are walking me home. Got that?" she said, bumping my shoulder.

The three of us walked through the double doors together and got the usual stares. The band warming up and the humming of conversation in the room created a din of noise. I could still almost hear the murmurs about me not having a date. Leaving Mary and Phillip on the dance floor, I headed toward the punch bowl. There was already a small crowd of mostly boys around the beverages. The unattached girls were seated along the wall in stiff chairs or standing in small groups just off the floor.

As I approached, I saw a large back bending over the bowl. It was Monster, his friend Butch nearby and noticing me coming toward them. He tapped Monster on the shoulder, and they turned to face me.

Something had started changing me over the previous couple of months and had morphed me quickly from a high school boy into a young adult. I had matured mentally as my body grew in strength, and I was more confident. This would go really badly for Monster if he chose to have a confrontation.

"Hey, Mike! Say, I want to tell you to your face that I was in the wrong last year, and I had it coming. What say we let bygones go and start fresh?" He looked sincere and offered his large paw for a handshake. I paused and looked between his face and Butch and saw no malice.

I took his hand and said, "Peter, glad to meet you. My name is Mike!" We shook and Butch slapped me on the back and offered me a fresh cup of punch.

"No, man, it's Pete to you, or you can call me Monster like my buddies do," he offered. "Say, I see that that sharp cookie you brought last time isn't here tonight. Do you expect her?"

"No, Pete, I don't, but you never know anything for sure. You interested in her?"

"Man, she set my brain on fire when I saw her dance. Then I heard the rumors. Does she work at The Farm like they say?" Pete asked.

I took a long sip of punch and looked around delaying my answer. "Yes, she does," I finally said. "I didn't know anything about it until after the dance. I was as surprised as everyone else."

Butch was listening intently and asked, "Does that mean we can just go out there and..." I knew what he meant. He almost spoke the truth, that he or his buddies could just hire her.

"I guess it does mean that, Butch," I answered.

"Would it bother you, Mike, if a bunch of us went out there?" Pete asked.

"Look, guys, there are some things you should know. First, I don't have anything to do with Janel. I don't even want to know what she does either. Remember that The Farm is run by Shark. Ever hear of him? Once you go out there, you put yourself at risk, because they will separate you from your money faster than you can think about it. They have all the cops bought and paid for, and they can get by with doing anything they want to do."

"You know what she charges?" Pete asked.

"Did you even hear me just now? No, I have no idea." They were blind with lust. Well, they were warned and that was all I could do.

We turned around and watched the dancers out on the floor. I could see Mary's face looking at us from a distance. Phillip was dancing along in simple discoordination, but at least I could trust him not to get personal with her.

"Say, Mike," Pete said. "Can I talk to you about Mary without you getting angry?"

"Probably not," I said without looking at him.

"Well, here goes. She looks pitiful out there with that little runt. I can't believe that she is having a good time. It's embarrassing, you know."

"And your suggestion?" I inquired.

"Look, Mike, we all heard that you knocked out a professional fighter in the first round. It's no secret that you can do the same thing with any guy here. We all know that you protect Mary with a vengeance. I sure know. The thing is that you are choking her. It isn't right."

"This is your attempt at asking if you can dance with her?" I asked.

"No, no, not at all. I am just a big ape. I know that. I'll never ask, because she wouldn't ever want to dance with me. But, if you say it's OK, then there are some fellows here who are good dancers who would love to give her a spin. I promise that I will personally supervise from a distance so she is treated like she should be. What do you think?" he asked.

I didn't like it. It was the start of giving her away, and it tore at my heart, but Pete was right. With this self-described big ape and me supervising, there wouldn't be anyone who would take the chance of getting fresh with her. "Yup, Pete, I'm choking her, I admit it. Go ahead and give the word, but I'll be watching. Tell them that too."

Pete held up his arm and gave a little wave to two guys hovering in the distance. Immediately they both started across the floor toward Mary and Phillip. Both looked normal and were well-dressed. I clenched my fist and watched. One of them tapped Phillip on the shoulder, and he looked around to see where I was. When he found my eyes, I shrugged, and he backed away from Mary. She also gave me a long and questioning look, but I smiled at her to let her know that I knew what was happening. We discovered that Pete was right. The first boy was an excellent dancer, and when they started in earnest, the other couples backed away to watch. As soon as the band changed pieces, the other fellow cut in like a smoothly choreographed routine of professionals. Mary was smiling, and her long golden hair flowed in waves as she spun and moved. She was dressed in a white, near floor length, dress decorated with scattered sequins that caught the light in a changing colored rainbow as she moved. Either boy was handsome and both looked like they belonged with her out on the floor. I couldn't watch the sight of this person I loved so much being happy in the arms of another. After I had enough, I had to turn away. Scanning the line of girls waiting to be asked, I realized that most of them were watching me. They smiled expectantly as I casually looked them over. I tossed the paper cup in the trash and walked over to the first one.

"Hi. My name is Mike. I was wondering if I could dance with you?"

She stood, leaving her purse on the chair. "I came tonight hoping that you would ask me. Sure, I would love to dance with you, Mike." She smoothly folded her arm in mine, and we advanced a few feet onto the floor. "My name is Julie Cranston, and I know everything about you." She smiled a sweet smile and brushed her long brown hair back over her ear. I took her hand in mine, and we started moving slowly to the music as we looked each other over.

"It's not possible, Julie," I said.

"What do you mean?" she said, surprised.

"That you know everything about me. All you know is rumors, whatever they are. I'll bet you that facts are different than rumors," I said as we moved closer.

"I know that you are the best looking guy in school, or anywhere for that matter. I know that you are smart and have the best grades in school. We all know how much you love Mary."

"Yes, that again. Does it bother you?" I asked looking at her face.

"Well, I have two brothers. We speak, that's about all. If I were to fall off a cliff, they might have more time in the bathroom and would secretly be glad. Your relationship with Mary is something else. You love her, don't you?"

"Yes, I love her. What is wrong with that?"

"Nothing when said that way, but you are possessive of her physically. You can't stand to see a boy look at her or touch her. That's weird. I was watching you a while ago when those two started dancing with her. I saw the clenched fist. You wanted to bust them, didn't you?"

"Julie, I love her. I don't have any explanation for it. We were born together, and she is all I ever knew or cared about. I couldn't bear to have anything happen to her, and I am overly protective, I admit it."

"You know what we are all wondering, don't you?" she asked.

"I can imagine. No. Never. Ever. Does that answer your wondering mind?"

"Well, at least it puts it to rest. We were actually pretty happy when you showed up with that girl at the last dance. She put the rest of us to shame, though. Such a looker and so well appointed. Then we found out more about her. Good for you, Mike. I pronounce you normal."

"Wait! Let's not start another rumor, Julie. I didn't know anything about her until she walked in that night. Notice that I didn't go with her when she left? Don't get that started, because I am innocent."

"I would love to find out how innocent, Mike. Care for a little stroll outside?"

"Did you see all the lovely girls who needed to dance. I don't have time!"

"Phooey. You won't go because Mary is watching. She hasn't taken her eyes off of us. She has it as bad for you as you do for her." At that comment, I searched for Mary and sure enough, she was dancing and watching. Her partner was better than I ever could be, and it looked like they were having fun. I pulled Julie in, and we embraced and danced a slow romantic number.

When the music died, I said, "You are a better dancer than I am. Loved it and thanks."

"You mean, we are finished?" she said, pretending to be surprised. We looked toward the wall and two girls waved.

"See what I mean?" I said and laughed.

"I'll be here when the dance ends. Can you remember that?" Julie remarked over her shoulder, just before she returned to her chair.

The next girl was also very attractive and batted her eyes at me. She stood up as I approached. There was something familiar about her, but I didn't think I had ever seen her before.

"Hi, my name is Mike. Would you do me the honor of this next dance?"

"I perfectly well know your name. Do you not remember me?" the girl asked, using a faint accent.

Her voice was familiar, and I looked her up and down. She was attractive, very attractive, and was wearing a rather expensive looking gown. Then suddenly it came to me, "Frieda?" It had been months since I last saw her and then only at a distance. This wasn't the same girl on the outside.

"Yes, it is me, Frieda. Surprised?"

I looked at her full bosom bulging and filling her low cut dress. No, this was a very different girl. She radiated confidence and elegance.

"For heaven's sake, Frieda! Yes! What happened to you?" I stammered.

"I guess that I'm not a little girl any longer. I woke up. Like the new me?" Frieda asked, knowing my answer, because it was in my eyes.

"I never told you how sorry I am that our evening was ruined last time we were together. It seemed like it was over before it started. Please forgive me for acting the brute that night."

"Oh, no, Mike. I was thrilled to see you in action. The events are still vivid to me, and I think of them often." She said in her cute Austrian accent. "I saw that you made up with the football team tonight, and I also see that Mary is out dancing, and you are not punching some boy in the face."

"Do you also have a problem with me looking out for my sister?" I asked.

"It is time you looked after yourself. After all, you are both destined to marry someone else and separate. It is the way it is."

There was something about Frieda. I didn't remember from our previous date having this feeling of being so comfortable with her, like I had known her for a long time. She just stood there smiling at me, and I got the feeling that she was waiting for me to talk. The clamor of people talking and the band playing disappeared in my head, and it was like we were standing alone somewhere in a quiet place.

"Can I tell you something in private, Frieda?"

"Yes, Mike."

"We only kissed once when we were children. Since that time, the only contact I ever made with her is touching shoulders. But, I dream otherwise. I can't help it, and it makes me ashamed when I remember it. I love Mary, and I'm afraid of my own thoughts. It isn't right, but like you just said, it is what it is."

"Well, that explains it. You are in love with her as much as you would be if you were not related. You want to be physically close, but you both know that would be wrong. This is destructive, is it not?"

"At times, I am destroyed inside, and I react with anger to everyone but Mary. It also gives me the drive to be the best at everything so she has respect for me."

"I have been around her enough to believe that she feels the exact same way about you. Are you absolutely sure that you and Mary are related?" Frieda asked.

"We recently had someone else ask us that question. He said that we look unrelated. After he said that, I realized that he was right. My memory of her goes back all the way, and we were raised as fraternal twins and have one father and one mother. We are brother and sister."

"Enough of that for now, or you will ruin my evening," she said as she took my arm in hers. "Dance with me, and I won't disgust you with my sweaty hands this time."

She was right about her hands. This time, they were soft and warm and delightful to touch. As we danced and turned, I saw Mary's eyes from across the room, just for an instant, but it was enough. We were keeping tabs on each other, and we both knew what the other thought. That we wanted to be with each other and not anybody else. I knew that I couldn't allow myself to think that way. It was wrong, evil, and stupid, and it could never come true. When I turned my attention back to the lovely girl in my arms, I saw that she was patiently waiting for me to notice her. We moved well together, and it was no effort at all, like we were tuned into the same channel. I felt more comfortable around her than anyone other than Mary. In Frieda's face, I could see no expectations, no demands, only acceptance of how things were. I had pent-up my problems inside of me, because there was nobody I could talk to, but I could see that perhaps I was wrong.

"Did we even dance together last time?" I asked.

"Only for a moment, then you were distracted," she answered and smiled.

Before I could respond, there was noise and commotion. I looked toward the noise just in time to see Monster pick a boy up by his shirt, belt him, and hurl him out of the door onto the street. There was a lot of applause and laughter. Frieda and I seemed to be the only ones who didn't know what was going on. I saw several faces turn toward me, and it dawned on me that it had something to do with Mary.

"Please forgive me, Frieda, I have to go see what this was about. I promise to return. I promise," I said. She just smiled and stood there as if she were going to remain in that very spot. I headed toward the crowd near the door. Pete was looking at me and obviously feeling smug about something.

"I told you I'd watch out for her, didn't I?" he asked from a distance.

"What happened?" I asked.

"Some bum tried to horn in without my permission. I fixed his little ass for him. He won't be back," Pete said wiping his hands on his pants as if to get rid of the dirt. I looked at Mary, who was still in the crowd, and I could see that she was shamed by rowdy males, in front of her classmates, again. I felt sorry for her, because I knew that she would feel that somehow she was at fault. Another dance ruined because of her.

I extended my hand to Pete, "Thanks, Pete. Thanks for watching out for her." After shaking his large hand, I turned and made my way through the crowd to Mary.

"Sorry, Mary. We can't seem to have a simple dance, can we?" I could see her moist eyes and the way she darted looks around to see that she was once again the center of attention. "Please, come with me, and we'll sit for a while and let the dancing resume." She nodded yes and wiped at her face. She allowed me to guide her back across to where Frieda was waiting.

Frieda hadn't moved since I walked away, and I took her arm and guided both of them to the chairs along the side wall where we all sat down.

"Seems that we have done this before!" I joked. The two girls were not about to smile at that memory, and so we just sat there and looked out. "We saw you dancing, Mary. You looked like it was a lot of fun. Those two boys really worked you out, didn't they?" Mary nodded ever so slightly but, otherwise, didn't respond. "Did you get anything to drink? Want some punch?" I persisted.

"Why don't you get both of us some, Mike," Frieda said quietly. "I'll stay here and talk to Mary while you are gone." She raised her eyebrows at me, and I got the message to take off and let them have a moment.

On the way to the punch bowl, Phillip came walking toward me. "You know, I didn't get a single dance with her. Every time I tried, they would cut in."

"Say, what actually happened?" I asked him.

"A guy from another school thought he should try to dance with the prettiest girl here, that's all. Monster came out of nowhere and picked him right off of the floor and tossed him. After seeing that, I'm scared to try again. After all, you and Monster have kissed and made up, and where does that leave me? I figure that Monster or his buddies can beat me up anytime they feel like it, because you won't do anything to stop them."

"I never said I was going to protect you, squirt. I only protect Mary. You are on your own, but I don't think you have anything to worry about. Pete is just doing that to get on my good side and to make up for what happened before. I also think he wants to visit Janel, and he thinks that he needs my permission."

Phillip had a shocked look on his face and said, "Does that mean that I can go visit her too?"

"Does that mean that you want to?" I asked.

"Sure. What red-blooded boy wouldn't want to," Phillip admitted.

"Well, that changes things, Phillip. Don't you dare go out there and even talk to Mary, because if you do, I'll toss you out the door the same way." I meant it and he knew it. As I walked away, I could see his shoulders sagging.

"Wait a minute, Mike," he called out. "How come you can go visit Janel anytime you want and still have this double standard for the rest of us?"

"That's because I don't want anything from her and you do," I answered. I continued to the punch bowl crowd who partially parted for me. Pete was there still grinning at his good deed.

"Did you see it Mike?" he asked.

"At least I saw the boy in the air on his way out the door."

"Yeah, that felt good," Pete said.

I had a sudden thought, "Pete, I think you are a man of his word. Is that right?"

"You bet I am. What can I do for you?"

"Can I trust you to sit beside Mary while I finish a dance with Frieda? You know not to do something stupid, right?" I asked.

"I would be eternally grateful, Mike. I never had the nerve to even speak to her before. There is no way I'll let you down, Mike. Thanks, buddy." He ambled faster, grinning as he made his way toward the girls. I saw Mary look up and put her hand over her mouth in surprise and then she looked around and found me. I smiled that it would be all right, and I held up the punch glasses to show that I was on the way. Pete beat me there and was already trying to talk to Mary when I came up with the two punch glasses. I looked at Frieda who was trying to suppress laughter.

"Frieda, would you please dance with me?" I asked, handing Pete and Mary each a glass of punch. She got up quickly and took my extended arm, leaving the two seated, engaged in a one-sided conversation.

"Remember, Pete," I reminded him, as we were walking away. He grinned and gave me a thumbs up and resumed his longing look at Mary.

"You are full of surprises, Mike," Frieda said. "What happened to Phillip?" We could see poor Phillip, by himself, leaning against the far wall looking at the floor.

"You know, I trusted him, but he let me down," I said.

"How so?"

"Turns out that he wants to go out to The Farm and see Janel. It makes me sick that he said that, and I let him touch Mary."

"Doesn't Pete want the same thing?" Frieda asked with a little knowing grin.

"Yes, I admit that he does, and he'll probably go out there, and Phillip would never have the nerve. The difference is that Pete is not allowed to touch Mary, and he knows it. I think that I can trust him a little farther, that's all."

"Oh, Mike. You can't just let it go. Let me ask you a personal question. Did you go out to visit Janel?"

She had trapped me, or so she thought. "Frieda, I don't want that kind of relationship with Janel. I haven't done what you are suspecting me of and never will. Don't think that way about me."

"Kind of sensitive about it, aren't you? Did you see her out there or not? It's just a simple yes or no kind of question, and you need to give a simple answer. Her gaze was steady even though we were moving to the music.

"Okay, I saw her out there. We were alone in her room with the door closed, but I didn't do anything. I swear it."

"Did you kiss her?" Frieda asked.

"What did you talk about with Mary?" I asked.

"First, you answer my question. Actually, I suppose you just did. You did kiss Janel," she said with finality.

"It was my first kiss. She offered, and I accepted. That was absolutely all there was to it."

"Did you enjoy your first kiss?" she asked, this time smiling because she found me out after all.

"It was pretty wonderful. Yes, I enjoyed it."

"So, now what do you think of Janel?"

"I feel very very sorry for her. I pity her. I wish..."

"That you could somehow save her." Frieda finished my thought for me and was right on target.

"Yes, I would like to see her out of that prison."

"You know that she never finished school. It's likely that she has no other way to survive. At least, I'll bet that's what she would say."

"Frieda, you still didn't tell me what you and Mary were talking about. This time, don't change the subject."

"You, of course," she answered. The tune changed, and we started moving to a different rhythm. She wasn't about to disclose what they talked about, and she was going to leave it to me to guess. After the dance ended, we walked back toward Mary and Pete. Mary was looking forlornly at us as we approached, while Pete was in an animated but one-sided conversation.

"Thanks, Pete," I said. He took my meaning, thanked us and left without complaint.

"Did you and Pete find anything in common?" I asked.

"We discussed football," Mary said flatly. I followed her eyes and saw that she was looking at Phillip, and he was looking back at her from across the floor. She abruptly stood and said, "I owe Phillip at least one dance. Excuse me," and she started toward him. Frieda put her hand on my arm to restrain me from also getting up.

"You don't want to do that, Mike. She is right. Let her dance with him. It won't hurt either one of them." I relaxed and patted her hand. Frieda was correct, of course. We watched Phillip light up and come forward, meeting Mary halfway.

"You want to protect everyone, don't you Mike? It's so sweet, but you ever think that there is nothing left for you? You can't ever have the thing you want most and you have to start looking another direction. You know that, don't you?"

"I guess that I do," I confessed.

"Something you should know. Mary feels exactly like you do. If something doesn't change between you two, you both will end up doing something you will regret the rest of your lives. You are being drawn in tighter into this vortex, and I think you both will reach a point where you won't be able to resist any longer. The reason I cornered you about your first kiss is to make you admit that you enjoyed the touch and feel of some female other than your sister. You love her, and she loves you, and it's wonderful that you feel that way, but you know in your heart that if you really love her, you can't violate her. You have to go one way, and she has to go the other. There is nothing else that can be said."

"Frieda, you are a real handful. How do you have such insight about something that is inside of me?"

"I am female," she said with a laugh. "The real reason is that you have forced yourself to never admit what you are thinking. It's obvious to the rest of us. I don't have to be a therapist to see it, just because you can't."

The dancing wound down and the band started packing up. Frieda and I stuck together for the rest of the evening to the dismay of the unattached girls along the wall. Mary's previous enthusiastic partners came back for more, but Phillip got at least one dance with her. She was still surrounded by a mixed group, but I could catch her glance occasionally. She still was keeping up with what I was doing, as was I for her.

"Frieda, is your dad coming to get you again?"

"Yes, soon," she said. "Want to go outside and wait with me?" she asked. We strolled slowly out of the door toward the curb.

"I really enjoyed being with you, Frieda. It feels like we have known each other for a long time."

"Like brother and sister?" she said mockingly but with a smile.

"No, funny Frieda. No, more like really good friends."

"I was thinking, Mike, that you might want to kiss me and see how I compare, since you are so experienced now." She put her head back and gave a little pucker. I did the wrong thing and gave a quick glance at the open door. She quickly retracted and gave me a little push. "I expected that. You are worried that Mary will see you kiss someone, aren't you? Or is it that you are worried that she will feel that she can do the same? Or is it that I'm not as appealing as Janel?"

I looked into those green catlike eyes set in an impassive face, and I couldn't decide if she was angry or still playing therapist with me. "I'm sorry, Frieda. Believe me, you are very appealing, very beautiful, and I am deeply grateful to have held you in my arms tonight, even if it was just for a little while. I feel so good around you, so free to talk. Please don't let us part like that." Just as I finished my little speech, I could feel the radiation from Mary as she and

Phillip came outside. I didn't have to look at her to know that she was nearby. Neither did Frieda, who never looked away from my face.

"It will take a lot to get your attention away from Mary. Don't worry, Mike, I knew what was going to happen, but I am still your friend. Call me sometime. Any time you need me." She turned toward the curb as her father's car came down the drive. I opened the door for her, and before the car pulled away, she gave me a last smile and a little wave.

Three days after we finished our junior year in school, Father died in the hospital. We buried him two days later, and then the grief hit me. At his burial, I flooded with tears that seemed to have no end. When it passed, I found myself thinking about him constantly. I always knew that he and I were not as close as he was to Mary. Since I loved her too, I could understand, and it really never bothered me. Father always treated me with respect, except for the frequent spankings when I was young, and we had a man's mutual affection for each other. He fed us, clothed us and gave us shelter. He was there when we needed him, and for that I was always grateful. Buddies, we were not. He never offered to play ball or go fishing with me or anything that fathers and sons do to bond. At the time, I never realized what I was missing. A child just takes and accepts life as he finds it, because he knows no other way. Now that I am an old man and looking back at what my father did or didn't do, I understand and forgive him completely. Now, I understand that he never accepted me as his true son, even though the facts said that I was. But he never once told me that he felt that way, and he treated me as though I was his son. I am sure that he never really loved me, but perhaps I couldn't expect him to ignore what he felt in his heart.

Mother took it very hard and openly fretted that there wasn't enough money to keep the house or afford to make repairs to the car. With the car disabled, we had no transportation and were forced to walk or ride the bus. There wasn't any social net in those days, and except for charity and the kindness of strangers, it was possible for a family to starve. I went back to the garage and the grease pit, and Mary went back to the dress shop. Mother took in laundry and kept children for pennies, but we got by.

One day that summer, I heard Billy shouting at me, and I emerged from the pit in the garage and wiped my dirty hands on a dirty towel. "Got someone here to see you, Mike," he shouted again. When I stepped into the light, I saw who it was. Shark was leaning against his long black Caddy, smoking.

"Hi, kid. Heard about your old man. Sorry." He blew a cloud of smoke into the air and turned to Billy. "How much you paying this kid?" he asked.

Billy stammered, "Gee, Shark, I think it's about three bucks a day. Something like that."

"Need some more cash, kid?" Shark asked, smiling at his smart question.

"Always, Mr. Cohen. I'm okay though, and Billy treats me good," I answered.

"Get out of those rags, kid, and come with me. Only, I ain't asking, kid. Billy, you have any problem with that?" The tone Shark used left little doubt about the futility of argument with him. I pulled off my dirty coveralls as I went back into the garage and went to the grimy sink and washed off what grease I could. I was left with my white undershirt, my cut off jeans and dirty shoes. When I came back outside, Shark looked me over like I was just out of the sewer. He motioned for me to get in his car, and he went around to the other side. We drove off leaving Billy standing helplessly in front of his pumps watching us leave. Shark drove downtown and parked at a meter in front of an upscale men's clothing store.

Shark pulled two crisp hundreds from his pocket and flipped them to me. "Go in there and get some clothes. Get a suit and shoes, too. Tell them I sent you. I'll be here waiting so don't take too long." I looked down at my hand holding the two hundred dollars and realized that this was the day I dreaded. I was part of the mob, and there was nothing I could do and had nowhere to hide. They would hook me on my family's need for money since they didn't succeed with using Janel. As commanded, I got out of the big car and headed into the air conditioned store. One of the clerks saw me come in and avoided my eyes and pretended that I wasn't there. I heard footsteps coming down a flight of wooden stairs and the door to the upstairs office opened. An older and stooped man in an expensive suit emerged.

"You're with Mr. Cohen, correct? I saw you get out of his car just now. Something we can do for you?" He motioned for the now alert clerk to come forward, and he did so with speed.

"I need some clothes and shoes and...a suit," I said. I had a couple of sport-type coats before and usually only wore them to church. My father's coats were good enough for the dances at school but a suit of my own! They hustled me off to the far corners of the store to pick out items.

"How much do you want to spend today, sir?" the clerk asked.

"No more than two hundred. That enough?" I innocently asked.

"That will do nicely, sir," he said, and we started picking up items. Pretty soon, I had a large arm full of brand new clothes and was wearing a shiny black pair of wingtips. I paid and put the remainder in my new wallet and hurried out to the waiting car. I hesitated when I saw a woman in the seat next to Shark. He had his arm around her, and they were in what appeared to be an intimate conversation. She saw me outside the car and rolled down the window. A quick glance showed her to be a young blonde in a low cut blouse. She couldn't have been much, if any, older than I was.

"Backseat, kid," Shark said. I opened the door and put all my clothes on the seat and climbed in. The blonde watched me the entire time as if I were doing something interesting. "Kid, meet Betty. She's one of ours, and we are just reconnecting. See you got some duds. Hope you look sharp in them, because I have a job for you later today."

"My name is Mike, Betty," I said and reached over the seat to shake her hand. She giggled and rolled her eyes but didn't shake my hand. I felt like an idiot for trying.

"Betty is a pretty hot number, Mike. She is usually down in this area if you ever feel the need. Feel free," Shark said and then started the car. Betty kissed him on his ear and got out giggling. I watched her walk away and couldn't help but notice that she wore a tight skirt and was blessed with a large rear end that she used to advantage. As the long car floated over the streets, I was aware that we were headed out to The Farm again.

"You drive, kid?" Shark asked.

"Sure," I said. He pulled the car sharply over to the curb and got out.

"No sense me driving you around. You drive me around. Get up there." I did as he said and soon found myself powering around majestically in the large heavy Cadillac. "To the office, kid," he said from the backseat. I was already heading out there. When we arrived, there were a few more cars in the lot than last time I was there. We could hear the music from inside the building as soon as the car made the last turn. I came around and opened the door for Shark and when he exited, I grabbed my packages. The front door opened by itself as we approached the bar, and on the way in, I saw Spiny grinning at me.

"Kid, go to Janel's room and get changed. Better knock first," Shark suggested. I made the turn into the bedroom area and dumped my packages on the floor in front of her closed door. I listened and could hear no voices so I knocked softly and waited. After I could hear nothing in response, I knocked again but louder. It seemed that I could hear a voice from a long way off, but I couldn't make out what she said. I opened the door and walked in and heard the shower running in the bathroom. I placed my packages on the rumpled bed and looked around. Same room, same odor of perfume hanging in the air. At least the noise from the bar area was muffled. Before I got organized to change, the door to the bathroom opened and Janel came out wrapped in a large towel, drying her long hair in another one. She stopped when she saw me standing there.

"I wondered when you would come back. They got you, don't they," she observed. I nodded yes. She continued to come closer and when she got to me she wrapped her arms around my waist and drew me tight. "Did you ever think of me, Mike?" she said into my shirt.

"All the time, Janel."

"But you never came back," she reminded me.

"I was trying to avoid the mob, not you, Janel. Did you think about what I said?"

"You mean, think about getting away from here? Of course I thought about it." She squeezed harder.

I pushed her gently to arm's length. Clean and without makeup she looked so young and innocent. I could see why all the men sought her out. There was nothing dirty about her, only purity and fragility. She looked like what any man would want to claim as his own.

"You know a detective named Smith?" I asked.

Janel frowned, "Yeah, I met him a couple of times. How do you know him?"

"He stopped me in the street after Shark's boys killed a dog and threatened some of the football team. We talked about you a little. He seems to think that you could leave at any time. Shark would just replace you. Is it true?"

"Shark would kill me if I left. He makes a lot of money from me. No, it isn't true. Anything else?" She was a bit harsh with her response. I thought I might as well get the rest of it out.

"Smith said that you use a lot of drugs. Do you?"

"Oh, that's it," she said, and her face took on a mean look. "They tell that story. Goes something like this, 'She gets a lot of money from men that she uses for drugs.' That sound like the tale?"

"Yes."

"Here is the truth, Mike. Some of them do give me money, and Shark and Spiny take it all from me. They laugh about it. I never use drugs. Want to see my arms?" She rolled her arms around, and I could only see perfect and transparent white skin. I told you the truth. What does it take to convince you?"

"I always believed you, but I had to ask. I'm sorry, Janel. I'm sorry that you are here, and I'm sorry that I can't do anything about it yet, but I still think about it, and someday I'll find an out for you."

"Oh, Mike. Seeing you is like seeing spring. Full of hope and newness. My life here...I don't want you to know about it. I hate that you are being drawn into it also. Why?"

"Why? Shark is making me. I don't want to. He is trying to buy me with cash and with you. My father died recently, and we are having some hard times. Shark knows this, and he is using it to get me to join them. He said I could have you any time, like you are something inanimate and not a person with free will."

"Now I feel sorry for you. It's true about you having me any time you want. I was given orders about that. I am willing, though, so you don't have to feel bad about it."

"I want to be your friend and someone you can trust, and I want to feel that way about you. If there ever comes a time that we both want each other, then we can do so with a clear mind, but I don't think that time has come," I said.

"You still in love with your sister?" Her question was, at least, blunt.

"Yes, that will never change, but she isn't here in this room. It is just you and me and what we decide, isn't it?" Janel didn't answer, and she started picking through the packages of new clothes.

"Any here for me?" she asked.

"Not this time. Do you need clothes?"

"Girls always want new clothes. It makes them feel better about themselves. I only get what they give me, which isn't much. Sure, I want new clothes, shoes or anything to remind me that there is something else in the world except this bed."

"I can see that you have to put on something. Shark told me to dress up, because we are doing something tonight. Want me to wait for you outside, then you can do the same for me?" I asked.

"No, I don't want you to wait outside. You just stand right where you are. Don't move," she said and then dropped the towel to the floor. I wish I could tell you what was going on in my mind at that moment. There just aren't any words which convey the sensation that was happening to me. Words like spectacular, wondrous, epitome are not enough. Actually, the reason I can't describe it is that my mind was not given to any rational thought just then. It was clearly the key that fit the slot or the combination that opened the safe. Evolution made sure that males like me have a reaction to that image. It insures the reproduction of the species and, frankly, drives a significant portion of human activity. We are nearly helpless before it. Is she beautiful or is it only that my brain is programmed to think that she is? No, she is beautiful and beyond any description. You have to be a male and see her as I saw her to understand. Janel didn't have to say a word, her body said it all.

"What are you thinking, Mike," she asked.

"I can't think just now," I answered truthfully. My eyes couldn't pull themselves away from her, and they went up and down and never settled on any spot, because all of her was beautiful, every last molecule of her. She chose that moment to unwrap her hair, and it cascaded down her back, completing the perfect picture.

"I am thinking that you should change also. Don't you think that it's a good idea? After all, we are really good friends, aren't we?" she asked.

"Yes, good friends," I answered robotically. It dawned on me that I had to leave the room or else succumb to her. Her nudity gave her just too much power over me to resist the pull. I started gathering my packages in a hurry.

"Don't tell me you are leaving? Am I not attractive enough for you?" she asked.

"You certainly are, Janel. Much too attractive for me. I have to leave."

"Mike, have you kissed any girl since our kiss?"

"No, Janel."

"Wasn't it exciting?" she asked.

"My first kiss. I'll always remember it."

"If you stay, I will open a whole world for you of firsts. Please let me show you," she said. There was a little desperation in her voice, not pleading and not anger. I could tell that this was something that she really wanted, and she wasn't just obeying orders.

"You know, Janel, I can't help caring for you. I like you. Your doing this to me is almost like forcing me, compelling me to be with you. It isn't right. I can't do it. I'm going to leave, but I want you to know that I'll still be your friend for life if you will let me."

"You don't understand, Mike. I want to have you as my friend too, but I have nothing else I can give you except myself."

"I'm sorry, Janel. No. Not now. Please don't get hurt. It's not a rejection of you. I'm just not ready for that." I left her crying and standing in the middle of the room with her arms straight down. She looked so helpless, small and alone, but I had no choice except to leave. I hated the men who put her in this place, and I hated those who would soil such a gift from the heavens as she was. I resolved again that I would somehow free her.

I went to the men's room to change and came out a different species. Now I looked like them. "Hey, Mike," Spiny called out across the room. "Nice threads!" Shark looked up from his card game and nodded his approval, then he waved me and Spiny to him.

"Spiny, tonight I want Mike to go with you. Show him the ropes, you understand?" Shark instructed.

"Sure, Shark. I show him," Spiny replied, giving me a knowing grin.

"Another thing, Spiny. We're getting pressure from some new guys in town. They might find you out there. Watch for them."

Spiny patted his gun under his coat and said, "I hope dat dey do, Shark."

The outing with Spiny was a series of pickups of small packages, probably cash. We drove from place to place and went inside. Some were small stores or barber shops, even a pool hall. Each time we went in, they seemed to know what Spiny was there for, and after a bit of chitchat, they would deftly pass a small paper sack over to us and then we were off to the next stop. At some, we got hostility, but they still gave up the little paper bag. Once back in the car, Spiny would pull out a heavy metal box from under the seat, put the sack inside and secure it with a key.

"Dis da small stuff," Spiny explained with a grin. I assumed that he meant that other places would give out larger amounts of cash, and I was right. He drove around in a large circle of connecting streets in the downtown area looking for something and suddenly found it, accompanied by a jerking stop of the car. I could make out a tall man standing in a dark doorway near three women in skimpy clothing.

"Lewishus!" Spiny commanded from the car. The man broke away from the girls and reluctantly came over to the driver's side while digging into his coat pocket.

"Spiny, my man. Come to collect or to get serviced?" he said with a guttural voice and leaned into the window to see who was in the passenger seat. Me. "New boy, I see. You need some action, new boy?"

"Just da bills, Lew. No jive." Spiny said. Lew pulled out a big roll of cash, quickly divided it in half and pushed one of the halves toward the window.

"I'll take the other half," Spiny said. I could hear a sigh from Lew and then reluctantly he gave Spiny the other half. "Any more rolls in da other coat pocket, Lew?"

"No, man. Dats all I got. I has to feed my girls, ya know, or dey get skinny, and it be hard on what ya leave me wid." He turned away shaking his head and walked back toward the small crowd of women as we drove away. I looked at the cash still on the seat between us. In the changing light, it looked like mostly tens and twenties and was about two inches thick.

"Now, da big stops," Spiny said as he drove. I noticed that he checked his pistol twice so wherever we were headed had some risks as well as cash. We drove into a darker part of town that I had previously only seen in the daylight. There were more than a few abandoned cars and a lot of roadside litter. Occasionally, I caught the glimpse of someone moving in the shadows. We parked in a dark alley, and I could hear loud, throbbing music coming through the wood wall next to the car.

"Mike, ya better stay here on dis one. Stay in da car and put that cash under da seat, got dat?" Spiny said. I grunted a yes and started looking around. Spiny got out and checked his gun again and headed for the corner of the building next to us. He turned the corner and disappeared from view. When my eyes adjusted to the dark, I spotted two shadowy figures start across the alley, headed for the same spot. As they crossed into the light, I could see the shiny suits. They were muscle from another gang, and they were after Spiny. I shrunk down in the car and quickly thought over what I should do. Most likely, when they finished with Spiny, they would come back to the car looking for the money and would find me. If I left Spiny alone and headed home, I would have to answer to Shark later. My only choice clear, I quietly got out of the car and rapidly closed the distance to the corner. I paused under the red glare of the blinking overhead neon sign also illuminating two men roughly ten feet behind Spiny. My mind raced with my limited options, and then I saw one of them reach for something in his pocket. I sprinted forward as fast as I could and called out to Spiny just as I crashed into the backs of the two thugs. The three of us went down together, and I came over the top of them and sprung to my feet first. The stubby revolver in one man's hand moved in slow motion just as my new black wingtip struck his face. The other one rose to his knees as the pop of his switchblade resonated in the dark. I hit him hard in the nose with my left hand as my right fist dove into the top of his head. Spiny pushed me aside, his glinting pistol aimed at the one with the gun.

"Get up, both ya or get it right here," Spiny said with malice. They both struggled to their feet, glowering at me. I bent down and picked up the knife and gun, then stood back, frightened to witness what was about to happen.

"Kid, go inside and tell da bartender to call Da Farm. Tell dem to send some guys over here like right now." I understood and left him guarding the two facing the wall with their hands over their heads. As I entered the dim, smoky bar, I felt all the faces watching me. I did as instructed and the fat bartender said he would call right away, and headed for the single telephone hanging on the shadowed wall. I wanted out of that place full of curious eyes and headed back outside to find Spiny frisking the two men. He extracted a pair of brass knuckles and another gun and tucked their wallets into his own pants.

"To da car, my friends," he ordered. As they walked away, I picked up the rest of the stuff on the ground. Spiny handed me the car keys and said, "Mike, open da trunk."

"We ain't getting in there," one man said.

"I can shoot ya right here and put ya in myself," Spiny observed. I could see that they were thinking of rushing us, so I pointed the other gun at them and moved back without saying anything.

"Look, gents, it's like dis. I want ya to have a talk with Shark before ya get shot. He always need new men. Ya might want to work for him. Give it some thought, huh? Better than catchin a bullet." That seemed to change the dynamics, and the two men relaxed a little and were about to get into the car's large trunk when two pairs of headlights appeared at the other end of the alley. We all stood in place as they came up and stopped. I hoped that it was our guys when we heard car doors opening and closing, but no one said anything. I could hear footsteps getting closer, and I held my breath but didn't take my eyes off of the two we had captured.

"Whatcha catch, Spiny?" a deep voice asked. The man came past me and towered over me by at least a foot with his hat on. Two more came from the other side.

"We got two wise guys about to make a hit on me. Mike here saved me, otherwise I'd be meat on a slab tonight," Spiny answered. I felt, rather than saw, the appraising looks come my way. I lowered the pistol and moved away letting the gangsters sort things out.

"You guys take off, we got this," the big man said.

"I got a pickup to make first. Don't leave yet," Spiny requested. He motioned me to accompany him back inside the bar, and we left the other five standing, eyeing each other.

"I owe ya, Mike. I won't forget dis," he said as we came through the bar door. As soon as we came in, the conversation died down, and we were watched by eyes from dark corners. Unconcerned, Spiny walked toward the rear and pushed past a small curtained opening into another room. A couple of rough-looking types sat at a wooden table and looked up as we came in.

"Got my present?" Spiny asked, and we all glared at each other. I pulled my hat farther down onto my face hoping to disguise the fact that I was still in high school. Without a word, one of the men produced a cigar box and slid it across the table. Spiny picked it up and hefted it to gauge its weight.

"Not bad. Shark will do the count. Better hope that he doesn't find anything missing," Spiny threatened in a low voice.

"It's all there. Who's the kid?" one burly man asked.

"New man. Named Mike. Ya'll be seeing him again." Spiny nodded and flicked the brim of his hat, and we left the way we came. In the alley, the two captives were already seated in the backseat of one of the cars and Shark's men were outside waiting on us.

"All done, Spiny? Any trouble?" the big man asked.

"No, we got it. See ya around." We got into Spiny's car, and he pulled out the strong box and put the pimp cash from under the seat inside the box. Then he opened the cigar box that contained mostly hundreds, lots of them. Spiny pulled out five bills and tossed them onto my lap.

"Bonus. Ya earned it. Ya can also keep what's in da wallets and ya can keep da gun and blade. Good night for ya, huh?" He pulled the cash out of the wallets and threw that on my lap, then tossed the wallets out the window. Another several hundred dollars plus change.

"What about the count? Won't that be wrong?" I asked.

"Yeah. I didn't like the attitude in dere. Dey got it coming, don't worry bout it."

"Are we done?" I asked.

"Yeah, I get da rest of it tomorrow. I'll take ya home now, unless ya wants to go to Da Farm and recreate for a while."

"No thanks, I'd rather get home," I said. "What will happen to those two?" I asked.

"Ya don't want to know."

Spiny and I drove back to my home in silence. When he pulled to the curb, he said, "Pick ya up tomorrow about two. Don't make me wait."

I had no idea what time it was, but the sky was black and most of the other homes' lights were out. Trying to be quiet, I pushed open the front door and entered the dark living room.

"Glad you decided to come home, at last. We were worried sick." It was Mary's voice, and I detected a small quiver.

"Is Mother there with you," I asked in a quiet voice.

"No, she couldn't take it and went to bed an hour ago. Are you all right?

I went toward her voice and knew from the direction that she was on the couch. Reaching out in the dark, I patted around and found that she was lying down, covered by a light blanket. "Nice of you to wait up for me," I said and knelt down near her head.

"Tell me everything."

"Well, that's a long story. It was an eventful day." I reached into my pocket and took out an impressive stack of cash and put it into her hand. I felt her roll to her back, and for a moment she was silent.

"This is a lot of money. How did you get it."

"I didn't do anything dishonest unless you count saving Spiny's life as dishonest. He gave it to me as a reward.

Shark took me down to Simson's this morning and bought me some clothes. I guess I am officially a gang member as of now."

"I've been waiting up for you because we always tell each other everything. There's a lot more to this story."

"There is nothing to hide, Mary. I'm just tired. Spiny is coming to get me tomorrow afternoon, but I still have no idea what they plan for me. We need to make a list tomorrow of all the places Spiny and I stopped at to give to Detective Smith. It will be a whole page of places that pay the mob in cash, and I'm sure Smith will want to know. Shark's boys took two men, that I knocked down, away in a car, but I don't know much more than that. I don't know who they were or who took them, but I'll bet they won't be seen alive again." I could feel the couch moving as Mary started to cry. "Please, Mary, don't cry. I'm all right, I didn't do anything wrong, and I brought back some money that we badly need." I reached out and put my hand on her shoulder.

"Mike, don't you see that you are involved now. You'll never get away from them, and pretty soon you'll be just like they are," she said through the sobs and tears. "I have to ask you this. Would you be doing this if I wasn't your sister, if you didn't even know me?" She put her finger right on the question that could only be answered "No."

"So far, it has nothing to do with you. I just got noticed by them, and they are determined to have me join up. You and I are going to turn the table by informing the police about everything they do. They will be sorry that they made me come in."

"If they find out you are an informant, what will they do?" she asked.

"We just have to trust Detective Smith. There is nothing else I can do. I am not going to become like them. You'll see," I assured her.

"What are we going to do with all this money?"

"I'm going to have you give it to Mother. Make up some story about where it came from. She'll believe it if you say it, and even if she doesn't, she will be glad to get some money and will look the other way."

"Did you see Janel today?"

"Yes."

"Want to tell me about that?"

"I want to tell you that we spoke briefly and that I feel more sorry for her than ever, and most important, is that I didn't do anything at all. You should quit worrying about Janel and me. You are the most important person in my life. There isn't anything I wouldn't do for you, and I'll never let you down. You know that."

She started sobbing again and reached out with an arm and pulled me down toward her. We were cheek to cheek, and on one side of my face was her wet, warm skin and on the other side was her hand still clutching the paper money. This was the first time since we became sexually aware that we had embraced. I wanted to for a long time, but I was afraid of what kind of feeling it would bring out in me. She felt so perfect, so alive and so natural to touch. I kissed her on the cheek and wrapped my arms around her. I realized that what I was feeling was love, not passion and not sexual desire, just love. When I hugged Janel, I had to repress an intense desire for her, but I didn't feel anything like I did at this moment with Mary in my arms. Frieda was wrong. There was nothing to worry about, because I loved Mary so much that I would even protect her from me. I just wanted to hold her and feel her warmth and take in her scents and her breath. My mind was empty of sexual thoughts. It was such a relief to me that I had to hold back my tears. It was all right that I loved my sister, and there was nothing evil or ugly about it.

Before Mary left for work, we worked on the list for Smith. I felt better after getting it down on paper, and I wrote another page describing what happened outside the bar. We decided that Mary would call and ask where and how he wanted it sent. Before she left, she turned to me and gave me a little kiss on my cheek. She had never done that before, and I also saw a little glint in her eye. We were closer than ever, and we had put our unnatural fear of physical contact behind us. I watched her walk away as if it would be the last time I would ever see her. It was strange to realize that in a few days, it would be our seventeenth birthday, and we had seen each other every day of every one of those seventeen years. But I still hated to part from her even for a few hours. I took a deep breath just as she was nearly out of sight. Yes, I loved her, and it felt wonderful to admit it.

Spiny's car took the familiar turn into the parking lot at The Farm. It was two thirty, and I still had no idea what I was going to be asked to do. When we entered, Shark was in his familiar spot and didn't look up from his card game until we were standing in front of him. When he saw me, he gave me his big gold-tooth smile.

"Well, the young pugilist has returned. I heard about last night. You got it, Mike. I always knew it. Here is what I want from you. You are to return to the boxing club every afternoon. Get at least three hours of training, then come here to eat with us. Then you can go on rounds with Spiny until you get the hang of it and our customers get used to seeing you. Eventually, you will do it alone, but not yet. Sleep until noon. Get paid big bucks. What more can you want? Oh, yes, that one." Shark looked over at the bar. I followed his eyes, and we both stared at the lovely bare back of Janel who was watching in the mirror. He gave her a "come here" wave, and she immediately got up. "Yes, that one," Shark said seemingly to himself.

Janel came up, and I perceived hostility from her when she glanced at me and then quickly looked away. Her face remained impassive, but there was something different than before.

"Janel, did you hear about our boy's exploits last night. How he saved Spiny's life?" Shark asked her.

"Yeah, I heard."

"Did you ever hear about him knocking out our boy King in the first minute of the first round?"

"Yeah, I heard that one too."

"Have you noticed how damned good-looking this kid is?" Shark continued, while looking down at his deck.

"If you say so," she responded.

"And you, Mike. Ever seen any girl as attractive as this one?"

"No, Mr. Cohen. She is tops," I said, avoiding the comparison with my incredible sister.

"Seen her without any clothes yet, Mike?"

"Yes, Mr. Cohen, I have."

"So, what'd you think?" he said, starting to deal out cards.

"It took my breath away. I couldn't think."

"Janel. Have you seen Mike without any clothes?"

"No, and I don't want to."

"You remember that I told you that you were to be nice, remember?" Shark said and looked at her hard.

"I don't care. You can't pay me enough for that. Don't send this little boy into my room again. Find a real man, if you can." This time her anger was right on the surface. She had been hurt and humiliated, and this was her way of getting back at me. She gave me a mean look, and I saw another side of her. Nothing soft about her this time.

Shark shook his head. "Try to do something nice for people, and this is what you get. Mike, your problem is that you don't know what you are missing. This girl thinks the world of you, and you have hurt her several times. I don't blame her a bit. You are the loser here, whether you know it or not. I've been paid a thousand bucks for ten minutes with her, and you get it for free. I worry about you, boy."

Janel shot me a fiery look of defiance. She knew that the very mention of men that she had serviced would bother me. This also was payback. And it was true that it hurt. I tried to force the thoughts out of my mind of any man with the right amount of money having her do anything he wanted. It was painful to think about, and I especially didn't want to learn that she was an avid and willing partner. I believe that I put my sister so high on a pedestal that I assumed that all women were like her, especially the beautiful ones. To learn that it isn't true is one of life's painful lessons. The moment didn't change anything regarding my sympathy for Janel. I didn't want, or expect to have, a sexual encounter with her, so her anger didn't disappoint me, and I understood completely why she felt that way. I refused to return her hateful look, and it seemed to calm her down. She had her moment of revengeful poking of a knife into me, but I could see in her eyes that she didn't really mean it.

Shark put down the cards. "You two go grab a table over there where I can keep an eye on you and talk this out. That's an order." He went back to concentrating on his cards, and we both left for a corner of the large room. I held the chair for her as she sat down, and she gave me a funny look of surprise.

"Janel, I am sorry if I hurt you. I apologize a million times, really. What can I do to get you to forgive me?"

"You won't make love to me, because you think I'm too low class or too dirty for you, isn't that so?" Her nostrils flared a bit as she spoke, and there was a flash of color in her face. This was, after all, the hot button item, not the sex, but in what regard I held her.

"I have treated you with respect and tenderness. You already know what effect you have on me physically, and you remember that I have told you several times how absolutely beautiful you are. You are angry because you think I have rejected you, yet you know that I haven't been with any other women and that you gave me my first kiss. Doesn't it seem like I hold you in high regard after all?"

"Yes, I guess that it does," she said and allowed some of the sweetness to return to her face.

"Thanks. Here is another question. Do you love me?" I asked.

"Well, I have never been in love, but I think that it could happen with you."

"I want to make love to the woman that I love in my heart. Is that stupid?" I asked.

"No, it's very special," she admitted and started to tear and sniff. I offered her my hanky, and she took it. "I guess I wanted to bring you to my level, and then I would have a chance with you because we would be the same. It's too late for me to better myself because I have ruined my life. You are correct if you thought that I wanted to ruin yours too." The tears began in earnest, and I could see Shark and Spiny watching us from across the room. I let her cry and just sat silently and watched her. It was a good lesson for me. I could never have any thought of sex with Mary because it would ruin her life too. It took a while, but eventually, Janel took a big breath and gave me a weak smile and sat back up.

"Perhaps I can do something for you, Mike," she said as she blotted away the last of the tears. "Let's talk about you and Mary."

"Let's not," I contested.

"No! You need to talk it out. No one is more qualified that I am to talk about sex. Now that we have gotten our sex thing behind us, we can freely talk about anything and everything. Like most men, you probably think about it, dream about it and wish for it more or less all the time. Right?"

"True."

"Honestly, what did you think when we were together in my room last time?"

"I thought that I wanted to stand there and look at you forever. I was awfully close to being on fire. I thought that you are the most perfect creature in the universe and that you were somehow made just for me."

"Do you feel that way about Mary?"

"I don't allow myself to think that way about her. It's off-limits."

"Ever dream about having her?"

"Only about two hundred times."

"No one ever hears this sort of saga about brothers and sisters. I heard that she feels the same way about you. Want to know what I think? To me, it means that something is wrong with the story that you are brother and sister. There was a mixup someplace. You don't even look like her."

"This is the third time that I have heard this theory. Mary and I have even discussed it. Problem is that I remember her before I can remember her. We have always been together, and we have always loved each other. We seem to be closer than Siamese twins."

"You hear a lot hanging around this den of thieves. Twice, I have heard of doctors being paid to do a switch. You know, wife and hubby had their hearts set on a particular sex and then have the other. A doctor on the take can easily switch one for what they want if he gets the right opportunity. What was the name of your mother's doctor?"

"I don't know his name. Listen, this is painful talk for me to hear because I have it bad for her already. This could make it worse. We would need some sort of proof. I don't want to start thinking this way. She is my sister and that's that. I know that I love her, but I am never going to have sex with her, and I refuse to be so low that I start thinking about it. I even try to forget my dreams. They shame me."

Janel reached across the table and patted my hand. "Mike, you are the sweetest guy I have ever seen. I'm sorry about what I said earlier. I was just hurt and angry. Given the way you feel about me, you are quite a man to turn me down, and possibly, you are the only man alive that would. You are tortured from all this pent-up sexual desire and here I offer you a release and you would rather continue to suffer. Such character! I know that I could fall in love with you."

"When I said that I wanted to be your friend, Janel, I meant it. Tell me again that you want to get out of here."

"I want to get out of here!" she said under her breath. "There is no way I can leave, even if I had the money. They watch me all the time. They search my room. They offer me drugs which would further imprison me. Spiny told me once that if I tried to leave, they would find me and pour acid on my face."

"How much money would you need, Janel?"

"Five grand and a little help and I'm out of here," she said quickly.

"Does this place bring in a lot of cash?" I asked.

"Are you kidding? They bring it in here from all over the place. Us girls, the gambling and blackmail bring in at least seventy five thou a week. Then there is the booze and the drugs. We guess that Shark is bringing in two hundred thousand a week. He doesn't pay out much, but I hear that he splits with the out-of-town bosses."

"Do you know what he does with the money?" I asked.

"No, not really. We think that his big goons drive it out of town and deposit it somewhere under some other name, but that's just a guess. I don't know what you are thinking, Mike, but it's dangerous just to think about it."

"I told you that we had to stick together, and this is what I meant. By comparing notes, we may be able to figure out something."

"You can't steal from the mob. They would hunt you forever, no matter how long it took. Think of another way," she said in a whisper. Her face was again radiant and beautiful. I felt close to her and desperately wanted to help her. Whatever I came up with, it was going to take some time and a better understanding of how things work. It wasn't going to happen soon, and she would be stuck here for the foreseeable future.

"You can come into my room anytime you like, Mike. In fact, I want you to. I forgive you. We are friends, and you are the only person I can talk to that I trust. If you ever want more from me, just ask."

"You are delightful to be around when you aren't angry. I love looking at you and, by the way, thank you for that view you gave me in your room…I still can't get over it. Every day that I'm here, I'll look forward to seeing you and talking with you." Half-standing, I leaned over the table and kissed her lips briefly. It seemed to mean a lot to her that I would do that in public, and she rewarded me with an incredible smile.

"Hey, lovebirds, the boss wants to see ya," Spiny shouted. We got up and went over to their table.

"Well, hell's bells, it worked didn't it? You two look good together you know. See what happens when you behave? Now, time for supper. Mike, you are part of our group now. They will be coming in shortly, and we all dine together. Janel, you can get back to work and earn your keep. Man, you look good tonight." Shark was in a good mood. There must have been lots of cash in that little box. Just as he said, men started drifting in, and I could always tell if they were part of the mob. They just had the look. A shout from a back room rang out, and we all started filing in. A couple of them eyed me suspiciously but kept quiet. The back room contained a long table surrounded by chairs. Two waiters circulated, supplying beverages and linen.

"Mike, come and sit with me," Spiny called from across the room. He was near the head of the table, and he pointed to a chair he was holding beside him. I made my way around and started to sit, but he restrained me. Then I noticed that everyone was standing, apparently waiting on Shark to arrive at the head of the table. He finally came rushing in and motioned everyone to sit down.

"Welcome to all of you. First things first," he said as he clanked on a glass with his knife. They all stopped talking and turned toward him. "Welcome a new man to our group. Mike, stand up." They all watched me but didn't make a sound. Shark continued, "Mike Condor is our youngest member. Remember the story of the kid who cleaned up King? This is the fellow we talk about. Last night, his first time on the job, he took out two of the Muretto gang who were about to polish off Spiny. By himself, he put both of the big guys on the ground. Give him a round." This time there were glasses raised and shouting all around. Shark motioned for me to sit down. "Mike is still a kid but give him respect. Money and girls wouldn't hurt either!" They all laughed and a few quarters were tossed toward me.

The meeting droned on with Shark doing most of the talking. He discussed various operations and expenses, who had cars and who needed cars. I nearly fell asleep. We could smell the food being cooked in the adjoining kitchen. Finally, Shark stopped talking and looked around. "Time to eat, drink and drink some more." More applause, then the doors shot open as the food trays were brought in. The noise level was high and got higher as the liquor flowed. The fellow on the other side of me slapped me on the back repeatedly, and as he got plastered, asked if I was keeping all the girls satisfied. I said that I was and was prepared for his next response, that I was to call him if I needed any help.

The thought struck me that I had no way home except to let Spiny take me and the way he was drinking, it wasn't going to be a very safe trip. I considered walking, but the distance was over seven miles, and it was pitch dark. I also didn't know that the high point of the night was coming up.

Shark stood up and motioned for someone out of my sight to do something. The doors to the bar area opened and a line of girls came in. As I found out later, the joke was that the girls were free to choose who they were going to be with that night. They came around cautiously peering at the assembled men who were whooping and laughing. When they chose someone, they would stand behind him with her hands on his shoulders. Some chose to put their hands elsewhere to the delight of the other men. Unexpectedly, I felt a pair of hands on my shoulders. I started to turn to see what she looked like, or if I recognized her, but she pushed my head straight ahead. Whoever the girl was behind me, she was getting a lot of attention from the men across from me, and they weren't laughing. Shark's face fell when he looked my way, and he didn't look very happy either. When every girl had made her selection, Shark dismissed the room and left by the side door.

I stood up to meet this person standing behind me. Before I completely turned, I realized that it was Janel. She was grinning at her little joke and was dressed up and made up like she had been at the dance. No wonder I got some frowns. The other men were jealous, because she looked like a movie star. Most of the other girls were pretty frumpy and the remainder looked cheap. Janel was a stunner.

"Thank God, it's you," I exclaimed.

"And thank him that you are you," she answered with a giggle.

"Now what?" I asked.

"You will come with me to my room. That's what they expect and that is what we will do," she said, and led the way through the crowd. I got several hard slaps on my back on the way out, and some were hard enough to feel more like a punishment was intended. We made a beeline for the hall leading to her room and quickly closed the door behind us.

"Hey, what's going to happen out there in the bar?" I asked. She turned and gave me a quizzical look.

"Can't you imagine what will happen when there are no rules, no supervision and no morals. If you can't, I don't want to describe it to you."

"It seems that I'm not getting home tonight unless I walk," I said.

"That's not much of a complement to me, is it? I'll have to pay for my choice of you. Better appreciate what I did for you, Mike."

"What do you mean, 'pay'?" She didn't respond, and I let it drop. Through the closed door, a woman's shriek could be heard, then loud laughter. Suddenly, I felt dog-tired. Janel noticed and led me over to the bed and pushed me down onto my back. She untied my new shoes and threw them across the room, then came around and lay down beside me, both of us looking up at the boring and dirty ceiling. I reached out and took her hand in mine.

"Glad to know you, Janel. By the way, you look ravishing tonight. You know, I just remembered that I don't really know what ravishing means. It sort of sounds like food or something and that would certainly apply to the way you look right now." She laughed and put her other hand to her mouth.

"Would it bother you if I laid my head on your chest, Mike?" I responded by pulling her toward me, and she curled up with her head on my chest and her hand and arm loosely over my abdomen.

"Could you tell me about yourself, Janel? As you said, we are close friends so we don't have to hold anything back. What about it?" I could feel her squirm as if the memories were unpleasant for her.

"It's not a pretty story, Mike. I don't want you to feel sorry for me."

"I just want to know everything about you because I care about you, and I want to understand, that's all. You don't have to tell me anything, if you don't want to."

She took a long time to start talking, and while I waited, I just listened to her breathing and the occasional animal sounds which made it through the door.

"My parents were never married. Where I grew up, that marks you as contemptible, just like you are the one who has done something wrong. What a way to start life. Few friends and most of those are in your same shoes. My father had enough of being with us, joined the Navy and left us without any source of income. We got some help from relatives, but they either ran out of money or got tired of helping us. My mother started bringing home men for money. She really wasn't like that, and it shamed her terribly to do it but she kept us alive that way. As I reached about twelve, her men started noticing me." She stopped for awhile, and I listened to see if she was crying, but I couldn't tell.

"May, that was my mother's name, finally found a man she wanted to keep around. The very first time he was alone with me...." This time I knew that she was crying. I stroked her arm and shoulder, and she got it under control. "Well, the short version is that when May found out, she blamed me and kicked me out of the apartment. I had nowhere to go and wandered around on the street for two days before the police picked me up. I ended up in a Juvenile Detention Center. Rough kids. I started to become attractive around then, and the male supervisors started passing me around. One day I fled back onto the street and hitchhiked my way to another city. This time I knew enough to say away from cops. Asking around, I found a Catholic church and a couple of kindly nuns who wanted to help. They could tell that I had been around, as they say, but they found a place for me in one of their orphanages where I went back to school and had a place to sleep. It worked for a while until their doctor examined me and reported his findings back to the nuns. They decided that a sexually active girl did not belong in the orphanage with decent girls. They planned to hand me back to the cops, but I ran away instead. I was back on the street again, and I fell in with a bunch of kids like me who were living hand to mouth. There were a few thieves, a few with temporary jobs and a few girls like me who had no choices except to sell our bodies when we had to. We all pooled our money and lived in abandoned buildings, moving around a lot for safety. Our little community eventually fell apart, and once more I was alone. One of Shark's men spotted me and pulled me in here where I've been ever since." She let out a big sigh and stopped talking.

"Compared to you, I've been very lucky. Thanks for trusting me with your story. I understand you better, and I appreciate you telling me about yourself. It was obviously painful for you to remember what happened, and it's also obvious that there have been very few people in your life that you could trust. I hope I can be different. As for me, I don't like being forced into the mob, and I'll have to break away at some point. I would like to get you away at the same time. I don't have a plan, because I don't know enough yet to make one."

"You better make a plan pretty soon, or they will never let you leave. Expect that they will get you to commit a crime, possibly a murder, and hold that over you to make you stay. It's happened before."

Janel and I snuggled close, and we continued with some small talk as the noise in the outer room eased off. I must have drifted off to sleep, because I woke with a start. Janel was turned facing away from me but still touching me with her back and feet. I didn't have a watch, and I looked around the room, spotting her big ticking alarm clock on the dresser. Four a.m. The place was silent as a tomb. I lay back down and thought about what I should do. My choices were simple. I could walk home, or I could just stay here and start my day at The Farm. As I mulled it over, Janel stirred, turning to see if I was awake. When she saw that I was, she rolled over and put her arm over me and pulled her face close to mine.

"This is the first time in my life that I woke up with someone I cared about," she said sleepily. She kissed me on my cheek and asked, "What is going on in that head now?" She started playing with my hair and winding some of it around her finger as she looked at me.

"Well, we are even. This is the first time I ever slept with a woman that I cared about," I said.

"You could have added that this was the only time," she teased.

"I always start at the top, and it took awhile to find her." This time she gave a little pout, likely telling me that I had gone too far with that one. I leaned over and kissed her on the cheek. "What time do you usually get up around here?"

"We usually are busy at night, and night can last until dawn for some of us. We get up around noon, and the bar opens at three."

"What happens if you get hungry before noon?"

"Oh, you can just go into the kitchen and eat whatever. Are you telling me that you are hungry?

"More restless, I think."

"You can chew on me. I'm very satisfying." She pinched me in the side and it hurt.

"Yes, I'm awake now," I said. I reached my arm under and around her head and rolled her on top of me. We were eye to eye. "You still look, what was it...oh, radishing! No, it was ravishing. You are ravishing!"

"So are you," she said in a very small voice and touched her nose to mine and held it there. I wrapped both arms around her back and gave a big squeeze, forcing the air out of her lungs, and she burst out laughing. "Well, you are full of life this early. Want me to go to the kitchen with you and help you find some food?"

"I think that sounds good. Suppose that room is still full?"

"Most have gone back to wherever they came from. There may be several still there, but they'll still be drunk and won't even see us. One thing you must agree to before I take you out there."

"Sure, just ask."

"You have to come back here with me. I need to touch you and hold you, and I hope you feel the same way."

"I agree. Holding you is very special, and I need it too." She rolled up to a sitting position and, with her back to me, fussed with her hair. I got up looking for where she had tossed my shoes and found them against the far wall. I came back and sat beside her, while I found the energy to put them on. I looked at my companion in the dim light and saw how utterly attractive she was. I started to say something, but she looked at me and I lost my train of thought.

"You remember what you said about making love to someone that you love in your heart?"

"I do."

"That is the right way. I see it now, and I never could before. What a wonderful thing that must be, to give yourself to someone you love and who loves you. My wish is that it will happen to you someday."

"Don't you wish that for yourself?"

"I would wish it, but it would be futile."

"Then, I will wish it for you. If you could get away from here, I'm sure you could start over and find happiness."

"Jeez, Mike, how I hope that happens."

We opened her door cautiously. The place was silent. We crept into the barroom as silently as we could, heading for the dining area. Janel had predicted correctly. The place was empty except for three men passed out on the floor. I didn't see any of the girls from last night.

"What happened to all the girls?" I whispered.

"Their pimps probably came and got them and put them back on the street." Now I understood better where they came from. Shark owned them too. We continued past the bottles on the floor, and in a couple of places what looked like vomit, continuing on into the dark kitchen. After Janel found the switch and put on the lights, she went to the large refrigerator and looked inside.

"There are some eggs and a big piece of beef. What will it be, breakfast or lunch?" she asked.

"Can you cook?" I inquired.

"If I didn't, I would have starved a long time ago. Want me to make you something?"

"Please. And I'll help you if you show me where the stuff is."

"You pull up a stool and watch. I'm fast at this," she said, giving me a big smile.

She began working, and in a few minutes, she had a plate full of smoking eggs and beef strips, and from somewhere she produced a large glass of orange juice. She beckoned me to sit on a chair beside her at the kitchen table.

"Did you get some?" I asked.

"No, I never eat until noon. I keep my figure that way."

"Say, I've never seen you drink any booze. Do you?"

"Very rarely and then just a little. I'm clean. No drugs, no alcohol and no cigarettes. Some of the girls get old quick on that stuff, but it's not for someone smart enough to know what it will do to you."

Janel was so attractive that she looked out of place in the kitchen, still wearing her dancing dress, and I felt bad that I didn't suggest that she take it off. She was keeping her word to me to keep sex out of our relationship so undressing in front of me would have been like before. I was growing to like her company more and more. As I ate, we talked, seemingly about everything and about nothing. When I was nearly finished, one of the kitchen doors opened abruptly and standing in the door was Shark. He looked bleary eyed, he was swaying slightly, his face a mask of hatred.

"What the hell are you two doing?" The question was sharply and harshly delivered.

"Hi, Shark," I said. We are grabbing an early breakfast, at least I am. Want some food?" I offered.

"When did I give you permission to call me anything other than Mr. Cohen, you pompous little kid? Another thing, I said you could visit with her. I didn't give her to you. Didn't you get enough of her last night? Do you still have to be with her now? The answer better be no."

"We were just getting food, Mr. Cohen. Where's the harm?" I asked.

"Look, kid, I'm revoking your privileges with her. You are not allowed to even talk with her from now on. Now get out of my place."

"Does this mean that I'm fired, and you don't want me around any more?" I said, hoping he would agree.

"It means get out of here. It means that you still do as you are told, and that means whatever I want, and what I want is for you to take your face out of here as fast as you can."

"You know that means I have to walk seven or eight miles in the dark since I don't have a car."

"You can fly if you want. Just leave right now or face the consequences." The message was clear, I had to leave. He was mad and drunk, and I feared what he might do to Janel. She didn't look worried, and I figured that she had probably seen this act before. I looked at her, and she nodded to me that I had to leave. Shark was still balancing in the door frame glaring at us. I stood up, shrugged and leaned over and gave Janel a kiss on the cheek. I left by the other door and walked outside into the dark and cool air. I didn't know it at the time, but that was the last time I would ever talk to the beautiful girl named Janel.

As I walked down the gravel drive toward the road, I had a sobering realization. I was wearing new, stiff, dress shoes. The long walk ahead was going to be memorable, and it certainly was.

I limped along on the last street before my home street, and my feet were shouting at me. Even taking the shoelaces out didn't help. I was going to be lucky to just make it. The dawn was giving way to morning about the time I arrived. I sat down on the stoop and pulled the shoes and socks off. The blisters were enormous. Behind me the screen door opened, and Mary came out and sat beside me.

"Hard night?"

"I got trapped at their drunken party. There was no one to take me home. Shark kicked me out the door about four this morning, and I walked home."

"Hmmm," she offered. "Let me get some salts to soak your feet. You could be crippled for a while it would appear." She left and went into the house. I could hear Mother's voice saying, "Did that bum son of mine finally make it home?" Mary's voice was low, and I couldn't make out what she said in return.

Mother opened the screen door and shouted, "Did you forget where you live, son, or were you having too good a time at The Farm with your criminal friends?"

"Please, Mother, the neighbors will hear you," Mary reproached.

"Well, everyone knows Mike has become a mobster. They might as well hear it from his mother," she said even louder. Mary escorted her back inside, but I could hear the muttering and occasional loud voice coming from inside. After a little while, she was quiet, and Mary came back with a pan of hot water and sat down beside me.

"What happened out there? Want to talk about it?"

"Some pretty ugly stuff, Mary. Some of the things that go on out there would disgust you. It did me. Shark was pretty rough on me this morning, but he was angry and drunk. I could be finished with them, I don't know."

"That doesn't tell me much," she said, holding her chin in her hands.

"I know that you want to know about Janel, and I don't blame you for wanting to know. She told me her very sad story last night. It would have made you cry to hear it. She has never caught a break in life, and it gets worse all the time. This will make you happy, though. Shark absolutely ordered me to not speak to her any more. You won't have to worry any longer about her."

"Why did he do that?"

"They had a big sex party planned. They brought in a bunch of hookers and made them choose a man to be with. I think Janel was slated to be with someone, possibly Shark himself. She was by far the best looking of them. Janel chose me instead, and Shark is really mad at both of us. She told me she was going to have to pay for that choice. I didn't discover what was going to happen to her."

"You mean that you spent the whole night with her until four this morning?"

"We hid in her room and talked. The rest of the crowd was doing something in the bar area, but we didn't see any of it. I fell asleep for a lot of that time. See the clothes I am wearing? They never came off. Never. Neither did hers. We never kissed, just hugged a couple of times. It was totally innocent, I promise. Her choosing me prevented her from being in that mess, whatever was going on, and prevented me from seeing it. You can look at it as though we saved each other."

"Have you gotten close to her then?"

"Oh, Mary, Mary. There is no one but you in my heart. I love you so much it hurts. Don't ever worry about me losing that and choosing somebody else to take your place. Janel is a poor little thing that needs help. I'll never be able to love her like I love you, but I, at least, can treat her like the friend she is to me."

"She is a loose woman and very attractive. Sure, I worry about you, because you are only human. There are temptations even you can't resist."

"That happened already. There couldn't be any more temptation than that, and I did resist it. Don't worry so much. You know what we usually talk about when I am with a girl? We talk about you or you and me. Everybody in town knows the score. I even heard the theory that you and I are not related again, this time from Janel. Even she thinks that we are not. I told her that I can't let that thought into my mind, or I would actually go crazy. If I didn't make a supreme effort every day to control my thoughts, I only would think of one thing. You."

"Well, brother, you have company on that one," she said and then got up and went inside.

With Mary's help I made it into my bed and fell asleep on my back. By the time I woke up the light from my window was fading into evening. I heard my door crack as it creeped open, and I saw Mary's almond-shaped eye looking in. She saw that I was awake and came in.

"Time to eat. Think you can get up and come to dinner?"

I looked at my feet and thought about it. "Let's see," I said and sat up and carefully put a foot on the floor. "Nope," I said. "Not without some help."

"Just as I thought. I'll help you in there. By the way, Mother has calmed down, and I think we need to tell her what is going on."

"She can't handle it, Mary."

"We need to try," she said, and let me put my arm over her shoulder. I limped along on my heels and sat down at the dinner table. At first, Mother ignored me, and as she sat the plates and food down, she started to look longer in my direction. I didn't say anything until they both sat down and had said the prayer.

"Mother, I need to tell you what I am doing. It's not what you think. Are you interested in listening?"

"Yes, Mike, I'm listening, and I'm listening for your father as well who wouldn't have let you get into this mess."

"This started when he was still with us. He just didn't know it," I said. She looked surprised but remained quiet.

"Before I tell you anything, I want you to promise not to tell anyone, and I mean anyone, about what you hear. Can you do that?"

"How can I promise when I don't know what you are going to say. What if the right thing to do is to call the police?" she said.

"Mary and I have already met with the police. We talked to a detective named Smith. He is aware of everything I do, but it's a secret and telling anyone about it could get us all killed. Do you understand how important this is to us now?"

"I didn't know, Mike. Go ahead with your story, you have my word that I won't tell anyone."

"First of all, Mother, I have not done any crime or any other bad thing. They forced me into joining them, but I am trying to figure out how to get away from them. They have implied a threat to Mary to get me in, and I know that the threat is real. They are capable of anything. Another thing you need to know. Smith said that a lot of cops are on the take and can't be trusted."

"How do you know that you can trust this Smith?"

"Frankly, we don't know for sure, but right now we believe him, because we have no other choices," Mary said.

Mother looked at the wall, in thought for a moment. "Have you thought about us moving out of town? We have some relations out west that would take us in and help us get started."

"It could work, but we would have to be sure that our trail could not be followed. We would have to walk away from this house in the middle of the night and not take anything with us. Could you do that?"

"I'll have to write them. Course, it will take money, that we don't have, to do it."

"If I could get the money and truthfully tell you that I didn't commit any crime to get it, would you take it?" I asked.

"Mike, it isn't possible for that to happen. I wouldn't be able to believe you."

"I see why you would think that. What about writing the letter and then we can see if we have any options?"

Mother didn't say what she was going to do, and we had a quiet dinner with all of us lost in our own internal world. I was about to ask Mary to help me get back to my room when we heard a screech of tires in front of the house. We all looked at each other for answers, and then there was a loud knock on the door. I had a sense of foreboding regarding who it could be, and Mother got up and opened the door as I tried to struggle to my swollen feet.

The door opened, and I could see the smiling face of Spiny standing under the porch light.

"Evening, Mrs. Condor, I am Gerald Spinnazzo, a friend of ya son. Is he here?"

"Sure is. You might as well come inside and see for yourself." She stepped back and Spiny walked into the small living room which was open to the dining room. He saw me standing there and waved as he came forward.

"Well, Mike. Sorry about da long walk dis morning," he said, then he took a long look at my feet. "Holy sh... I'm sorry folks. Wow, ya feet look pretty bad, Mike."

"They feel like they look Spiny. Dress shoes," I offered.

"Well, I have a gift to ya that might make ya feet feel like clicking. Come over here and look at da curb." Mary took my arm, and I hobbled over to the front door. At the curb I could see two cars. One of them was a convertible Ford, a two seater with a rumble seat.

"Here's da key to dat job. Shark said it might make up for da yelling last night. He feel pretty bad bout it. Ya can't tell in this light, but it's bright red and really sharp."

"Where did that come from?" I asked.

"Shark won it in a poker game a couple days ago. Thought ya would like it, that's all. Ya like it, don't ya?"

"Does this mean that I am still working for you?"

"Sure does. Ya drive that car out to Da Farm when ya feet feel like it and talk to Shark. Let's make it tomorrow about midnight. Okay?"

"Why midnight?"

"Dats a counting night. Nobody but us. You guys can get straight. Shark said to tell ya that ya can see Janel afterward."

I took the key from him, and he tipped his hat, smiled, and left in the big Caddy.

Mary was the first one to speak, "I don't like it. First Shark kicks you out and now gives you a car and Janel. And the midnight thing."

"They are different. Who knows? I expect that they could just kill me anywhere, instead of luring me out there. Besides, I have done nothing to them, and Shark has pursued me for two years to get me out there. He even introduced me at his meeting."

"Are you going, Mike?" Mother asked.

"I have to. If I didn't show, Spiny or the big thugs would show up at the door. Maybe it is as Spiny said, Shark is making amends because he was angry and drunk that night."

My feet improved enough the next day to take Mary out in the little V8 Ford, and it was a blast. I let her drive most of the time, and she got the hang of it really fast. We cruised by Phillip's house and let him drool on the bright red paint, and afterward we all went to the malt shop, with Phillip riding in the rumble seat. It was one of those innocent happy times that you always remember the rest of your life.

On her way into her bedroom, Mary kissed me on the cheek, "Mike, that was a great way to spend a day. I can't wait to do it again." Yes, it was, but that was the last day we would have together for years to come. If I could relive one day in my life, that day would be high on the list. Mary's shining and happy face, with her hair blowing freely around her head, is still fresh in my mind. When she tried to shift and stalled the car in an intersection, we laughed so hard I almost fell out of the car. I thought about that day many times when I was alone and frightened, and I would often wish I could be transported back in time to be there with her again.

I pulled on my father's old leather coat and managed to get my feet stuffed into my now well-worn new shoes. Just as I was about to say goodbye, I had a strange impulse and opened the top dresser drawer. From in the back, I withdrew the sock which contained the gun I picked up in the alley when I saved Spiny. I had never fired a gun, but this one seemed simple enough. I opened the cylinder and saw that it had six rounds in the chambers, then I tucked it into my waist and zipped the jacket over it. After supper, I had thought out what I should do tonight, and I came to the conclusion that I would give the car back to Shark and ask him, even beg him, one more time to let me go. I figured that I owed him some money for the clothes, and I could pay him back a little at a time. The money Spiny gave me was between us, and I wasn't sure that Shark even knew about it. It would mean another long walk back home, but if I got out of the gang, it would be worth it. Before I left the room, I pulled on my hat and looked around. I didn't own anything worth keeping, and if we left in a hurry, I wouldn't miss much. The small bedroom that had been my private sanctuary for several years looked very small and old that night. Mary was standing up, as was Mother, when I entered the living room.

"Please, son, be careful, won't you? Promise me that you will get away if they mean you any harm tonight," Mother pleaded.

"Don't worry, Mother. It's just a meeting, and it's the way they do things. I'll try to get back as soon as I can. I plan to give Shark back the car, and it's a long way back here on foot, so don't wait up for me."

Mary just stood there with her eyes glistening. I turned to face her, and we both just looked at each other. There were no words necessary between us. It was a long tender, but silent, moment, and then I opened the door to leave. When I closed it behind me, I could hear Mary crying.

Just as I slowed for the turn into The Farm's gravel drive, I thought I saw movement behind one of the bushes and I slowed. It was a woman. She stood erect and walked toward the car as I rolled down the window.

"Mike? she said hesitantly.

"Yeah, I'm Mike."

"You remember me. I'm Gale, Janel's friend," she said and put her hands into the open window and clutched the sill. The light was just enough that I recognized her as the girl who usually sat beside Janel at the bar.

"Sure, Gale, I remember. Why are you out here this time of night?"

"I'm waiting for you, Mike. There are things you have to know, and Janel asked me to tell you before I left."

"Janel? Is she all right?"

"No, Mike. Shark beat her after you left night before last, and after that, she told him that she was through with this place and that she was never going to work again. He and Spiny went to work on her and beat her until she couldn't get up. I think she is going to die, but they won't let her get any help and won't let her leave. I'm leaving this place tonight, and I'm never coming back, but I promised Janel that I would stay long enough to warn you."

"Warn me about what?"

"Janel told me that they were going to let her die and blame it on you. She thinks that they are going to kill you when you come in tonight."

"Who is in there right now?" I asked.

"Shark and Spiny and the big guy, Martin. They always make us leave when they count the money. Only Janel is left, and she is in her room. Two of Shark's muscle boys just left, but they might be back at any time. What are you going to do, Mike?"

"I have to go in there and try to rescue Janel. I promised her I would get her out of there, and I guess this is the night that I'll try."

"They are too much for you, Mike. You're just a kid. You should get your family and run away from here tonight, before they start looking for you."

"I know, Gale, that is what I should do, but I can't leave Janel in there to die. They will blame her death on me anyway, and then I'll have both the cops and the mob chasing me. At least if they kill me, my mother and sister will be rid of them."

"No wonder that Janel is in love with you. I can sure see why, Mike. I have to go now, before they see me. I hope you can save her."

"Janel said that she was in love with me?"

"Yes, couldn't you tell? Good luck, Mike." Then she slipped into the night, and I was alone with The Farm's neon light blinking in the night. I crept slowly into the drive with my lights off making as little sound as a car can on gravel. I left the door open when I got out and walked quietly up to the entry door and listened. I could hear men's voices but couldn't make out what they were saying. Other than that, the place was dead quiet. There were three cars in the parking lot, and I recognized Shark's and Spiny's. The other one must have belonged to Martin. I unzipped my jacket and pushed the gun over to my side so that it couldn't be seen and then I opened the door. The talking stopped suddenly, and when I got inside, I saw Shark and Spiny sitting at their usual table, with a large stack of cash in front of them. The big guy, Martin, was seated midway on the other side of the room and had a glass of beer in one hand. A large black handgun was lying on the table in front of him.

"Well, if it isn't Snow White, come to pay his respects," Shark said, and Spiny started laughing. Both of them had a mean look about them. A quick glance at Martin told me that he was waiting for orders from Shark.

"I want to see Janel, first," I said and started moving quickly toward her room. Spiny started rising to his feet, but I heard Shark say, "Let the kid see her," and pushed him back down. I nearly sprinted to her room and opened the door to see her lying in bed.

"Janel!" I called. She didn't move, and as I got closer, I saw her swollen face. Her eyes were hidden behind massive swelling of her eye lids, and her lip was split open in two places. Her beautiful nose was twisted to one side, and her hair was matted with blood. I carefully touched her face and found it cold. Poor lovely Janel was dead. My eyes filled with tears, and I felt my knees partly give way. I held myself over the bed with one arm and gave her a last look. The evil in the other room did this to her. They weren't satisfied with making her a virtual slave and robbing her of her dignity and her youth, but they felt that they could kill her without remorse when they were done with her. My heart flooded with rage, and I felt a hatred more intense than anytime in my life before or since that moment. I knew that I was going to have to kill Shark for what he did to Janel, and I resolved to do it that night.

I walked slowly out of her room and toward Shark's table, and I could see the smirks on their faces. "You killed her," I said. Behind me I heard Martin get up and start moving toward us.

"No, kid, you killed her. You made her want to get out of here. You made her believe that you were going to 'rescue' her. Hey, the stupid little girl even loved you. You couldn't just accept her as she was. You had to fill her head with crap about how she had some worth. I want you to know that she was valuable to me. She brought in a lot of dough. I am going to have to replace her with another chick who looks as good, maybe better. Your sister, kid. We are going to use your sister to replace her."

The revolver came out of my belt, and I twisted just in time to see Martin, his hands already extended toward me. I pulled the trigger and the bullet struck him in the throat. Before I turned back toward Shark, he was in the process of pulling his own pistol from his belt. I was just on the other side of the table from him, and when my weapon came around, it was just two feet from his head when it discharged. Spiny froze with panic on his face and pushed himself back against the wall.

"No, Mike. We buddies! Don't shoot!" were his last words, and I fired two shots into his chest. My ears were ringing from the gunfire when I stopped and listened. Martin was gasping for breath and was still alive. I went over and saw that he was motioning for me to come closer. I bent down and saw blood rapidly pooling on the floor beside his neck.

"No hard feelings, kid. Just business. You did good," he gurgled, then his eyes rolled back and his labored breathing stopped. Standing up I tried to think, but I was disoriented. I was the only one in the room alive, and poor Janel was in her bedroom, dead. I had let her down after all. Shark was right, I had helped kill her with my innocence. The weapon in my hand felt heavy, then I remembered where I got it. This was a goon's gun from another mob, and no one but me knew that I had it. I picked up a cloth and wiped it clean of my fingerprints and left it in plain view on the table. The money. There was a big pile of it and a leather satchel was lying on the floor beside the table. I scooped the cash into the satchel, and as I did so, I found a folded paper in the stack. It was the title to the little red Ford, and it was unsigned. I put it in my pocket and closed the bag, stood and looked around. I was starting to think clearly again and realized that the scene was going to look like a hit from another mob. Gale had said that two of Shark's men might come back at any time so I had to get away while I could. I rushed for the car, tossing the bag in the rumble seat and closing the lid. I started the car and, to my relief, saw no other cars in sight on the road ahead. Taking the long way back home, I was alert to avoid any sign of the police or anyone behind me. I parked at the curb in front of our house and rushed inside. It was two a.m. Mary came out of her bedroom while pulling on her robe. When she looked at me, she put her hands in front of her face.

"Oh, Mike! You made it home!"

"Look, Mary. You have to get Mother up right now and get out of town."

"You mean, right now? Leave? In the middle of the night?" she gasped.

"Yes, Mary. Right now, and I mean right now. Go get her up. Don't pack, just get away. You use the Ford outside and head west to her family. Now go do it."

"Aren't you going with us?" Mary asked, her hand still partially covering her mouth.

"No, I have to stay here and meet with Detective Smith. I'll catch up with you later. Trust me, Mary, you have to get away from here."

Mary ran toward Mother's room, and after a few minutes, they both came out with clothes on and both were tearing. Mother was shaking.

"Can you tell us what happened, son?"

"No. I can't. Just listen carefully to what I have to tell you," I said, and I pulled out the title of the car. "Here is the title for the car. Just register it in your name when you get there. It belongs to you now. There is a satchel in the back seat that has all the money that you will need. I want you to use some of it to send Mary away to a dancing school. The money is not stolen, and no one will be looking for it, but don't tell anyone how you got it. There is enough in there for new clothes and anything else you will need for the trip and for later."

I walked them to the car and handed Mary the keys. "Don't stall it in the intersections. I am counting on you now. Drive far away from here before you stop. Do you understand?"

Mary put her arms around me and kissed me on the lips. When she pulled away, she said, "I don't believe it any longer, either. I love you, Mike." She looked at me for a long time then said, "We will both be waiting for you at Aunt Audie's when you get there, and don't take too long." At that moment, my head was so full of what had just happened at The Farm and trying to get my family away from danger that it took a few moments to really realize that Mary kissed me and what she had meant.

I closed her car door after they got in and leaned inside, "I love you both with my whole heart. Keep yourselves safe until you see me again, please. Mary, thanks for what you said just now."

I stood there until the sound of the car was gone, then reluctantly turned to go back into the dark empty house. After I pulled my shoes and socks off of my painful feet, I fell across the couch.

There was a loud noise which finally woke me. I rubbed my face with my hands and looked around. The morning light was pouring in the room as was the pounding from the front door. I got up and peeked from the side window. It was Detective Smith, and he was alone.

"Well, I thought I was going to have to kick the door in. Glad to see you are alive, Mike."

"Did you think I was dead, Detective?"

"From what we just saw, yes. Is your family home this morning?"

"No. They left earlier for a family visit. I'm alone."

"Well, thank goodness you weren't out at The Farm. It looks like there was a reprisal for the two you told me about earlier. We found a gun at the scene, and we think it belonged to the Tony Muretto gang. They sent a clear message last night. Cohen, Spinnazzo, and his hit man, Leuchesie, are dead. That girl, Janel, was beaten to death. The same would have happened to you if you were out there." Detective Smith was looking at me in a funny way as if trying to figure something out. "Mike, I have to ask you. Do you know anything about this?"

"No, Detective. I was last out there two days ago. I had to walk home, and it ruined my feet. I was just trying to recover."

"Mind if I see your feet?"

"Of course not," I said, and I held one of the them up for him.

"I see," he said. "No, I would stay home too if my feet looked like that. By the way, the letters your sister has been sending me pretty well clears you of any involvement with them, and now that Shark is gone, looks like you are out of there."

"Too bad about Janel," I said.

"Did you do what I said and stay away from her?"

"Yes, I never got involved. I only talked to her on occasion. She was a very nice person, Detective."

He sighed and looked at me like he was going to ask me something. "If you say so, Mike. Say, mind if I come in?"

"Of course I don't, please come in." I moved away from the door and watched as he looked carefully around the room. The women had left so fast that everything was in place and was tidy.

"Do you have a gun, Mike?"

"My father had one. It's still in his closet. I don't remember ever seeing it fire. Want to look it over?"

"If you don't mind," he said. I got up and found the gun where it was always kept and handed it to Smith. He pulled the toggle back and smelled the chamber, then handed it back to me. "Sorry, I had to do that," He settled in to a chair and seemed to have something to say.

"Before I forget, Mike. I had a look at your birth records and did some poking around. The physician who delivered you was a man named Walter Sessions, and when you were born he was mostly working at the hospital full-time because he was just out of school. He is gone now so I couldn't talk to him, but I did check him out."

"Did he leave town?"

"No, he committed suicide about five years later. Turns out that he had a gambling addiction and back at that time his loan shark was none other than the recently deceased Lennard Cohen. Now you understand why they called him 'The Shark'. I think Dr. Sessions would have done nearly anything for money, including a switch of babies."

"Funny you should say that, Detective. Janel told me that she overheard that it was still being done recently."

"Well, to make a long story short, I tried to find out what other babies were born in that hospital at the same time, but it's going to take a court order to get that out of them. I ran out of time, but I'm thinking of another angle so it isn't over yet."

We sat there and looked at each other in silence. I could tell that he was thinking something through, and I became more worried the longer it lasted.

"Can I make you a cup of coffee, Detective," I offered as I got up.

"Yes, Mike, black please," and he got up and followed me into the kitchen. "Say, there is another possible explanation for the shootings at The Farm. Want to hear it?" he asked. No, I didn't want to hear it, but I didn't want to say that so I remained silent and worked on making the coffee. He leaned on the kitchen table and watched me work.

"It goes something like this. Someone out there at The Farm beat this Janel girl up, eventually causing her death. An unnamed individual heard about it and took it personal and decided to take matters into his own hands. This person, and we don't know who it was, had a gun that came from the Muretto gang that he more or less got by chance. This gun was used for the killings and then planted to blame it on this same out-of-town gang. There may have been a lot of money present which is now missing. What a good deed this fellow did by killing the lot of them, because they deserved killing, if anyone ever has. The problem is that if the rest of Shark's gang figures this out, that person is in a lot of trouble. Get it? It might also trigger a gang war, which is all right by us unless some innocent people also get hurt. If the Muretto gang can convince Shark's boys that they didn't do it, they will start hunting everybody even remotely connected. Get it?"

"It seems pretty clear, Detective. What do you think this person should do?"

"Well, he shouldn't admit that he did it, because he would have to be sent to prison, and the gangs would get to him in there for sure. By the way, where did your family go for this trip, and how long are they staying?"

"They are going a long way west, Detective but I don't know when or where, and I don't expect that they'll be back. It's pretty hush-hush you understand."

"Yes, I do understand. Do they have enough money to get by, you suppose?"

"They have some savings. I think that they will be all right."

I finished making the coffee, and we sat across from each other at the little table in the kitchen, looking at each other over and through the steam.

"You keep up with the news much, Mike?"

"No, we couldn't afford the paper after Father died, and my mother and sister don't really care about news anyway."

"Everybody thinks that there is going to be another big war. You know that you have to register for the draft this year, don't you?"

"I heard that they send you a notice through the mail, but I haven't gotten one yet."

"Turns out that there is a bus scheduled to leave town for induction into the Army this afternoon. I think that when we finish our coffee, you should grab some personal things, and let me take you downtown to enlist. You'll just have time to catch the bus. The good thing is that you will beat the crowd who will just get drafted anyway. It'll look good on your service record that you enlisted. Give you an edge, you know. The other good thing is that no criminal can ever touch you in there, because the U.S. Army will be your mother, and she wouldn't like it."

I settled back in the hard seat and looked out at Detective Smith, who was waiting patiently for the bus to pull away. In the time of less than a day, I had lost Janel, murdered three people, said goodbye to my mother and sister and the town I grew up in and was now, and for the foreseeable future, part of the rapidly expanding American Army. That was the day I grew up.

Chapter 5

THE CONFERENCE

Mr. Burns!" Jill called out as he walked by her cubicle. She heard a grunt, and his footsteps returned toward her. He stood in front of the opening with a pencil stuck behind his ear, his usual wad of papers in one hand. He shrugged as if to say, "What?"

"Did you have a chance to read my manuscript about the Condors?"

"You mean that stack of papers three inches high? No."

"Well, can't you help with the direction it is going?"

He came forward a bit and said, "You are writing a book, Jill. This is a newspaper office. We can't print a four hundred page novel in the newspaper. So what is your question?"

"Mr. Burns, I guess I want some indication from you that the work is interesting and that my writing style is satisfactory. You know...encouragement?"

"Jill, Jill, Jill. I did look at it, and I thought the story was really interesting, and you have done a marvelous job putting it down on paper. If I wasn't such a he-man, I would probably have cried. Does that help?"

"Are you serious, Mr. Burns? You did read it?"

"Some of it. I thought it was pretty good." His voice trailed off as he headed down the hall. That was all she was going to get, she supposed. Well, next she was going to spend some time with Mary and try to record her point of view. Aside from typing in all the recorded part of the story and trying to read the mother's extensive diaries, she had lost most of her personal life. She badly needed some other person to bounce ideas off of and the only person who was interested was Lilith. Jill picked up the phone and punched Lilith's number.

After a short wait, Lilith answered, and Jill explained what was going on with the interviews. "Your grandfather and I finished his story up until he went into the Army. I am going to spend all my free time on Mary next, and we can get that down. I would like you to go over what I have written and give me your perspective."

"I would like to do that, Jill. Were there any surprises?"

"If a triple homicide and escape from the Mob in the middle of the night is a surprise, then yes."

"You don't mean that?" Lilith exclaimed.

"You have to read it for yourself. I put it down just like he told it. He was very frank and left nothing, and I mean nothing, out. Quite a guy, that one. Wish they still made his model today."

"Is this going to be a problem with the law?"

"According to his story, the ones he killed were mobsters bent on killing him and making a sex slave out of Mary. He had justification. Besides, there is no proof. The thing happened seventy-three years ago, and from what he said, the police knew about it. I see no problem unless you do."

"You are right, I better read it. Can we meet?" Lilith asked.

"I am scheduled to start with Mary tomorrow about ten, and I hope that will be an everyday thing. We badly need her view of this, because so far it is from a male perspective. I am working on the diaries at night and trying to do some correlation. Are you still pursuing your work on what happened to the sister who was taken?"

"I'm starting to think that your PI boyfriend could be useful, especially if he can circumvent the rules."

"Want to play dirty, he is your man. I'll get hold of him and see if he's interested and let you know when we meet. One thing interesting about that subject. According to Mike, there was a policeman, Detective Smith, who suspected that the babies were switched and identified a Dr. Walter Sessions who probably took a bribe for doing it. He died many years ago so there may not be much to go on after this much time. Seems to me that we need someone on the ground that can dig into the hospital records and find who was born at the same time and try to track that."

"All right then, I'll get over there tomorrow. Thanks again for all of this. I hope it pays off with a book for you someday."

Jill waved to the desk clerk on the way back to Mary's room. By now, just about everybody who worked there recognized her, and she was even starting to feel like part of the staff. She knocked softly on Mary's door and got a "Come in" from inside. Mary was indeed ready for her and was sitting up in bed with her hair groomed.

"Are you feeling well today, Mrs. Condor?" Jill asked.

"Oh, I feel fine, Jill, and please call me Mary. Did Mike give you a good story?"

"He sure did. It was fascinating. The thing that came over most clearly was his love for you that started early in life and just grew and grew. Women like me just can't imagine having a man like Mike feel that way about them."

"He was telling you the truth, you know. He loved me so much and that never changed. The lowest time in my life was when we were separated during war and of course we never knew if the soldiers would even come back."

"I need to know, Mary, if you have any feelings about trying to find your actual twin. I got the feeling from Mike that he was happy with the way life turned out for him, and he seems to not want to know any more."

"It's different for Mike, dear. He was the one abandoned by his parents or at least by his mother, and the baby that was switched was my twin. I would love to know more and even meet her if she is still alive. If we were identical, Mike would certainly be in for a surprise wouldn't he?" she giggled. "Two of us to love!"

"That's good enough for me, Mary. Lilith and I will get busy and see what we can discover."

"You mean, before it's too late, don't you?"

"Yes."

Chapter 6

MARY'S STORY

My memory for detail might not be as accurate as Mike's, but there are my feelings to remember, and I have a lot of them. When I was getting ready for my interview, I had plenty of time to recall the past and cry again where I cried before and to relive the happy times. Mike was so much a part of everything I remember that sometimes he is all I remember. He was always there, never angry, never impatient, and always ready to do anything I asked, no matter how small or how big. It was like having a personal servant except that I loved him as he loved me. My father used to say, "Two peas in a pod," so often that we tired of it.

They dressed us in the same colors and outfits for a long time because we started out the same size. We slept in the same bed, and I remember curling up to him and putting my nose up against his shoulder. I had to touch him or I couldn't get to sleep. We developed our own language, you know, and they said that they had a hard time getting us to stop and just speak English. More often, we communicated by looks, and I don't mean sign. I used to think that we could speak to each other that way, you know, actually read each other's thoughts through our eyes. It would only take an instant to do. I still believe that we could do it. When we went shopping with Mother, we would hold hands. If mother wanted to hold one of our hands, it was always mine, because Mike would never let go of my other hand to hold hers. Mike was never a bad kid. Never actually did anything wrong. He took a lot of beatings, though, and most of them were instead of me. I was afraid of a spanking, but I hated almost as much to see him struck. He wouldn't have it any other way, and usually, Father could not make him cry, no matter how hard his blows were. Father and I were very close, and he would hold me and cuddle me and tell me stories and let Mike just stand there and watch. Mike would never complain as long as I was getting attention. All he seemed to want was to make me happy. I ended up with most of the toys, because he would always give me his if I wanted them, and it was the same way with food.

Mike grew in size and strength quickly, and when he did, he found he could decide who I played with. It was never other boys, at least not for long. Mike didn't mind playing girl games as long as it was when I was present, otherwise he ignored girls. The boys soon learned not to kid him about it, or they would be chased down and taught a lesson. There was no boy that could hit him as hard as his own father would so he was completely unafraid of fights.

When we went to school, Mike insisted that he sit next to me, and he was so persistent about it that he usually got his way. When it came time for tests or homework, he would help me when he wasn't supposed to, and eventually we had to be kept apart. He was placed in the back of the room, usually reserved for troublemakers. I could feel his eyes on me, and it was comforting to know that he was watching me.

We had some friends who had brothers and sisters so I knew how it usually went. In our case, we never fought and always wanted to do things together. I don't know how old we were when Mother finally wouldn't allow bathing together, but I was old enough to remember being in the tub with Mike before we stopped. I remember that we would touch our bodies together while being toweled off to keep warm. In fact, I remember the first bath I took without him. I cried the whole time. It was like a part of me was missing. We usually slept together, and I think that only stopped when we were about six or so. At our first separation, we were given our own beds which were apart only by a couple of feet, but by morning, we were usually in the same bed. Eventually, we moved to a larger house, and we each had a small room to ourselves. Mike would sneak in and lay with me until I fell asleep and then try to get back to his room before we were discovered. He continued to make sure I was asleep by coming into my room and telling me goodnight until that day we were separated by fate at age seventeen. He still does the same thing every night here!

Mike may have told you about our snowman wedding, or perhaps you saw the old photographs. It was so much fun! One day, I was looking at pictures of my mother's sister's wedding and asking her about it. After that, I knew I wanted to get married, and I asked her who I should marry. She said, "You always marry someone you love!" That made it simple. I loved Mike so I wanted to marry him. We were so young and innocent that I know Mother just took it in fun, and she helped organize it, even taking the photos. I was serious, however, and after that day, I always felt that I was married to Mike. The day we were actually married many years later brought back memories of that day in the snow with Mike when we kissed for the camera.

There was a day, somewhere back in time, that I first looked at Mike as a boy. He was impressive and strong for his age, and I finally noticed. That moment changed a lot for me, and after that I could see the beauty in his shape, his masculine mannerisms and his strength. At the same moment, perhaps, he also noticed me in a different way. He sought me out with his eyes, and I could feel the affection and interest. It was kindly and almost reverent, the way he treated me, as if he considered me a fragile piece of glass that could break if mishandled. At the dinner table, he would steal glances at me, and I could almost feel his gaze on my hair or neck or almost any part of me. Another change was when we started to refrain from touching or contact. It wasn't that I didn't want to. There was such a pull inside of me toward him that I was afraid of it, and at the time I didn't understand it. Somehow we both knew it was wrong but still we wanted to be close. In some ways, our attraction was subconscious, and there was something internal about it, like a force of nature which could not be silenced. About this time, our parents noticed and became alarmed. They arranged a visit with a very strange doctor who interviewed us and afterward nothing changed. We didn't think about it at the time, but later, I wondered what he had told them. When I was about fifteen, I asked Mother what it was about. She said that they were told that nothing at all was wrong and that nature would sort it out. In that regard, I suppose that he was correct. The pressure on us built up by the day, both from the guilt of our attraction and the increase in intensity of it. Looking back, having Mike that close was both hell and heaven, but I wouldn't change a day of it or give up a precious moment of time.

After I passed puberty, I started to become more attractive to boys. They were interested and increasingly friendly. That is, before they met Mike. He had a way of intimidating them from a distance, but I think it was mostly because of his reputation. I knew that he would pay visits to some of them or wait for them after school, but I was so flattered that I didn't complain. He was in constant trouble about it, but nobody could change the way he felt about me and that was the real problem. He would accept any punishment but would turn around and do the same things again the next day. Just a boy talking to me would sometimes trigger anger in Mike, but if they actually touched me, they were sure to get a bloody face for it. Word got around, and soon, I couldn't get one to even look my way. My girlfriends were all enthralled by Mike. He had the best grades in school, and he was attractive and quiet. Not one of them could get his attention, no matter how hard they tried. Mike probably thought that I was somehow keeping them away, but it was all about him. He only had eyes for me, and everyone knew it.

When I started taking dance lessons twice a week after school, Mother would pick me up, drive me over and wait on me. Of course, Mike wanted to go also, but every time he was there was chaos for our poor instructor. Mike didn't do anything wrong and never said a word, but the girls were watching him instead of dancing, and they finally asked him not to return. He was crushed, and I knew why. All he wanted to do was to watch me move. He was so utterly and helplessly drawn to me that he never got enough of being around me. Mike would just sit there, mesmerized every time I was on the floor. Our parents felt like they should give him some lessons too, but the only thing they could come up with was boxing. Before entering high school, he started going to a seedy boxing club and had to ride his bike over there, even in winter. He both enjoyed it and excelled at it as he did everything he tried. It wasn't good for the other boys, however, because Mike became much better at fighting, and none of them wanted to try him out.

I remember that I did something naughty when we were still young, but I don't remember how old we were at the time. The truth is that I can't fully explain why I did what I did, but looking back, the reasons were probably obvious. One night, I had an urge to break rules and have Mike see me naked. I had thought about it for weeks, and it grew into something so important to me that I was almost consumed by it. Was it wrong? No harm came of it, and I suffered no loss of respect for myself or by Mike, so perhaps it was not. When it happened, Mike never said a word, and he never made reference to it later. Afterward, he treated me with the same respect and tenderness that he had always shown me. Instead of feeling dirty about showing him my body, I felt glad that I had. It was, I think, my way of paying him back for all the things he did for me, and above all, it was a statement of trust between us. After we were married, he did say that he carried around in his head that image of me without clothes and that it came back many times over his lifetime. What better gift could you give someone?

Some time in the ninth grade, there was a school-sponsored dance. It was a big deal at the time, and students were sort of expected to go, and if you didn't it was because you were a social outcast. Mike relented just in time, allowing his only friend, Phillip, to ask me, with the understanding of good behavior. That meant that Mike was going to come and supervise. Phillip was a small boy with a head full of bright red unruly hair, but he was my only choice. We ended up good friends over time, but he was never an exciting date for me. I pressured Mike into accompanying a nice unassuming girl called Frieda. She was a good choice at the time, because I could never imagine that Mike would be attracted to her. Later, she blossomed in her figure but also her personality, and I think she would have done about anything to get close to my brother. It might have been possible except our high school years were cut short.

At the dance, Mike got into it with three big, boorish football players and knocked two of them out cold on the floor. What a commotion! I felt like hiding in the broom closet because it was all about me, and I felt all those people looking me over. We sat out the rest of the dance, and when we were ready to go home, Mike expected trouble. I know that he would have taken on the whole football team by himself, but he was worried about me getting hurt or frightened and arranged for the school principal to drive us home. That was when the real trouble started for us, and it was not to be undone, changing our lives for the worse. Mike talked to a gangster named Shark he knew from the club, and Shark had his men threaten some of the football team. The members of the team took it serious because it probably was no idle threat. After that, Mike was indebted to the gangsters and couldn't avoid slowly being drawn in. They used every trick to get him to join, but the one that worked was that they threatened to do something to me. If Mike was then the man he was when he came back from the war, he would have killed all of them right then and there. He was only a youngster at the time, and he had nowhere to go to get away from them.

I was partly to blame for the biggest ruse they played on Mike. There was a teenage girl working as a prostitute for the mob named Janel Cicero. She looked young and innocent when she made friends with me, and I admit that I was taken in by her. That was certainly not what she was in real life. I suggested that she come to a dance as a blind date for Mike, but when she showed up it wasn't the same girl at all. The Janel that came to the dance was the most sexually aware creature that any of us had ever seen. She could have enchanted any boy there, but she focused on poor Mike. He was no match for her charms, and we all witnessed his embarrassment while they were dancing together. We all knew what was happening to him, because we could see it. Every time she got close to him it would happen again, and they sat out much of the dance because of it. I saw her trying to entice him into her car after the dance, and you can imagine my relief when he didn't go with her. In some ways, though, she hooked him. He liked her, and in the months to follow, he spent a lot of time with her. He always was scheming to get her away from the mobsters, but I never felt it would happen, and in the end, it didn't .

Mike and I wanted to be together as much as we could, and at the end of each day, we always did our homework on the little kitchen table. We didn't converse much but having the comfort of having him across from me meant a lot. A glance exchanged can mean anything, but in our case, it usually meant love. Love to me means something different than it does to people who really mean lust when they say love. I have experienced lust, and at times, I had lust for Mike. Love is different. It means that this person whom you love is someone you just can't think of living a day without. It's that someone whom you would be there for no matter what it took and love is your feeling for that special someone whom you can trust enough to tell your darkest secrets. Love puts the wants and needs of that person above your own. Love is much more about giving than it is about getting. That was the case of Mike and me. Because of our relationship as twins, we were restrained about expressing what we felt about each other in words, and we couldn't show it physically. The only way we talked about it was in our eye contact. It was enough. Neither one of us thought that we could live without the other.

After Father died, both Mike and I returned to work because we had to. I worked as a part-time seamstress and model for a dress shop, and I rather enjoyed it. Mike worked as a grease monkey at a service station. He did, that is, until Shark came around one day and plucked him out of the pit and put him to work with the mob. I knew that he was seeing Janel out there at what the locals called "The Den of Sin" but was actually named The Farm. Janel was so attractive that she was the talk of the town, and since I never saw The Farm with my own eyes, I dreamed up what it looked like, and what I saw, I didn't like. In my daydream, Janel was scantily clothed, or sometimes not at all, and I imagined the effect on my brother was like a moth to a flame. I was fearful for him and jealous at the same time. He always told me what happened when he went out there, and I believed him, but I think that he was a little in love with Janel from the kind and respectful way he would talk about her. I suspected that Janel had also fallen for Mike, but I never saw her after that dance so I couldn't be sure.

An example of the love that Mike had for me came at another dance. Again, I was officially with Phillip, but when we were actually there, I suddenly found myself dancing with several boys and, believe it or not, with Mike's approval. I know that he didn't want any boy to get close to me, but that night he looked the other way so I could have fun. He was there without a date, but so many girls pursued him that there was an actual line waiting for him to ask them to the floor, or to anywhere else. That night he made friends with the football guys, and he seemed to be at peace with the world. He kept a hawk's eye on what I was doing, and I did the same to him. Frieda was the one who captured him that night, and she had changed so much in the nearly two years since they had seen each other she didn't seem to be the same girl. She had developed a spectacular figure and a lot of poise and self-confidence. I wanted to see pimples and fat when I looked at her, not ample breasts. They looked good together, and I could see them talking constantly and smiling at each other. I was so jealous that I felt the blood rush to my face, and I couldn't help it. There was only one man in my life, ever, and that was Mike.

Other people kept suggesting that Mike and I were not related. It just didn't make sense to them, because we didn't look alike. It struck me that they were right. I was fair with blonde hair and blue eyes, and Mike was toned with dark hair and eyes. He didn't look at all like Father or Mother or anyone else related to our family. We discussed it a couple of times, but I think we didn't want to allow ourselves to think that way, in case we were related. I decided to pursue this topic with Mother after Father died. She admitted a horrible thing to me that I never told Mike. Father didn't see the relationship of Mike to him either, and he was convinced that Mother had slept with another man, and Mike was the result. No matter what Mother said, he remained unconvinced, and for that reason, he never actually bonded with poor Mike. It never occurred to either of them that Mike could have been switched for my twin sister. Near the beginning of the eleventh grade, we were shown a nature film in class. They talked about a cowbird who lays its eggs in another bird's nest, and the hatchlings are raised by the other mother bird. It struck me between the eyes, and I couldn't get the thought out of my mind. What if that had happened to us? After that, I slowly found myself not believing that Mike and I were twins, and I stopped trying to suppress feelings of love for him. I admitted to myself what I already felt. I loved Mike with my whole being.

There are two days in my life that were the most memorable and made my life change direction abruptly. One, of course, was the day I married Mike, and it was the happiest. The saddest day, and the most traumatic, happened one summer day before we were to start our senior year in school. The preceding day started early when I heard Mike groaning, and the sound seemed to be coming from the front porch. He had not come home the night before, and I went to sleep that night with tears, because I thought either something bad had happened to him or that he had spent the night with Janel. Both were true, but were not as I feared. When I went outside, he was trying to peel his socks away from his foot blisters. His feet looked terrible, and the skin was coming off in sheets. He spent much of the day in bed, and I had to assist him when he got up. That night, one of the gang members, named Spiny, came by and dropped off a snappy little red car and ordered Mike to be back out at The Farm the next night at midnight. I was alarmed and had a premonition that something bad was going to happen. Mike felt that he had no choice except to go and refused to consider any other course of action. The next day he felt well enough to take me out in the new car, and what a good time we had driving around with the top down. I wished that the day would never end. It seemed then that time was running out on us, and it made the good time we had seem all that more sweet. And it was the last day...before everything changed forever.

Just after two a.m. the front door burst open, and Mike rushed in. I could tell at a glance that something bad had happened. He was in a rush to get Mother and me out of the house and out of town. We had no time to gather any belongings or even pack clothing. We put on what we had, grabbed our purses and piled into the car. Just before I got in, I held Mike in my arms and kissed him on the lips. That was the first kiss we had since childhood. He looked stunned, and I think he would have reacted differently if he wasn't busy trying to save our lives. I also told him that

I no longer believed that we were twins. I don't think that by that time he believed it either, but he was so honorable a person, he never let it change how he treated me. He didn't say anything but thanks at the time, because he was so anxious for us to leave and drive west, and we did just as he asked. As I drove away, I saw him standing alone to face whatever was coming at him, and I cried so much that I couldn't see the road.

Mike said that there was money in the trunk, and when we stopped for gas, we needed to pay and found a leather satchel back there which was full of money. The next night, Mother and I counted over one hundred twenty thousand dollars in various bills. We were staggered. Both of us cried again, because we knew that Mike would have to have someone after him and the money. We didn't find out for over a month what happened to him when a letter came from an Army training base. He was in the Army, and he told us the story of how Detective Smith helped him get away. The same Detective Smith had all our belongings at our house boxed up and stored for us. Mike never told us what happened that night, and I assume that it was better that we didn't know. I never heard about Shark, Spiny or Janel again, and that was good.

We ended up in a small town in Washington State. I finished high school there, and I thought about Mike a thousand times a day. War was officially declared before Christmas, and we knew that Mike would be involved in the fighting. He was gone until the summer of 1945, and all I had was a few letters from him during that time. I wrote to him every day, but he told me later that all he got were maybe a couple of dozen of them during the whole war.

Our new physician was a very nice young doctor who would take the time to listen. During one visit, I decided to talk to him frankly about my brother and me. After he comprehended what I was trying to tell him, he paused to think about it.

"Mary, there are discoveries being made every day in the field of genetics but first something simple. Have you both been tested for blood type? Often, the test will not prove anything since there is one predominant type, but it might be worth looking at. Do this first, write to Mike and tell him to look at his dog tag and find out what blood type he is and write you back. I'll test you right now, and we can compare the two later. It'll help if you can find out what type your parents are."

It was a start, and I wrote Mike that night. Mother got Father's medical records and had herself tested. Both of us were type AB, and Father was an A. Dr. Edwards explained to me that the only type which would not be possible as a relation was an O. We held our breath waiting for Mike to write back. It took nearly three months, and the letter was the last before he shipped out to fight in the European war.

One fine day, the letter came that I was waiting for and the first line of the first page said, "I am O positive. Does that tell you anything?" It did. It told me that the man that I loved all my life was not my brother and that my love for him was pure and right and that he would belong to me the rest of our lives. The only problem was that he had to get back alive first!

Chapter 7

THE REST OF THE STORY

Lilith sat down and started flipping through the now thick manuscript. "Jill, this is amazing. You have really worked hard to accumulate this much from them."

"However much work it was for me, it was very tiring on both of them, especially Mary. She is weaker now than when we started. There is a lot she didn't say, and things I would like to know more about, but I think she is close to being unable to continue. Some of it is very emotional for her. Then she gets distressed, and we have to stop for another day. You can see what you think, but I believe that she is done."

"What was it that you needed to know, in particular?" Lilith asked looking up at her.

"Like what she and her mother did for the three and a half years that Mike was gone."

"I can tell you some of that. After finishing high school, Mary went to New York and attended Juilliard. She was there for two years and then went on to have a short career on stage in New York. She was trained as a modern dancer and, with her beauty, could have become famous. She actually was famous but for a short time. When Mike came back, they married and she performed locally while he

207

went back to school. When my mother was born, she retired for good."

"What about men in her life? Were there any?" Jill asked.

"Men? I heard that they chased her constantly. If you have seen the photos of her, you know why. She could have had almost any man she chose at that time. The men were wasting their time, though, because there was only one man in the world she could ever love."

"Mike said that she sometimes teased him about the other men in her life so I thought..."

"Oh, that! That's just pillow talk with them. My grandfather doesn't believe a bit of it and neither do I," she laughed.

"Did you read the part about when Mike shot those three gangsters?"

"Yes, it was most interesting, and I never heard before what happened that night. He never told Mary a word about it. I don't think we have a problem with the law on this issue nor about the money that he took. All that money was from illegal activities, so there are no claims on it."

"I have to complete Mike's story about what happened to him in the war and then summarize your great grandmother's diaries before the book will be finished."

"That by itself is a big undertaking. Mike was a very decorated soldier, and he was in the war from when it started to when it finished. I've never heard any stories from him about his adventures over there. A lot of soldiers like him won't discuss it. They don't consider that it was glamorous and seem to want to forget it. The diaries are full of mundane events coupled with revelations that she would have never discussed with a living person. She died before I was born and before Mary and Mike were married, but her writing shows a complex and thoughtful person that I would have like to have known."

"Yes, that's the impression I got also. She held things together and raised a son that even she thought was a stranger, but she never mentioned it and treated him like her own," Jill said.

"By the way, your old boyfriend is interesting. Such a flirt. I had to set him straight the first time I met him. He seems qualified to work for us, and he certainly won't be restrained by what is legal. Right now, he is down at the hospital where Mike and Mary were born and is pretending to be an inspector for an accrediting agency. I saw his fake credentials, and I thought they were the real thing. If he can come up with anything, I'll have him follow it up, and if my aunt is still alive, we'll find her."

"You can see why he doesn't share my bed any longer. Shifty is as shifty does. He makes a good investigator, though."

"May I ask how you plan to write about what you have found in the diaries?"

"Like you said, a lot of it is just everyday life, but the parts that relate to her marriage or to the children will be quoted just as she wrote them. I see no need to editorialize on her work or even comment it. Is that satisfactory to you?"

"That's what I'd hoped that you would say."

Chapter 8

CHARLOTTE'S STORY

Book 2 Page 133

The doctor told me today that he heard two heartbeats so we are having twins! Joe will want to know, but I don't think he will be ready for two children at one time! I'm excited, and now I have to start looking for a place to put both of them. I wonder if they will look alike?

Book 2 Page 195

I had some contractions today which frightened me a little bit. I called to speak to Dr. Ross, but he went out East for something, and they don't think he will be back in time to deliver my twins. His nurse said that there was a doctor on duty full-time at the hospital, so we don't have to worry at all. We decided on one large bassinet that Joe found for a good price, and we will put them in there together. After all, they are together right now, so they might not want to be apart!

Book 2 Page 204

I delivered twins late last night! A boy and a girl and both are healthy! I haven't seen them yet, but the nurse says that they both are fine, and I can get them for feeding in a little while. The young doctor is very nice, and after I had the second one, he had them give me some gas while they finished with me. I didn't get to see much of the babies at that time, and I am most anxious to have them in my arms. Dr. Walter Sessions, that was the doctor's name. Last night when we arrived, there was another woman in labor at the same time, and she looked as scared as I felt. I didn't get a chance to talk with her, because we were both very busy!

I'm exhausted and supposed to be resting now, but I'm waiting for Joe to come back and tell me about the babies!

Joe came in this afternoon and seemed to be distressed about something, but he wouldn't talk about it. He said the babies were fine, and we discussed names for them. Ten more minutes and then I get them!

Book 2 Page 205

We decided on the babies names: Mike Andrew Condor and Mary Jasmine Condor! They both are healthy and beautiful. You can tell at a distance which one is a boy and which is a girl, because Mike has dark hair and has slightly darker skin. More masculine! Mary has scant blonde hair. I am so happy!

Still waiting on Joe to come back. He is troubled, but he said that this is not the time to discuss it.

Book 2 Page 206

Problem. Joe called Dr. Sessions to meet with both of us and told him (us) that he noticed that Mike looked different than Mary, and he wasn't sure that Mike was his. I started to cry when I heard what he said. Dr. Sessions assured us that, since they weren't identical twins, they could look very different, and it was common for it to be that way. He seemed to not see a problem. Joe was not satisfied and said that little Mike didn't look like any of his relatives. Right in front of me, he asked if another man could be the father. I didn't know what to think when he said that. He knows that I have been faithful to him. It really hurt. Dr. Sessions told him that he had never heard of a woman having babies by two different men at the same time and didn't even think it was possible. After he said that, Joe seemed to calm down and apologized to me. I can't get over it though. It was the worst thing anyone ever said to me. Right now, I don't even want to go home.

Book 2 Page 280

Our babies are healthy and cute as buttons. They share the same little bassinet and cry immediately when one is picked up without the other. So adorable! They have started to gain weight, and we have matching outfits for them that my mother made. Diapers everywhere!

They do look different, and so much so that I have decided to forgive my husband for what he thought. I can see now what he saw. They are both mine, came out of me and were fathered by Joe, so if they are different it is God's way.

Book 2 page 356

We had a good Christmas even though money was tight this year. The babies are so cute to watch. They are five months old now and will smile at you when you talk! They are very aware of each other, and they hate to be apart, even for a few moments. They always sleep touching somewhere, usually their heads! I have had to try to nurse both of them at the same time. So tiring on the arms! But it makes them quiet. I would love to have a picture made with them both on my nipples at the same time with their little legs touching each other and their eyes rolling around looking at everything.

Book 3 page 210

The twins are walking this morning all by themselves. Each seems to hold the other up, and they stagger around together, giggling at each other. They are never far apart, and they communicate by some method I don't understand. They still are sleeping in the same little crib, and when I come in the morning to get them up, they are usually already playing with each other and both in a good mood. I watched them for a while, and I noticed that little Mike never lets his sister out of his sight. Mary is very independent and will wander around the house, and little Mike just trails along. It's like a miniature version of the wedding vows "Wither thou goest..."

Book 4 page 101

Mary has her father's eye, and he seems to favor her. I know that fathers and daughters sometimes attract each other, but I feel sorry for Mike who is left out a lot. He just stands there and watches them play and never complains, as long as Mary is within his reach. They have to touch when they are sleeping, no buts about it. I sometimes come in and find them intertwined with their heads facing each other.

Book 4 page 175

Joe and I had an argument this morning about Mike. I told him that he should try to include Mike more or even give him some special attention. Joe told me that he still didn't really feel that Mike was his baby. That again. It really hurt me to think that Joe still believes that I was unfaithful to him. I can't seem to convince him that Mike is his. Even if he somehow isn't, it shouldn't matter, because he is only a little baby that needs care, and we are raising him and owe him the same love as Mary.

Book 4 page 247

I have been making excuses why I can't sleep with Joe any longer, and I often continue to fuss around, pretending to do some late chores until he goes to bed, then I sleep on the couch. The truth is that I can no longer love a man who insists that I was unfaithful to him. If that's the way he feels after all this time, then it will never change.

Book 4 page 301

Some early Christmas shopping today, and I took the toddlers with me. They hold hands and walk together attracting so much attention. Can't remember how many oohs and aahs I heard today. They are in their own little world together. Mike holds his sister's hand and has to be scolded to allow her to eat with both hands. She never complains though.

Book 5 page 172

My twins are still sleeping together in the same bed. Both are getting ready to be potty trained, and I can see some problems ahead. Both of them fuss at any attempt at separation. They both talk well, but they also have their own language. It's like a real language, and they both understand each other and say the same words. I talked to the doctor about it, and he seems unconcerned as long as they both are progressing in English.

Talk about cute is when they take their bath together in the tub. Splashing and laughing, they sit with legs intertwined and facing each other and have a ball doing it. I get them out (together) and dry them down, and they use every opportunity to rub up against their twin while I'm doing it. None of my friends that have small children have ever heard of anything like it.

Book 5 page 212

We are nearly there on the potty training (no more diapers!), but I have uncovered a small problem. They want to go at the same time, and we only have one little potty chair. They don't fight for it but try to sit on it at the same time! It's so funny.

Book 5 page 352

The end of a year. The twins are three and are inseparable. At Joe's insistence, we purchased separate beds for them and have them apart by just enough to walk between. Mike is starting to become larger and slightly more dominant, but he does everything he can do to make his sister happy. You can see him looking at her frequently, and I wish I knew what goes on in their minds.

Book 7 page 260

I give up. We make the children go to bed in their own separate beds, and they do, but come morning, every morning, they are cuddled together in the same bed. Sometimes it's his and sometimes her's. Grrr!

At this age, no more community baths! The children don't like it, and it's more work for me, but I think it must be that way.

Since the start of kindergarten, I have been trying hard to get them to play with other children with mixed results. They will do it but only if both of them are together doing it. Never changes. Miss Jensen says that it's the same way at school.

Book 8 page 285

Back from the psychologist today concerning the children and their closeness. He listened to me about what I felt the problem was and talked to the children together, out of our sight. Later, he explained about the Westermarck effect which was described by a Finnish anthropologist in the last century. Apparently, there is a biological barrier between people who are raised together from an early age. There is almost no chance that they will be sexually attracted when they get older. He also gave us the example of the Chinese who used to use the Shim-pua marriage which was selling a girl child at a very early age to family so that she would serve as a servant and then later marry the boy child. He said that the marriage almost never worked. Whew! That was a load off of my mind. I guess our twins closeness is a good thing and not a bad one. I am very happy tonight.

Book 8 page 320

We had a snow storm today, and it left us with a good deal of the kind of snow that makes a great snowman. I took the twins outside, and I showed them how to roll the balls, and we ended up with a nice sized one. Mary wanted to make him more real so we gathered up some vegetables and an old hat and presto...a snowman! Mary got a twinkle in her eye and said, "I want the snowman to marry us!" Mike just stood there and looked blankly at her. I'm sure he never heard of marriage. I paused for a moment, then thought it would make some good pictures. The children went inside in a rush to dress, but all they had were flimsy summer clothes! I posed them in front of the distinguished snowman and hoped that the picture wouldn't show little Mike shaking from the cold. "Now, give each other a kiss!" and they did, right on the lips, and then put their red cheeks against each other and smiled. What a great photo. Hope it turns out.

Book 9 page 232

Mike hit a neighbor's boy in the face today and bloodied his nose. I can't find out why it happened, but I'm guessing that it had something to do with Mary. She claims that the boy tried to hit her, but I know that she is lying. Those two really stick together.

Book 9 page 301

Poor little Mike got another spanking from his father today. Some little knickknack was dropped and broke, and Mike said he did it. I saw his sister playing with it earlier, so I'm sure it was she who dropped it, and I told Joe that, but it didn't make any difference. I think Joe is too quick to spank Mike because... I can't bring myself to say that any longer. If it wasn't for the children, I would leave Joe and go live with my sister in Washington. My problems with

Joe are one thing, but he takes it out on little Mike. The child is very tough and getting tougher, because he never cries any more, no matter what Joe does.

Book 10 page 123

Mike sent home again today for fighting. I called the teacher, and she says that the principal likes Mike because of his grades and good behavior, but they are frustrated at all the fighting. They think that he is protecting his sister in some way. I know he is, and I also know that he won't stop. He is becoming a problem child, but he is so loving and tender with Mary that I don't have the heart to say anything to him. If the boys would just learn to stay away from her, they wouldn't have to worry about Mike. Someday.

Book 10 page 355

Took Mary (and Mike!) to buy her a new dress for the holiday. She is becoming so attractive that people are starting to notice. We need to give her some lessons in dancing or singing or even a musical instrument. I don't know what Mike will do if he is separated from her for even an hour. Sometimes I see them holding hands under the dinner table! Mary can give him such a look with her long eyelashes and her little shrugs. When we have a family meal, they sit as close as possible, and if you watch, you can see that they touch shoulders frequently. No accident there, and they both do it.

Book 11 page 234

Moved in to our new home today. More room but more cleaning and care also. The twins have their own bedrooms, and we will have to keep our fingers crossed that we can enforce the rules. We were never able to keep them apart in the old bedroom, because no matter what we said or did, they would always end up together in one bed. They seemed to have to touch each other to get to sleep. It's always been that way, but I'm hoping to change it now.

Mike has shot up in size, and you can see the little man in him starting to come out. Mary gets more beautiful by the day.

Joe promised me some extra money next year for Mary's dancing lessons.

Book 13 page 23

Mike expelled today for knocking a boy's front tooth out. He refuses to say why he did it. Mary won't say either and pretends that she doesn't know anything about it. Those two!

They do their homework together, and I'm glad, because Mike is a straight A student, and Mary needs his help. They use the time talking in a low voice so that we can't hear them. No idea what is in those little heads.

Book 14 page 52

It's been dawning on me that Mike is different. It's not that I don't love him. I do, but I feel like his chemistry is somewhat different than ours. He does look different, and the older he gets, the more you can see it. He is special and dear to me, and I don't know why I even think about it, but I do. I know that I didn't have any man in my life other than Joe, but something must have happened. I started thinking about the other woman who was having a child at the same time I was. I wonder if I could discover her name and take a look at her child, just to be sure. Would I give Mike up if I found that he wasn't mine? No, I don't want that, because he is my child now and for always. Besides, taking the children away from each other would be heartless. I have never seen the like of the love between my children.

Book 14 page 301

Another year is drawing to a close. My children are twelve now and are going thru the changes. Mike with his big feet, and Mary with her little breasts. They are so precious! The bathroom is never empty, because Mary is always in there doing something to her hair. This is the time I have been fearing, because children start to become sexually aware at this age. I hope that psychologist knew what he was talking about.

Book 14 page 355

Joe got up early today and checked on the children and found them in the same bed. He got really angry and accused Mike of some horrible things I know he wouldn't do. He got another violent spanking, but the look on his face took Joe back a little. A little more size and I don't think Mike would take a beating any longer. After Joe went to work, I asked Mary about it when we were alone. She admitted that they frequently slept together and didn't understand why that was wrong. I know that they didn't do anything, because they love each other so much. I explained the best I could, without a physical description of sex, why it was wrong. Mary listened, but I could tell from her eyes that nothing I could say or do would change the way she or Mike felt. I think that Joe and I are the ones with a problem, because we simply can never feel that depth of love for another person. Threatening them, ordering them and explaining to them hasn't worked. We need some help. After talking to Joe, we decided that our physician should be the one to explain this thing to the children, if he would agree.

Book 15 page 21

Our doctor is an older and wise man who has seen a lot of the world. He listened to me explain our problem very patiently. He has seen the children since they were born, and I think he might have had his own feelings about them already in his mind.

"Mrs. Condor, I have been watching your children grow up to be a couple of the finest young people I have had the privilege to know. Part of it is your excellent parenting, and it shows how much you care about them. Your husband came to me long ago with the feeling that Mike wasn't his child, and I know that this comes as no surprise to you. Have you ever had such thoughts?"

I admitted to him that I have come to the same conclusion, but I love Mike all the same.

"Long ago, I had the same opinion, and after Dr. Sessions died suddenly and we were apprised of his gambling problem, we opened all the records of his cases and your's came up also. To make a long story short, there was a woman who gave birth within a few minutes of your births. We tried to track her down and found that she had entered the hospital under an assumed name, and there was no way to find her. This doesn't mean for sure that she took your baby for hers. The question you have to answer is do you love Mike as your own now and would you give him up?"

I told him that is what I thought happened, and I couldn't give the boy up, but I would like to see my own child and make sure he or she is all right.

"Well, if you want to do that, I will inform the police. Be warned, however, that I can't predict what will happen if they were to find the woman and the child, and it's still very possible that Mike is yours after all."

After thinking it over, I decided to let it drop for now. I couldn't bear to lose Mike, who has become part of my heart, and he is everything to Mary. I decided to keep this matter to myself, because if Joe found out he was right, I think it would be unpredictable what he might do. He might as well go on thinking that I am just a whore, since he has thought that for several years anyway.

Dr. Ross made an appointment to talk to the children about sex and why they shouldn't sleep together. I have had a change of heart about them, though. I don't want them to experience sex at this early age, but their love for one another is probably the most wonderful thing I have witnessed in my life. I am jealous of it.

Book 15 page 25

Mike and Mary visited Dr. Ross today and went in there without me. When they came out, I couldn't read their faces and was glad when I was called in to talk to him.

"First of all, Charlotte, I want you to know that they have not had any sexual contact. The fact that they love each other is obvious. I don't even see newlyweds who have more affection for their new mate than your children do for each other. I went through why all cultures don't allow reproductive activity between close relatives and how it even is a prohibited activity among animal species. They clearly understand that it would be wrong, and I think that they always have known that. Their love is above that level, and it, frankly, is the most blessed thing I have ever known in my professional or personal life. You couldn't change how they feel even if you wanted to, and I don't."

I asked Dr. Ross if he had ever heard of the Westermarck effect that the psychologist had talked about. He said that he remembered hearing about it in medical school, but my children haven't and obviously don't believe it anyway. After this, I refuse to worry any longer about what I can't change.

Book 17 Page 234

Joe home from the hospital. He has less chest pain than before, but I see that he is weak. Unable to work say the doctors. How am I going to feed this bunch?

Book 17 Page 240

My wonderful children stepped forward and found jobs. Mary will work at City Fashions which is a nice upscale dress shop. She could learn some useful things there! Mike said that he will do deliveries of groceries on his bicycle! Such sweet children.

Book 17 Page 270

Mary just handed me a wad of cash, and I counted fifty dollars! She gave me a concocted story about finding it behind the dresser. I don't believe her for a second, and I think that it came from Mike, but I can't imagine what he did to get it. I hope he didn't get into crime or something. We can use the money, though, and right now I have no choice except to trust them.

Book 17 page 290

Had a visit from the police today. A nice Detective Smith and his partner. They wanted to talk about Mike! My heart almost fell out, and I remembered the fifty dollars. They assured me that Mike had done nothing wrong, but some local criminals had decided that they wanted to recruit Mike and might show up at the house. They wanted me to call them if anything was amiss or if I felt threatened.

I spoke to Mike when he got home, and he assured me that there was no problem. I wonder.

Book 17 page 345

Mike came home bruised in the face, and there was a cut above his right eye. We all thought that he was done with boxing, and he said that was a one time fight and that, although it didn't look like it, he won.

Book 19 page 130

My neighbor, Millie, who is the mother of Carol, one of the children's classmates, told me that Mike had a prostitute at the school dance, and everyone was talking about it. I am humiliated, if it is true.

Spoke in private with Mary about the dance, and she said that it was her fault, and she was the one who set up the blind date. She says that Mike knew nothing about it, and they only found out later who she was. Mary said that Mike acted the gentleman and refused a ride in the girl's car. I believed her, but it is most embarrassing that it happened. Mary said that it might be the work of the gangsters who were trying to get Mike in.

Book 19 page 149

Joe back in the hospital with sudden chest pain. The doctors told me to prepare for the worst and looking at Joe, I think that they are right.

Talked with my husband at the hospital this afternoon. He was in pain but was clear in his mind. He asked me if I would finally admit that I slept with another man, because now that he was dying, he wanted to know the truth. I told him that I never did, and that Dr. Ross and I both felt that a crooked doctor switched Mike for our baby in the hospital. I told him that I never said anything, because I was afraid that they would take Mike from us, so I let him believe what he wanted and that I never expected him to believe the truth anyway. It was a sad moment for us both when it struck him for the first time that I have never strayed from our marriage and our boy, Mike, was born to another woman.

"I've been such a fool, Charlotte. I know that it's too late to make up for all those lost years that I neglected you. All the time we've lost together. I won't ask you to forgive me, because I don't deserve it. You have been a good wife and a good mother and better than I could have ever asked for."

Joe started to cry and, God forgive me, I just sat there and looked at him, because I had nothing left to give him. He died alone that afternoon at four o'clock while I was home feeding the children.

Book 19 page 210

Mary just handed me a roll of cash so thick that my jaw dropped open. Heaven knows that we need the money, but I know that it is criminal money. Mike came home wearing new clothes yesterday that must have cost a lot. It looks like he has joined the bad people, and we have probably lost him.

Book 19 page 212

Mike stayed out all night for the first time. Mary said he was probably at The Farm, and I remember that the prostitute he dated works there. We are both worried about him, and she said that she would wait up all night for him, but I had to retire.

Book 19 page 213

We have finally stopped for the night. Mike came in at two a.m. this morning in a panic to have us get out of town. We assumed that the criminals were coming for us or him, and even though we were frightened, we had no choice. Mike didn't come with us, and he kept insisting that we get away fast. We don't know anything and assume the worst. He said that he would take care of the house and all our belongings, and all we had was our purses. We didn't have but a few dollars with us, but he said that all we needed was in the trunk. When we stopped for gas, we found a leather bag full of money. Tonight, in the motel, we counted it, and it was over one hundred twenty thousand dollars! We assume that it's stolen, and we don't know what to do. Mary insists that we trust him and keep moving away from town. I know my sister will take us in, but it's a very long trip. There is no way to contact Mike to see if he is all right. Mary cried off and on through the entire day. This is the first time they have ever been apart, and it is tearing her up and me as well.

Book 18 page 216

We arrived at Gladys' home midmorning. We called yesterday, and she was very happy to hear that we were coming and said that they had plenty of room for us, and we could stay as long as we liked. Mary and I discussed it, and we felt that we would wait to hear from Mike before deciding what to do after we arrived. Gladys' two boys are gone now, with Bob in the Navy and Ray married with his own farm. There is plenty of room, and Gladys and her husband, Tommy, seem to enjoy the company. We waited up late tonight for Mike's call that never came. I heard Mary crying in her room, poor child loves him so.

Book 18 page 246

Finally, a letter from Mike. He is in the Army(!) and on a training base in Georgia. He said that Detective Smith helped him enlist to get away from the mob and that we are not to try to come back home for now. Mary was so glad to hear from him that she couldn't read his letter, and I had to take it out of her hand. No word from him what happened that night, and I guess we don't want to find out.

Mary started assembling all the letters she has written to Mike now that she has someplace to send them. We talked it over, and I think it is time to register the car Mike gave us, in this state, because it looks like we will be here for a while. Mary will need to finish high school, and we will keep the money, I guess. Mike wanted her to go to New York for dancing but that decision is a year away. We at least can breathe easy that Mike is safe in the Army, if you can call that safe.

Book 19 page 141

Senior prom tonight and Mary isn't going. She had at least a dozen offers from boys and turned them all down. She was going to be Prom Queen, but now I don't know what they will do without her. I don't know if there is a runner-up Prom Queen but if there is, she will be a happy little girl.

Since Mary was home with nothing to do, I decided that we needed a long talk. I know that she has been working with a young doctor and has discovered that Mike and she are not related as we always somehow knew. The last letter we got from Mike confirmed his blood type, and we think he probably shipped out because he said that would be the last letter for long time. He is going to Europe into that war. Mary did write him right back with the good news, but we don't know when or where he will get the letter. She is broken and in the dumps right now, and this dance brings back a lot of memories for her when Mike was there. She said that they never got to dance even one time together. It is sad when now we know that they could have been together as they both wanted so much to be. She found the man of her dreams was always the one she loved, and now he may be lost in another crazy war.

Book 19 page 264

Took Mary to the train station to send her off to New York. She is to study dance at the famous Juilliard school.

She has all new clothes, and the tuition is paid in advance, thanks to Mike. If only he were here to go with her in to the big city, instead of all by herself. I would go too, but my health is not what it was. Now I've lost my babies and my husband, and except for my sister, I am all alone in the world. We got a couple of letters from Mike, but we can tell he never got the letter telling him that he and Mary are free to do what they always wished. That is to be together forever. I've stopped talking about him to her, because she breaks down at the thought of him in danger. We see the news about the war and hear it on the radio constantly, and we always think of our little Mike walking around behind his sister keeping close watch on everything she did. I wish he could see her now, because there is no living woman as attractive as she is at this moment in her life. She stops traffic, and I'm not kidding.

Book 19 page 340

Mary sent word that she is coming for Christmas! We are so happy for her success in the Big Apple! My health is not good and just hope that I can make it to Christmas to see Mary again. No letters from Mike for a very long time. I dread seeing the Western Union boys, and I keep fearing to receive the telegram that no one wants to see. If only the war could end so I could be there for Mary and Mike's wedding! I think of the snowman wedding all the time now, and I cherish the photo of it that we finally got back out of storage. The only wish I have in life now is to see that photo recreated for real.

Book 19 page 360

To whom may reading these diaries:

My mother, Charlotte M. Condor, died the day after Christmas, aged 54, of ovarian cancer. She was buried according to her wishes and attending the funeral were myself and her sister, Gladys, and her brother-in-law, Tommy.

This closes her diaries of nineteen years which started soon after she and my father, Thomas J. Condor, were married. My father died of a heart attack sixteen months ago. Their children are myself, Mary Condor, and my brother, Mike Condor.

My mother was a fine person and did the best she could do to raise and protect her children. Mike and I will miss her very much.

Mary Condor   December 28, 1942

Chapter 9

PAPER CHASE

So what do you have for me?" Lilith asked Paul for the second time.

"That's what I've been trying to tell you. I have nothing! I got into the medical records okay, but they have a note on the only other woman's chart that delivered that day saying that the address was fictitious. There is no way we can track her down."

Lilith looked at Paul and leaned back in her chair with her pen tapping on the desk. She thought about what Jill had told her about him. In a word, sleazy. Describes him perfectly, she thought. She could add lazy also.

"Well, my dear investigator, you are supposed to know what to do next, aren't you?" Lilith asked sarcastically.

"I have the birth certificate of the child in question right here," he said as he pulled from somewhere a photocopy and held it up like a prize. "The child should have the same name unless it was legally changed. You should know more than me about that. My understanding is that if a name is changed, there is a court document someplace."

"Yes, that's true. Unfortunately, this happened ninety years ago and not all old records are on the Internet. You would have to know where the court was located first.

Have you tried running down the physician who we think was taking bribes from the mob for the switch?"

"You mean this Dr. Sessions? Well, I am just getting started on that one. How about a little cash advance? That would help give me some incentive."

"How much? You already got five hundred in advance. What about an accounting of that first?" Lilith said.

"I'm thinking another two bills. I might have to do some bribing, you never know."

Lilith pushed the intercom button. "Yes, Miss Roberts?" the voice said.

"The gentleman is just leaving. Please issue him two hundred dollars and get a receipt." Lilith looked up at Paul and said, "Anything else?"

"No. I'll get right on it and get back to you. I'm sure we will find something eventually."

"I'm not giving you any more money unless you produce results. Got that?"

"Notice that I got the birth certificate right? That's results."

"Bye, Mr. Jones," she said and watched him reluctantly leave.

Lilith hit the intercom button again. "Yes, Miss Roberts?" the voice said.

"Call the reporter, Jill Longly, from the Newtown News and Commentary."

A few minutes later a telephone button lit and Lilith picked it up. "Hi, Jill."

"Hi, anything up with Paul?"

"He's sort of working on it and mostly working to get more money out of me. I have my doubts if he can find anything we can use, but I'm going to see how this next search goes. How are you doing on the diaries?"

"I'm all done. I'll run them over to your office tomorrow, is that all right?"

"Sure, but what's next after that? Are you finished then?"

"No, not quite yet. I would like to talk to Mike about the war, if he'll do it, and I'm heading that way right now. After that, we need to find Mary's sister, then the book will be finished."

"Oh, yes. I remembered what you said about getting some snapshots for the book. Mary had a collection of professional photographs made during the war, and I think that my mother has them put away someplace. Think you can use them?"

"I saw a couple in the scrapbook the first day I was over there. She was gorgeous during those years. One of them would make a great back cover."

"All right, I'll look. See you tomorrow."

Chapter 10

MIKE AT WAR

Somewhere Over Western France August 1944

Stand ready for deployment," the voice said over the drone of the aircraft's twin motors. The ready jump light came on, and the jump master pointed to an airman who opened the jump doors with a bang, and the noise grew intense. Backdraft from the passing air entered the cabin and shook them, viciously flapping their loose clothing. The air was cold, and looking out the door, nothing was visible except the dark night. Mike looked at his men to make sure they were all attached to the jump line. Each man checked the one in front of him to see that all straps were tight and the parachute rip cord was clipped in. They looked heavily burdened and had grim determined faces. This was not the first jump behind German lines for any of them, and all had seen extensive combat. Twelve men, including Mike. That was all the mission planners would allow. Stealth, they said, not force.

Mike could remember the Captain's words, "You will be behind German lines until Allied forces overtake your assigned area. Try to avoid contact with the enemy who is likely to be looking for you. The mission is of utmost importance. Killing the enemy is not. Free French forces will assist you on the ground. Most of all, be patient, we are coming for you."

The jump light changed color and started to flash. Mike took a last look at his men and signaled that the first man was to jump. He instantly went out the door and so did the rest in rapid sequence. Mike took a last look around and jumped into the darkness.

Falling, the rush of air obscured any sound but the noise of the plane they had just left, which rapidly faded in the distance. Looking down, he could make out parachutes which diminished in size as they floated downward to the black earth below. There was a sparkling of light below, and Mike realized that the first jumpers were coming under machine gun fire. He pulled hard on his lines trying to direct the chute away from the ambush. There was a slight change of direction but not enough. He could see return fire from the two or three men who were down first. All of a sudden an entire line of tracers started coming from the left. There were several machine guns firing, and he started to be able to hear the reports. He could tell which were German guns because of the rapidity of fire. Who were the others? The ground was just ahead, and he dropped his weapons bag just before he hit. Tracers flew over his head, tearing big holes in his chute before he could unbuckle. He fell against the cold ground and looked around. He was within sight of three men who were on their elbows and were firing into the woods. Tracers went over their heads and were coming from the other direction. There were some heavily armed allies behind them, Mike realized. He signaled for the men to pull back toward the woods behind them, a distance of about two hundred yards. Mortar fire whistled in, and the ground lifted them up and put them back down, hard. Earth and grass fell over them like a dark rain.

"Faster, men," Mike shouted. "We have to get out. They have our range." Smoke from the explosions helped obscure the retreat through the darkness. Mike pointed to the source of the tracer fire, and they headed that way at a jog, stopping and lying flat when mortar rounds came in. Finally, they reached the edge of the woods, still not knowing what was waiting for them. Mike counted heads quickly. Eight men, four lost. The machine guns continued, and he could hear motors running from somewhere.

"English!" a voice called out. Mike crouched lower and made ready with his Thompson. He could make out someone crawling toward them in a shallow gully. Four guns turned toward the newcomer. "English!" the man said again and waved for them to come to him or to follow. The man turned around, and Mike signaled his men to go that way. They crawled through deep mud for a distance and then the man stood.

"Safe here. We assist, no? Must hurry!" The man led the way into the deeper woods as the gunfire died out. The motor sound was closer and then Mike could make out the outline of a German transport. Was it a trick? As he squinted to see around him, a figure appeared in the back of the truck and jumped off. The shadow seemed to be a smaller person, and it approached where Mike was standing, with its arm raised in salute.

"Allies!" a female voice called out. As she got closer, Mike could make out a woman's face. When she pulled back her hood, he saw the glint of blonde hair.

"You are the American paratroopers we were here to assist. Too bad the Bosch found out, but luckily it was only a patrol, and we had the better guns. For now." She gave the Gallic shrug and waved them to the rear of the waiting German truck.

"Who are you, Miss, and why are we riding in a German army truck?" Mike asked.

"My code name is all you get *mon soldat élégant*. Nichole. We stole the vehicle two hours ago. Now if there are no more inquires, please, we *échapper* before more Germans arrive."

Mike gave his men the signal, and they quickly climbed into the truck and held on. After the truck drove a few hundred yards, it stopped again and ten men in civilian clothes got in. They exchanged handshakes and backslaps with Mike and his men, even though there was a near total language barrier. Mike stationed himself near the rear of the truck so he could watch the road behind them. He felt someone take his arm, and he turned to see Nichole smiling up at him. He leaned toward her to hear what she was saying above the ambient noise of the truck.

"Ten kilometers, then we stop. Walk four kilometers, then another ride. *Comprenez-vous?*" Mike nodded and gave her a thumbs up. In the far distance was the flash on the horizon of the big guns near the front. Occasionally, they could hear the low rumble even above the other noise. The road was dirt and rough, and they bounced along holding on to the hardware while trying to keep their guns ready. The men in the dark rear were only visible because of the occasional light reflection from their eyes, and it gave the impression of a truck load of raccoons.

There was a roar of the motor, and the truck accelerated and then veered suddenly and stopped. Overhead, Mike heard the shriek of a fighter plane passing closely. He squinted his eyes and held his breath, waiting for an explosion, but the plane passed over.

"German," Nichole said with a grin, then yelled, "*allons*," and the truck started moving. "This is why we are using a German truck. When your people come after dawn, we must be gone from this vehicle. Understand?" Mike nodded that he got it.

After another hour, the truck pulled to a screeching halt, and they all dismounted. Nichole led the group in single file with Mike bringing up the rear. They headed toward the woods just as the sky was beginning to get light. Just before they were all inside the dark and protective forest, another airplane appeared suddenly with deafening intensity. Machine gun fire from the plane seemed briefly to flicker some light into the trees and then the truck that they had been using exploded with a massive fireball and large pieces of it fell noisily to the earth.

"Aah, you see that our timing is perfect, no?" Nichole shouted to the group. The march brought them in and out of the tree line. Mike's men were wary and alert in the open, but their French colleagues seemed to be relaxed and nonchalant. Eventually, they reached the outskirts of a small village, and the group crouched behind some shrubs and studied the town in silence. Nothing seemed to be moving, and the only sound was a rooster making his morning calls.

"Fredrick, *allez voir!*" Nichole ordered, and a man in a battered tan great coat started walking slowly toward the town. His shoulders hunched as if in resignation to his fate. They all watched as he disappeared down one of the small streets. They waited for the sound of gunfire, but saw Fredrick waving to them to come forward. They all got up, hesitantly at first, then filed down the small hill toward town.

"Amazing!" one of the men muttered as they could see that the town was deserted except for a few chickens.

"Where are the people?" Mike asked her.

"Fled. The front, you know," she said not looking at him. As she spoke, thunder rolled back up from the west. The group stopped at a small barn, and the Frenchmen shook hands with the troopers and started to walk away. Mike looked confused and waited for an explanation.

"They go home. We haven't far to go now, you see." She opened the barn's double doors and two old battered farm trucks were partially visible under enormous piles of hay. The soldiers pitched in, and soon the trucks were fully visible. They pushed them into the street and then one started and one didn't. Mike held up his hands in frustration.

"Sergeant, let me give it a try," said Corporal Serge Evans. Without waiting for an answer, he said, "Give me a push, guys!" and then jumped behind the wheel. After gaining momentum for fifteen feet, Serge let the clutch out, and the motor coughed to life.

"Where are we headed?" Mike asked.

"Woods, then we wait for dark," she said. They headed out the main road then veered onto what looked like a cowpath. Mike estimated that the trip was four to five kilometers when they finally stopped on a signal from Nichole. The woods were indeed deep and little light came through the canopy.

"Rest, my friends. We travel tonight by foot," she said.

Mike stationed guards, who would shift in four hours, in a triangle from their position. The rest quickly got busy trying to sleep after a quick bite of rations. Mike and Nichole sat apart from the rest and struck up a conversation.

"You have the case for sure?" he asked.

"*Oui, monsieur*, it is safe. You will have it in your hands tonight."

"How did your people come by this find?"

"Oh, *mon soldat élégant*, your people really did it. An Allied plane found a German column and strafed it. Most were killed, and we French got the rest. Good work, no? We encountered a dead General with his case locked to his wrist. A sign of being valuable, no? Some of our people felt that it was something you Americans would want to see and here you are, no?"

"I was told that it was of utmost importance that it not get away from us. I was not told exactly what the case contains. Do you know?" Mike asked her.

"Bomb. Big Bomb. Plans for building a bomb for the master race. That is all I know." Mike mulled this over. He had heard the rumors of an atomic weapon that the Germans were supposed to be working on which would end the war in their favor. He never believed any of it, but perhaps it was true after all. If so, the briefcase could enable the Americans to build one or prevent the Germans from building theirs. The mission had been assembled in great haste, and Mike and his team were pulled off the lines only four days ago. All were hardened, experienced men and were dependable and self-reliant. A good choice except for their chosen leader, himself. True, he had been on or near the front lines of fighting from North Africa to

Sicily and then on into Italy. He was pulled away to join the invasion forces at Normandy but remembered that he had seen most of his comrades killed or wounded. That experience didn't make him feel he was qualified to lead even more men to their deaths. All these men with him had similar stories and experiences. Any of them could lead. Perhaps that was the point after all. No matter who died, someone was there fit to take charge.

"Where do you come from, Sergeant?" Nichole asked.

"A little city not far from Chicago. Ever hear of Chicago?"

"*Absolument*! All that jazz!" she said with a smile.

"And you, Nichole?"

"I am not able to discuss that presently. You will understand. Are you married then, Sergeant?"

"No, Nichole. Are you?"

"No, sadly," she said and gave a pout. That moment, he realized that she was a very attractive girl. There had been too much going on to really look at her before.

"You are so attractive. Surely someone would have asked?" Mike commented.

"This is my secret. A girl never tells, you know." She gave another cute pout. "Sergeant, do you have someone at home that you love?"

"Sure. My sister, Mary. I love her."

"No, *mon soldat élégant*, you know that I meant someone else. Do not play games with a French girl. We know about love, you know."

"So, I've heard. My sister is my twin. We were together every day since birth, and I haven't seen her for nearly two years. I miss her more than I can say."

"Does that mean that you were romantic with your sister?"

"Of course not in the way you are thinking."

"*Oh Dieu de remerciement*," she said wiping her brow. "I was starting to think you Americans were crazy, you know."

"What about you, Nichole. Anyone special?"

She looked away and stared into the darkening woods. "Not any longer, *mon ami*. The Germans captured and shot him. After that, I hated the Germans so much that I took Roland's place in the Resistance. Since your people are over there making so much noise, perhaps the Germans will run away and we can have peace. No?"

"It's going to take awhile. Can you tell me where we are headed tonight?"

"We walk just past these woods, and we will find a farmhouse belonging to a *loyal la France libre*. The case is there, secreted in the well. Can you tell me what you are going to do with it?"

"We have a short wave radio. I'm going to transmit as much as I can in case we can't get back to our lines. One of my men reads and speaks fluent German."

"This is a bad idea, *mon* Sergeant. The Germans will find you. They listen for radios such as yours, and they can find you very fast. Do not transmit. Hide and wait for your army. It is coming, I can hear it."

"They are in a rush to get this information. It might lead to preventing the Germans from using this weapon. These are my orders, I have to transmit."

"I have seen these papers, and they are many. Too much time to transmit. You will get us all killed." Mike thought this over, and it did seem that Nichole was right. He decided to look at the papers first and then decide. While he was lost in thought, two fighter planes went over the woods very close to the trees. They were overhead for only a couple of seconds. Could the trucks be seen through the trees, he wondered. Nichole seemed to read his mind.

"Relax, for this moment, we are safe. Later? Anyway, I thought they were yours, probably searching for tanks."

The planes didn't return which meant that they couldn't see below the tree tops. He relaxed again.

"What will you do if you get home?" Nichole asked.

"First, find my mother and sister. Then back to school, I think. Afterward, college. Something like that. You?"

"I want a good man to love and care for. That is all. Simple enough."

"I hope you find him, Nichole."

"Sometimes these things just happen, you know. It is the French way."

"Life doesn't go as planned very often, does it?" Mike observed.

"No. Now I just try to survive another day. I can't think past today and perhaps tomorrow. You must have discovered that also, no?"

"For the last two years, yes. Most soldiers, like me, think that we will never live to see the war end. It helps thinking that you are already dead. That way they can't kill you, and you can face what you have to face."

"You look like a man who would be a great lover. Have you been a great lover yet or is it still to be?"

"When I joined the Army, I was still seventeen. I was too young to have a lover and too busy since to be one. Anyway, where I've been there have been no women, only Germans trying to kill me."

"Oh, but you are wrong. You have met Nichole. Everything is changed. Your luck is with you after all." She smiled a devilish smile, and then her face fell. Mike could hear the noise as well. There was a rumbling, clanking and screeching noise getting louder by the second. Tanks. Lots of tanks. Mike could see one of his men signaling and alerting him to the noise. He and Nichole stood and looked around. There were no tanks in view, but now they could catch some German words. The column was very close, just outside of the trees. Mike signaled his men to take cover and move away from the trucks and away from the Germans. They scattered into the woods, and Mike and Nichole followed. They hid behind some thick bushes about two hundred yards away from the trucks and waited. The German column was big and continued on and on. Mike signaled, and the group fell back even farther from the German columns. So far, there were no signs of troops in the woods. They hunkered down for a long wait. Another noise could be heard now from another direction, and the tank motors got noticeably louder, and there were shouts in German. Then above the trees, more airplanes. Fighters, from the speed they were traveling. The sound diminished and then returned.

"There's going to be an attack on the tanks. They will come this way to get out of sight," Mike shouted and waved the men to follow him. They ran away from an increasingly loud series of explosions and gunfire. They could see columns of flame rising above the forest and feel the heat through the trees and then heard the sound of motors coming their way amid the sound of crashing trees. The tanks were heading into the woods to avoid Allied aircraft.

The aircraft overhead changed tactics and started dropping incendiary bombs into the forest. The whole place was lit with yellow and red flames and obscured by smoke transforming a green peaceful forest into Hell. Running was no longer an option, because they would now be easily seen. Staying risked being incinerated by Allied forces determined to eliminate the tanks before they could get to the front. This is the end of it, Mike thought, then he saw one of his men anxiously waving to get his attention. He was pointing to a small hill in front of him and from that position the man was out of view of the rapidly approaching German armor. Mike had simply no options. He helped Nichole stay low, and they crawled as fast as possible toward Corporal Taylor, who seemed to be guiding the other men into the hill. Mike understood. Taylor had discovered a cave. Just before Mike and Nichole arrived, Taylor disappeared into the hill as a sudden white light to their left followed by a violent blast hurled both of them into a stand of trees. When Mike recovered enough to look around, he saw that Nichole was unconscious and lying face down in the leaves. He could hear the shouts of the German soldiers getting closer. He pulled Nichole along on her back toward the cave and finally was assisted by one of the men to get her inside. Not more than five-seconds later, a clanking sound rapidly approached them and a dark mass obscured the opening. A German tank had stopped directly over the cave entrance.

"Anyone got a light?" a voice asked. One of the men found a small flashlight and turned it on. The cave seemed to be eight feet high in spots with a very small entrance which angled steeply up and was now obscured by the massive tank. Rearward, the opening tapered but didn't close completely, and cool air could be felt coming from between the rocks. The floor was rocky and laden with bat droppings and wood fragments. Mike pulled Nichole to the center and held her head away from the floor. She was breathing regularly, and he could see no injuries. One of the men suggested water and dripped some on her face to wash away the dirt. Her eyes fluttered open, and she started to cough.

"Looks like she'll be okay, Sarge. Just knocked out," someone said. The ground shook again, and dirt and dust fell from above. The tank directly above them was still running but remained stationary.

"What a break," Sergeant LaMarka said. "If it wasn't for this cave, we would all look like a used matchstick. Good find, Taylor. You just earned your pay for this month."

"We sure aren't going anywhere for now. You guys settle in and get some food, and we'll just have to wait this out," Mike said to his men. He turned his attention to Nichole who was now sitting up and looking around.

"A cave. How fortunate! This part of France is full of them. How did I get in here?"

"You were knocked out. We pulled you in," Mike said.

"You mean that you pulled me in, don't you, *mon ami*?"

"No, Nichole, we all did," Mike said.

"I remember one of your old cowboy movies I saw once. There was an Indian in it who was saved, like me, and he told the cowboy that he owed his life to him and that from then forward, he was going to belong to the cowboy. Did you see that one?"

"I don't remember that one, Nichole. Don't worry, I won't hold you to anything like that."

"It's not for you, soldier, to decide that. It is for me to decide, *comprenez-vous*?"

Mike sat down beside her and said, "Want some food? It's only rations and not French, but it fills your tummy."

"It's cold in here. Could I sit on your lap while I eat, *mon soldat élégant*?" The question drew chuckles from the men.

"If he doesn't want you, honey, you can sit on my lap all night," a voice said from the darkness.

"Sure, Nichole, it would be nice," Mike said and patted his lap. She got up just as the bulb in the flashlight flickered, indicating not much more time before total darkness returned. She sat down and wrapped an arm around his neck and positioned her face and lips close to his. Mike remarked to himself how light she was. He caught the faint odor of French perfume about her and felt her breath on his face. Another close explosion and more falling dirt. She pulled harder on his neck and moved her lips closer, touching his cheek.

"Remember food?" Mike asked and found her hand, pressing a bar into it.

"You are my protector. No?" she asked into his ear.

"I don't think you need much protection, Nichole. You were supposed to be protecting us, weren't you?"

"One never agreed to protect you from German tanks. That is too much, even for Nichole, *n'est pas*?"

Outside the cave the sound of explosions stopped. The cave was deafeningly quiet, except for the idling diesel above the entrance of the cave. Mike felt Nichole push away slightly, and he could hear her munching a biscuit from his K ration kit.

"What's next Sergeant?" someone asked.

"Go up there and push the tank off and then we can get out of here," Mike said. "Otherwise, you can get some rest. They have to leave for the front soon, but I expect they are picking up the pieces right now. Be patient. We weren't going to leave until dark in any event."

Nichols lips found his ear again, and she said, "Just what I would have said, *mon soldat élégant.* Now we have time to talk."

"Are all French women as sexy as you, Nichole?" Mike asked.

"*Mon Dieu, Non!* Just Nichole." She turned his head toward her and found his lips with hers. The kiss lasted a long moment, and he could feel her eyelashes fluttering against his cheek. Contact with this strange woman felt good, and in spite of the impossible surroundings, while it lasted, it took him away from the war.

"Did you enjoy my lips, *mon soldat élégant?*" she whispered.

"Yes, very much. Thank you."

"No thanks needed, *mon soldat élégant.* I belong to you, don't you recall?" She kissed him again, and he felt her tongue exploring his mouth. An unexpected and previously unexperienced sensation swept over him. Mike started to laugh.

"What is wrong? Are you having sport with Nichole?" she asked.

"No, it was wonderful. You are wonderful. It's just so improbable. A beautiful French girl on my lap sealed in a black cave with seven heavily armed men and a German tank over our heads. Isn't it funny?" he asked.

"Now you know to expect the unexpected with Nichole, *n'est pas?*"

"Life has gotten more interesting since you arrived."

"Sergeant, do you have a first name? I feel that I can get a first name if you can get my kisses."

"Mike."

"Well, Mike. Have you kissed a woman before me?"

"Two. Have you kissed a man before me?"

"One never tells, *mon ami,*" she said, and he felt the warmth of her face as she drew closer again.

"What are you going to do after we retrieve the briefcase, Nichole?"

"Sadly, I must leave you and return. You won't need Nichole any longer, and I must get away before the war comes here."

"You will be safe then?"

"There is no safety until the Krauts leave for good. And the Americans and their bombs," she added. She kissed him on the lips again, this time harder and longer.

"If you belong to me, why must you leave?" he asked.

"I will still belong to you, but I belong to France first. After the war, you must find me."

"How can I find you? I don't know your name or where you are."

"Love will find a way, *vous ne pensez pas?*"

Before he could think of an answer, they could feel the rocks of the cave vibrating. The sound of the tank above increased, and it moved slowly off the opening. Enough light spilled into the cave so that they could see each other. The sounds gradually faded as the German armor traveled west toward the American forces.

"I almost feel sorry for them headed that way. Patton's Army is in that direction, and he will be very happy to see them come to him," Sergeant LaMarka said.

"Cyrus, stick your head carefully out of the cave and see what's happening," Mike said.   Cyrus did so, and when he came back down, he said, " There are a few stragglers trying to repair the tanks. It's going to take a while yet."

"Good, good. I have you to thank for my life, and I'm not done thanking you yet," Nichole whispered into his ear.

"The others can see us, you know," Mike said.

"I am French. We don't care what people say about us when we make love."

"You are a real package, Nichole. I must say that it's been interesting."

"You haven't seen interesting yet, Mike."

"I can only imagine. The war, Nichole. Remember the war?"

"The war can wait. I belong to you right now and not the war, *comprenez*?" She grabbed his wrist and moved his hand down to her hip. "Does that feel good to you?"

"Heaven, Nichole. Like it was meant to be," he answered.

"Doesn't it feel good to own a French girl?

"Well, I would guess that no man will ever own Nichole," Mike said.

"Perhaps you are right, Mike. What time is it?"

"About 1800 hours."

"I don't understand this hours," she said.

"6 p.m." he said.

"It isn't dark yet. Are the *Bosch* gone?" she said looking at Cyrus. He took a quick peek.

"No. Some are still here."

"If the Germans came up the road, then they must have passed through the farm we seek. I hope that they didn't use the well."

"I hope so too, Nichole," Mike said.

"You know that the *loyal la France libre* often poison the wells for the Germans. The *Bosch* know this and don't trust the wells. They piss into the French wells they discover to get even. Such an ugly war," she sighed.

"We should get some sleep while we can, don't you think?" asked Mike.

"*Oui.*"

"Rotate guard on the opening. You first Cyrus. Alphabetical order. The rest sleep where you can," Mike ordered. They all made do with their pack under their heads, including Mike. Nichole settled into Mike's arms with her head on his shoulder. The hours passed and at 2:00 a.m., the watch called out, "They are gone. It's clear."

"We go," Nichole said and got up and stretched. A last check by Mike showed that the forest was empty except for a couple of burned out tanks. It was dead quiet.

"No noise, we don't know if any of them are still around. Take it slow," Mike ordered. With Mike and Nichole in the lead, they crept forward very slowly, trying not to make the leaves give away their position. The forest was empty, and the Germans had all gone west. They picked up the pace and soon found the other edge of the forest. Nichole held up her finger to her mouth, and they squatted and watched the moonlight-bathed farm for movement. Nichole was patient, and it paid off as they watched an armed German soldier walk slowly out of the farmhouse and stretch.

"The *Bosch* are still here!" she said in a whisper. As they squinted trying to see into the shadows, it was apparent that several tents were scattered around. Hidden in the barn, except for the long protruding muzzle of its rifled cannon, was a Panzer tank.

"Where is the well, Nichole?" Mike said in a low voice. She pointed, and he followed her finger to a shadow on the side of the farmhouse. On the western horizon, there were flashes and rumbling.

"In the morning, the Allied fighters will be out again looking for German vehicles. I wouldn't want to be in that tank if I were in their shoes," Sergeant LaMarka said.

"It will live as long at they keep it hidden. I'll bet they have tanks like that one scattered all over the area," Mike said. He studied the terrain between them and the well. There was only one area that was entirely in the open. The rest had shadows and bushes. "I think that one man could get to the well without being seen and get out again. You could back him up with fire if they spotted him," Mike said to Sergeant LaMarka.

"Going to ask for a volunteer, Mike?" LaMarka asked.

"No, I'm going to do it myself. You command if I don't get back. Right?" He turned to Nichole "How is the case hidden in the well?"

"There is a thin wire tied to the handle. The wire is hung on a small nail inside the well about one foot from the top edge. Just pull it up."

"How long is the wire?"

"Ten meters. Promise that you won't get caught, Mike. Promise."

"Believe me, I don't want to get caught. Nichole, are there any dogs on the farm?"

"Long ago eaten. The Germans often bring dogs of their own. Big dogs."

Corporal Larry Wiggins spoke up. "Sergeant, dogs will always bark at other animals, no matter how well trained they are. I can imitate two raccoons fighting. Can I show you?"

"Better not sound like a bunch of GI's imitating raccoons if you don't want that tank to start up. If you are sure, go ahead. " Mike said.

Wiggins sat up and put his hands to his mouth and let out a series of very believable raccoon sounds. After a moment, they heard distant barking getting closer. With a nod from Mike, Wiggins did it again, and this time they saw a German soldier being pulled by a large Shepherd dog round the corner of the house. The dog was looking directly at their position and barking violently. The dog was very strong and even though his handler protested, the dog was dragging him forward toward the edge of the woods.

"Get ready. Bayonets only," Mike warned. They spread out, knives flashing in the moonlight, crouching down and merging with the shadows. Mike pulled Nichole back into the woods and readied his machine gun. As they waited with tense muscles, the dog was winning and pulled along his handler who was dragging his boots and protesting. Two of the men started circling the pair as they came forward. When they were close enough, Mike dropped his hand and six men leapt on the soldier and his canine from cover. There was a muted yelp and then silence. They all held their breath and waited. Nothing happened.

Mike said, "We got the guard. It's time to go before someone misses him." He handed his gun and pack to another soldier and started creeping toward the farmhouse and the German camp.

Mike wished that the moon wasn't so bright or that it was raining. If he could see well, so could they. He was depending on a small window of opportunity with the canine patrol down. No way of determining how much time this was to give him. He quickly covered the ground up to the open field, then got down and crawled using his elbows and knees, stopping occasionally to listen. If he got in trouble, all he had was his pistol and two grenades. He would count on the riflemen behind him to give deadly fire, and he knew these men would. Finally, he reached the corner of the house and stood up beside it and listened. He could hear snoring in the house. At least several men were inside. Then there were the tents they could see and, of course, the tank. At least thirty, perhaps more. He concentrated on the well which was about fifteen feet away. He inched forward, ducking under the windows, and finally made it. The well was covered by a heavy oak lid, hinged in the center. He carefully opened the lid and laid it over its mate. He felt for the wire. Nothing. He decided that it must be the other side. He closed the lid and carefully moved around to the other side. Someone inside coughed, and he could hear voices. He froze in place listening. After a few moments, he couldn't hear any more sounds so he opened the other flap of wood. This time he found the wire as Nichole had described. He started pulling the wire up slowly, hand over hand. Whatever was down there was heavy, and the wire cut into his hands. In the moonlight, he saw the tan leather come into view. Just as he untied it, he heard footsteps in the gravel in front of the house. He crouched back down clutching the briefcase and waited. It was another patrol. This time it was two soldiers armed with machine pistols. They talked in low voices, walking slowly. Gradually, the footsteps faded, and he started moving back the way he had come. At the field, he dragged the case, but he knew that it was very visible if someone was watching. Behind him he heard someone calling for Horst. Again the voice rang out. Bets were that Horst was the man lying with his throat cut near the woods. Mike tried to hurry but was making more noise. Just as he got to the clump of bushes, a loud voice cried, *"Halt. Nicht bewegen!"* Just then, there were two rifle shots from the direction Mike was headed. Then there was an ascending chaos from behind him. He got up and ran toward the woods.

"We have to go. Move out!" he commanded. They headed back into the dark, traveling as fast as they could. A machine gun opened up from behind them and tracers arced all around, searching for a target. Overhead a flare erupted, but the canopy kept the light from the woods. Behind them, they could hear the tank start up. They ran for their lives. Rifle fire started, and they could hear the whine from bullets and the "whack" as the trees stopped the rounds.

"Keep moving," Mike said, and he grabbed Nichole. They veered and changed directions, looking for some protection. More dog sounds. Excited whining and barking. More than one.

"Condor!" called Sergeant LaMarka. "Keep moving. We'll set up a line of fire and keep them from you as long as we can. Just make it out of here with that case."

Mike could hear LaMarka shouting orders, and his men started returning the fire from behind them. Mike and

Nichole slogged their way into the thick woods, being torn by branches and constantly running into trees. The sounds of battle faded as they went forward, and finally they stopped for breath.

"Do you know this area and where we are?" he asked between breaths.

"Yes, there is a farm about two kilometers in that direction," she answered pointing.

"Will they take us in?" he asked.

"For sure. It is where I live."

"Will you still be Nichole when we get there?"

"Now I am Marie. You will be my retarded brother named Jules. We work the farm, you understand?"

"I think you should go home without me, Marie. If they find me there, they will kill you and everybody else."

"No, Mike. This is to free France from Germans. We are to continue together, or we die together. I live there alone. The others were killed or fled months ago. Come."

"I can't go without my men."

"You should want to protect that briefcase first. If the Germans produce a super bomb, all is lost. Your men know what to do. If they survive, your army will eventually find them or else they are dead anyhow."

Mike knew that she was right. The mission was first, and the briefcase was the mission. It had to be hidden away from the enemy until he could get back to the American lines. They could never hide that many men on a farm if the Germans came. One, perhaps, if he was lucky and had someone like Marie to cover for him. Maybe. He followed her, and it was apparent that she knew the woods and the area very well. In the near distance, he could hear the tank's main gun firing. His men were scattered or lost, but the tank would be in the open when dawn came in two hours. The Germans inside were as good as dead. Along the western horizon was the never ending flash of heavy weapons or bombs.

Marie and Mike entered the farmhouse. She found some clothing for him, and they both changed outfits. Mike was given a tattered straw hat and torn and faded coveralls, complete with hobnail boots. Marie's clothing was so baggy that it hid her young female physique and face. Marie instructed him to start pitching hay as soon as the dawn came up. They decided to hide the briefcase in the well using the same technique as before and quickly rigged it up. In the predawn light, the case was so deep in the dark hole that it could not be seen, but just to make sure, they draped a black cloth over it so no light could be reflected back up. Mike, as instructed, left for the fields and started working in plain view. Just as dawn came, so did the low flying fighters hunting for prey. He stood and waved to one which was passing low, just above his head, and saw the plane dip its wings as it pulled up and away. There were several terrific explosions just over the rise, and he assumed that the tank had been spotted. He hoped that it was. After a small period of quiet and sweaty work, he looked up to see two heavy German transport trucks headed his way, kicking up a cloud of dust behind them. Now it comes, he thought. He was willing to face death but standing here waiting on it was hard. As they got closer, he saw the back was bristling with troops, and he could see rifle barrels over the roof of the cab. Nowhere to run and hide this time. He hoped that Marie could escape when the action started. He leaned on his pitchfork and watched them get closer. Something caught his eye, and he glanced away from the Germans to see two dots getting larger on the horizon. Fighters. The blinking started before he could hear the plane motors. The ground around the German trucks erupted in dust and small explosions, and troops started diving off as fast as they could. The second plane seemed to hold back a little and then came in low and then seemed to head nearly straight into the blue sky. The trucks and soldiers were caught in an immense inferno of flames which encompassed them all. The fire stood straight into the air like a yellow tornado, and after it consumed everything combustible, there was only the blackened frame of each truck surrounded by black matchsticks. It was over. He and Marie were safe from the Germans at least today. He threw down the pitch fork and headed toward the house, and as he got closer, he saw her standing by the door ready to let him in.

Rome Italy, November 1944
Intelligence Assault Forces Headquarters

Mike walked up to the desk in the lobby and saluted crisply to the Lieutenant on duty. "Sergeant Michael Condor reporting for duty, sir. " He was dressed in a freshly pressed dress uniform, and his campaign medals and his new Silver Star decorated his chest. The lieutenant lazily returned his salute. He was in battle fatigues and the only decoration was the two bars on the lapels.

"At ease, Sergeant. Transfer papers?" He waited for Mike to hand him the packet. The Lieutenant flipped through the stack and sat down at his desk. A stream of officers and enlisted men from the British and American armies streamed around them, all in conversation.

Finally, he checked a clipboard and then looked up at Mike. "Welcome, Sergeant Condor. We have you on the list. Do you have knowledge about T Force, and what we are about?"

"Not much, sir. Just rumor."

"Well, we'll take care of that shortly. There is an indoctrination course for you, and the next one begins in two days. Checked into barracks yet?"

"Yes, sir, this morning."

"Your mail has been forwarded to us, I see," he said, looking at another list. Check with Sergeant Samson, and he should have something for you. It's the first desk at the end of G corridor to your left."

"Yes, sir."

The Lieutenant opened a locked drawer and took out a packet of square envelopes and opened one. "Here are your passes and your ID card which must be on your person at all times. Dress for us is casual with no visible rank or group insignia. Helps to be invisible at times. We can use an experienced combat man like you here, because we often need to use force to do our job. You will be issued your gear and assignment after the two-week orientation course. You are to report back to this desk at nine sharp in forty-eight hours. Until that time, you have a pass. Enjoy Rome, there is a lot to see here."

Mike saluted and turned to find G corridor. The building which had been requisitioned had been built for the Mussolini government and for the most part was modern, new and very large. He finally found the correct corridor and found Sergeant Samson at his desk.

"Hi, Sergeant, I'm reporting for duty today, and I'm told that you have my mail."

"We just might. You see some action before you came here?"

"Two years of it. After I got the Silver Star, they seemed to want me to get into the intelligence side of this war for a change. So here I am."

"Got a little free time before you dig in?"

"Forty-eight. That's all."

"Listen, when you are in Rome you'll see that the Italians like us being here. You'll get a lot of respect and cooperation. This city didn't get torn up like most of the others, and the Romans, in particular, are grateful. You'll have to fight off the beggar children and the prostitutes, but there is no particular danger. A few dollars American goes a long way here. Lots of nice girls, also, who would like you to take them home to meet the folks. Can I see your ID, and I'll try to get your mail and let you get out of here." In a few moments, he returned with a white sealed envelope with Mike's name on the front.

"Sign here, Sergeant, and catch up with home!"

On the way back down to the lobby, Mike tore into the envelope and found six letters. Two were from his mother, and the rest were from Mary. All of them were at least two years old. He sighed and put them in his shirt pocket and tossed the envelope. He was anxious to read mail even this old. He had gotten two letters from Mary before he left the States, and in them, she told how she and their mother made their way to the West Coast safely. The letters were with him until they got repeatedly wet and fell apart. He wrote constantly to Mary hoping that at least a few got to her. Now that he was stationary and out of the front line combat, the rest of the mail should get to him. Two years worth must be a big stack. Something to look forward to.

At the curb was a green military bus with the door open, the driver inside was a PFC who was smoking and waiting for something.

"Where is this bus headed, Private?"

The man jumped up, startled, and said, "Anywhere you want to go, Sergeant. That's what I'm here for."

"You mean a whole bus just for me?"

"Yes, Sergeant, since you are the only one here, and you are ready to go. Where can I take you?"

"I just want to see the sights, Private. Do you know your way around?"

"Better than some. Are you interested in ancient Rome, modern Rome or religious Rome?"

"Ancient Rome, I think."

"Trust me, Sarge, I'll start you off right. Come in and make yourself ready to get educated." Mike came in and as the bus rolled away, he pulled out the letters from home. He decided to save Mary's for last and started with the oldest from his Mother.

Dear Son,

We don't know if you get our letters, but we keep writing. Mary the most. She writes every day, and now that we have been here two months, that makes sixty or so that are coming your way. Please write her back if you get the chance, because every time the postman comes and there is no mail from you, she dies a little. Mary is back in school and finishing her last year. I wish you could be here also and protect her like you always did so well. We used to scold you and worry about what you did to all those boys, but now I miss everything about you. I am sorry that we ever said anything to you about it, not that you paid any attention to me or your father.

The money you left for us makes life easy, and don't worry, there should be a lot left for you when you get back home. Home is here in our little town in Washington now, and we have forgotten the past very quickly. The only thing we miss is our Mike.

Love, Mother

P.S. Got a letter from that nice Detective Smith and a receipt from a storage company who has all our things. He (Smith) said not to go try to get anything until you get out of the war, but he would try to find anything personal for us if we told him what we wanted. I think the only thing I want is our scrapbook full of the old photos, and I'm going to see if he will send it.

Take good care of yourself and come home safe. We love you.

Mike folded the letter and put it in another pocket and opened the second one.

Dear Son,

I know that what you want most is to hear about your sister instead of what I am doing, which isn't much. Mary becomes more beautiful each day, and she is the hit of the school she is attending. She is in plays and in the choir and still takes private dancing lessons. She is making good grades and seems happy until something reminds her that you aren't there. I think that it bothers her most at night when she is doing her homework. She seems to keep busy so that she doesn't have time to be sad.

I know that the last letter she got from you advised her that she should date some boys and try to forget you for now. She won't date any boy, and she gets offers all the time. To hear our neighbour tell it, the boys are pining away, but it makes no difference to her. The minute that she gets home, she sits down at the table and writes you even though she knows that you might never read her letter.

I got the scrapbook yesterday from Detective Smith, the dear man, and Mary got hold of it, and I haven't seen it since. If she wants, I will take out all your photos and just give them to her as long as I get to keep the snowman wedding one.

Hope that you are safe and well and can remain that way. We both love you and think of you all the time.

Mother

As the bus jogged along, he tuned out the chatter from his driver turned tour guide, and he finally opened the first of Mary's letters. His hand was shaking a little as he started to read.

Dear Mike,

First and always, I love you and I miss you. I always did love you, but before you were always right there to touch and talk to, and I never imagined that we would ever be apart. My dreams at night are about you, and when I wake, it seems almost real to me. I swear that I can see you clearly then and even touch you and feel your warmth. Oh, could it really be so.

School here is different. There aren't so many rough people and, as far as I know, the town is free of hoodlums. The folks here are hardworking, and for the most part, very honest. They won't believe my stories about the mob back at home. It's just as well that they are innocent. There is a new Army Air Base near here, and when we see the men all dressed up in their uniforms, I think of you. I stay away from them, though, because they pester me a lot. I feel sorry for them that they are far from home and are headed to war, but not that much.

We are doing what you wanted, and I am applying to dancing school for next year. If that happens, it will mean that I have to move away, clear across the country. Mother is gradually losing weight and doesn't look good. She sits alone a lot of the time, lost in her memories. It would mean a lot to her if you get leave to come home for a while. It would mean a lot to me, also.

Love, Love, Love,

Mary

Mike carefully and tenderly folded that one and put it away in a different pocket. He wiped his face with the back of his hand and sat up and looked around. Rome was a city of history, and you could see it on every street. Every corner was from some different place back in time, and it looked so beautiful and so unlike what he had seen previously after cities were liberated. The driver's voice came back into his consciousness.

"We are near the Tiber, and just across this next bridge are some famous monuments. There is the tomb of Augustus and right next to it is the famous *Ara Pacis*. That one was favored by Mussolini. You really should see it. Ready to stop, Sarge?"

"Yes, you can stop. Are you planning to wait for me?"

"I'll be here unless some brass gets in and orders me to leave. That could happen."

Mike got out and stretched. The waterfront was visible, and the first museum was newer looking. He thought that he could find an empty corner in that one and read the rest of Mary's mail before going on. Above the door he read *Ara Pacis* and went up the stairs to a well-lighted foyer in a mostly glass building. Inside was a squarish block of grey marble with carvings on the outside face. There were very few people around, and he could almost feel the history. A bench was there waiting for him, and he sat down and opened the second letter from Mary.

Dear Mike,

Have I told you today that I love you? I still do, and I think more than ever. There is something I am burning to tell you that will have to wait for a while yet. I'm sorry but it's pent-up in me, and I always could talk to you about anything, but I have to wait.

Mother is not as well as she was and mostly stays home with Aunt Gladys. They talk about the old times so much that I have to get away. I worry about her, but there is nothing I can do to turn back the hands of time. If I could, I would turn them back so that you and I were together again. I finally got a letter from you, and I know that you write me often, but that's what I thought was happening. Very few of our letters are getting through. If this is happening while you are still in America, I don't know if we will get any when you leave. I am afraid for you, and when I see the news, I know that you will be away for a long time, and I can't help but cry.

Mother got our scrapbook, and I took all the photos that had you in them and stuck them up all over the walls of my bedroom so that I could remember you every time I opened the door or woke up. It works, but it also breaks my heart.

Love you, love you, love you,

Mary

Mike wiped another tear and sat up looking at the huge carvings but not seeing them.

"Interested in history, Sergeant?" an accented voice asked. Mike looked up to see a British Major smiling at him. He stood quickly and came to a salute.

"No, no, my good man. Not here. Right now we should be on a first name basis and forget rank. Is that all right with you?" he said. Mike could see the kindly face, but he also saw the jacket heavy with medals. "I see that you were given the Silver Star. Impressive. My name is Johnson, Peter Johnson. And you are?"

"Mike Condor, sir. Glad to meet you."

"Now Mike, if we are to be proper friends, there will be no sir, just call me Pete and I'll call you Mike. Satisfactory?"

"Sure, Pete, but it feels awkward."

"Son, this war can't last more than a few more months. The Jerrys are beaten, and when they realize that, I'll still be Pete and you will still be Mike. We might as well start now and get used to it, don't you think?"

"I, for one, can't wait for the war to end so I can get back home," Mike said while he shook Pete's hand.

"Got a girl waiting for you?"

"Something like that. My sister."

Pete drew himself up and pointed to the monument. "I was a history professor at Oxford before the war, and I always wanted to see this thing firsthand. I can tell you all about it, but this is my first time here too." They started to stroll toward the structure which seemed to get larger the closer they got. As they approached, Mike could see the incredible detail in the carvings. The figures were life-size or perhaps larger.

"Mussolini and the Fascists brought this over from the excavation site north of here in thirty-six. They wanted it to symbolize how the new Italy was like the old. The monument was dedicated originally in 6 B.C. and stood by the riverbank for perhaps two hundred years, but was eventually buried by river silt. It was rediscovered in the early Middle Ages, and now is here for us to enjoy for the first time in two thousand years. It was a monument dedicated to Caesar Augustus for the peace that he brought to Rome. Today, Rome is at peace again, and the meaning of peace is as clear as it ever was before."

They moved over to the left side and stood before an elaborate work carved out of a solid block of stone. Mike saw that the central figure was of an elegant woman holding twins. The sight took his breath away.

"Pete, do you know who that woman was or what that means?"

"I can tell you that there are varied opinions, but the majority of Roman historians feel that the woman is symbolic of Tellus, or Mother Earth, and the twins are the Roman people. Every item, however small, in the sculpture has meaning. It was always my favorite of all Roman art, and I give thanks that I am standing here in the flesh to view it."

"You remember that I spoke of my sister? Her name is Mary, and we were born as twins. I was with her every day of my life until I left for the Army. You can't imagine what seeing this piece of stone does to me."

Pete looked at Mike for a long time before speaking. "There is more to this story, isn't there?"

"Yes, I love Mary, and she loves me. She is all I think about, and she was the only thing that kept me going when I thought I was about to die in battle."

"You and Mary are from the same mother, Mike?"

"We were raised that way, but eventually we thought that something was amiss. We have no family resemblance at all. Brothers and sisters are not supposed to love each other in that way, but we do. Neither one of us believes that we are blood-related, but I left before it could be proven."

"Have you checked your blood type? Sometimes that tells something."

"She wrote to me before I left asking me for my type. It's on our dog tags. I wrote her right back but never heard from her after that. It was two years ago. I figured that was why she asked. It won't mean anything, though. I talked about it with a corpsman, and he said that my O positive was common and that most people are that type."

"Well, I, for one, hope for the best for you. Want to continue on inside with me?"

"If it's all right with you, I want to read Mary's other two letters that I just got and then I want to just sit here and study that carving. Thanks for your explanation of it to me."

"The very best of luck to you, Mike. I hope that things work out for you, and if you try to stay alive for the next several months, I'm sure that it will."

"You too, Pete."

The Major ambled on inside the monument leaving Mike alone in front of the stone wall. He continued to look at the central figure and the two infants on her knee for a long time.

Dearest Mike,

We have settled in and are trying to make this new town our home. We are still living with Aunt Gladys and Uncle Tom, and they are very nice to us. It's a good thing that we are here because Mother often seems tired and even misses supper. We have seen a doctor, but he isn't open with me about what he thinks.

I am well and school is going well. Thank you again for the money because it makes all the difference for us now. I drive that cute little Ford around and get whistles all the time. I wish you were here to see it (or maybe not!). I haven't stalled it in the intersection since that first day, and you would be proud of me.

There is a trick that I have developed to get to sleep. I take a hot water bottle, or sometimes two, and put it in a pillow and go to sleep holding it like I used to hold you. When I get sleepy enough, it is almost like having you there like I always did. I wake up and feel the pillow and even talk to it at times. Silly right?

I am waiting for your letter with your blood type. Even if it doesn't help clear this thing up, I am going to tell you what I tried to do the last time I saw your face. I don't believe any longer that we are related. I feel it to the bottom of my soul, and nothing can convince me that it can't be so. The feel of your lips against mine is still with me, and once was not enough. Please come home to me. I love you.

Mary

Mike put the letter down beside him and tore open the last one. He was afraid to see this one, especially this one. Before reading it, he looked again at the carving of the mother of earth and her twins on her knee. He remembered all the times that Mary and he shared together. The baths, the wedding, the warm clothes straight from the iron. He remembered waking up and looking at her sleeping face just inches from his own. He remembered her hair shimmering in the light, and the way her ponytail swayed back and forth just for him, and the eyes that gleamed at him from across a crowded room meaning a million different things, and the smile from her that lit up the world when they passed in the hall.

Dear, Dear Mike!

The news! WE ARE NOT RELATED!!!!!!!!!! Your blood type is O positive and mine is AB. Father was A and Mother is AB. THERE IS NO WAY WE ARE RELATED! I am the happiest girl in the world, and I want to have you in my arms without any guilt at all. You are mine forever, and I am yours forever, and I can't wait to kiss you a thousand times on the lips or anywhere I can get at. This makes my life complete, except for one minor thing. You are somewhere other than here. Small problem!

I have been planning secretly and now openly, and I might as well tell you that the snowman is ready to do it again! He sent you a message that you are to hurry home to my arms, because you are never going to leave them again! I have been jumping up and down and running around so much since I got your letter that my legs are sore! I can't wait to go to bed and hug my Mike pillow. I'll get up in the morning and do the same dance as today. I LOVE YOU! Can I make that any clearer? Well, here goes. I LOVE YOU AND I WILL LOVE YOU FOREVER AND EVEN AFTER I DIE!

Love, and I do mean love,

Your Mary

Mike couldn't stop the flow of tears this time. His hand with the letter hung straight down, and he looked up at the ancient carving and wept. He felt a hand on his shoulder.

"Mike, was there bad news in the letter?" Pete asked with sympathy in his voice. Mike handed him the letter to read but didn't otherwise move.

"I dare say! Well, this is good news indeed and just what you wanted to hear. Congratulations, Mike! Well, this changes everything, doesn't it? Makes me want to cry with you, old man. Good show!"

Chapter 11

ΠΕΑΡ ΤΗΕ ΕΠD

Lilith dropped the heavy package on Jill's desk. She looked angry, and Jill sat back in her reclining chair, surprised.

"Problem?" she asked.

"I can't take ownership of this work, because it's all yours. Your idea, your time. And I have grown to like the idea of telling my grandparents' story, and more so than ever, thanks to some of the things that they told you that none of us have heard previously. I wonder what you are thinking writing it like this," Lilith said.

"I have no idea what you are talking about. You liked it up until Mike finished his war story. What do you see as an issue?"

"Well, Jill, it strikes me that Mary and Mike's stories are in the first person and so, in a way, is Charlotte's. It makes sense, because that's the way they told it to you. You just wrote it down. The war story is in the third person and reads like a novel. It's good, but why does this one have be different. It just sticks out."

"I thought that we had a friendship going, Lilith. If we did, you would think before you spoke. You weren't in there when they told me their stories, were you? I'll answer that for you. You were at work knocking down big bucks while I sat there day after day trying to pry the story out of these ninety year olds. If you think I just wrote down what they said verbatim you can look at my notes. I assembled them, Lilith. I coaxed the stories out of near chaos. At that age, they don't do linear thinking. They jump around as they remember. I made the story coherent, because it is a literary work, not a dictation. About Mike's tale of the war, he really wouldn't talk about the war. He talked around the war. He did give consent for me to obtain his service record and much of the story about the recovery of German nuclear secrets is there. He got a Silver Star for it, and the Army was very careful about details. I found and interviewed five of the eleven other men from that mission who are still alive. Two were killed by the Germans after Mike and Marie escaped, but the rest made it back to the American lines and lived to tell about it. It was a very celebrated mission, and it might have changed the outcome of the war. Yes, just that one mission. Did you know, by the way, that Marie Villerous wrote a book after the war giving details of her exploits in the Resistance? Well, she did, and an entire chapter is devoted to Mike. She doesn't call him Mike, but it's him. Go read it. I pieced the story together by hook and by crook, and there was no other way to tell it. Mike didn't tell it in a first person way. The letters from Mary, though, are the actual letters that Mike saved and carried around with him until the war ended."

"You are right, I didn't understand at all. I had no idea what or how you have done this. My humble apologies."

"I accept that, and we can go on from here as before."

"Well, now that we are back on a sound footing, I have a couple of questions that are nagging at me," Lilith said.

"Shoot."

"What happened between Mike and Marie after they were alone?"

"You think Mike would tell anything like that to me?"

"What did Marie say happened in her book?"

"You heard that she said that girls never tell? She didn't tell."

"What do you think happened?"

"I know your grandfather by now. He would never do anything that Mary couldn't know about. No man was ever as loyal. The record shows that they were there for about a week, and then the Resistance came and escorted Marie to a safer location since the American Army was rapidly moving that way. Mike stayed and waited it out. More risky than you might think," Jill added.

"Weren't there a lot of letters from Mary after Mike was stationed in Rome?"

"Yes, hundreds of them. Boxes of them. Mike couldn't save all of them, but we know the story from there. Mike became a highly valued member of the early G2 division and then moved over to OSS and then CIA. When he was director of the CIA, he was forced to hide any of his past that might harm him, and he became secretive by necessity. Mary became a raving beauty and was sought after by seemingly everyone in New York until Mike returned. You can imagine what would happen to any male that gave her undue attention after that. She could have been world-famous, rich and headed to Hollywood, but she wanted Mike in her life and nothing else. He couldn't be married to a star if he was also married to the intelligence community. Now I have a question for you."

"I know. It's about your old boyfriend who acts like he's my secret agent. He isn't worth the ink used to print the money that I have paid him. There is next to nothing that he has discovered that we can use."

"Is there any hope of finding Mary's sister?"

"Nope. It's over. Too bad because it would close your book and help close out the details of their lives," Lilith said.

"Well, I have a personal suggestion for you, Lilith."

"Such as?"

I have spent the better part of two months over at the nursing home, and I have watched both of them go downhill, especially Mary. It could happen at any time. Better start spending more time with them, or you may regret it later."

Chapter 12

THE FIND

Jill heard a noise and looked up from her computer. She saw the end of a magazine wiggling over the top of the cubicle divider. She reached out and grabbed it, and as she pulled it down, Tommy's face appeared.

"Hi, Gorgeous! Thought you might like to look at this old Look magazine from the forties. I ran across it looking for some background for a story the old man put me on. Lots of pictures about the Broadway people of that era. You might find something in there about the old folks you spend so much time on. Are you done with that yet?"

"Thanks for the mag, Tommy. No, I'm not done but almost. A few loose ends yet."

"The story going to appear in the paper someday?" he asked.

"I doubt it. Right now, I'm hoping to get a book out of it. Such a great and touching story."

"When are you going to let me read it?"

"I had no idea that you wanted to. Are you for real about it?"

"Anything that touches your hand touches me."

"Oh, brother. Get a new line, and I might consider it. Got to get back to work. Thanks for the magazine." She threw it on the chair by her coat. The cover was facing her, and she saw that several faces were showing and looking out, captured in black and white. In the back of her mind, there was a nagging something about.... The telephone buzzed at her, and she picked it up.

"Hi, this is Lilith. I thought I would update you on my grandparents if you have a moment."

"Sure do. Anything for those two. I feel like they are my own grandparents sometimes."

"Well, Mary has more problems with her kidneys in the last several days and is retaining a lot of water. She can still talk and knows where she is, but I think that she can only go downhill from here. If you get some free time, you might want to stop over and tell her goodbye."

"I'll do that. Thanks for letting me know. I wanted to talk to you anyway about the book. I've put most of it together, and my boss is going over it as a favor to me. I know he won't publish it, but if he likes it, he might put me in touch with someone who will."

"He should like it. I do. Good luck with that."

"Thanks. We'll have to get together soon. Lunch?"

"Sure, just call me," Lilith said.

After she hung up, she paused. Something was bothering her, and she didn't know what it was. Something she forgot? She adjusted her chair and her keyboard and got ready to type. No, there was something she was supposed to do. She looked around the cubicle. Was she supposed to be somewhere? She checked her calendar. Nope. She stood up and thought as she looked around. The old magazine. That was what was bothering her. She picked it up and looked at the cover again. There in the lower right corner was the face of Mary when she was young and beautiful. They had the wrong caption!

Funny for a magazine of that reputation to make a mistake on the cover. She opened it and sat back down as she flipped the pages.

"Holy Shit!" she said out loud. Tommy's face appeared above the partition.

"Hurt yourself?" he asked.

"Wow, come in here for a minute!" she said.

When he came around, she was standing again. "Look at this face! It's Mary Condor but it's not!"

"Looks like they made a mistake. It happens," he said.

"No, it's her but it's not. They talk about a Laura Jackson who was apparently a singer. A famous one looking at the spread they gave her. Laura Jackson? Ever hear about her?"

"What kind of singing did she do? I never heard that name as far as I know."

"Opera. Here is a photo of her on stage performing in Carmen. Wow, she was a big deal. My God, she looks exactly like Mary Condor," Jill said excitedly.

"They say that we all have lookalikes out there somewhere. It's interesting. Why are you so excited?"

"We have been looking under rocks for Mary Condor's twin. I think that we just found her! That means that they both were working in the limelight in New York at the same time but in different circles. I'm amazed that no one noticed it at the time. Both women were spectacular. Surely, they would have had someone notice."

"I'm no expert on social circles in the New York of the forties, but I'm betting that the opera-goers rarely went to Broadway and vice versa."

Jill sat down at her keyboard and after a few clicks did a search for Laura Jackson. There were thousands of hits. A few more moments and she sat up. "She's still alive!" After a few more clicks, she said, "Laura Jackson has a website!" She started browsing the pages and came up with a number at the bottom of the page. "She has no contact information, but here is one for an agency. The Rolland-Morris-Fienly Agency," she read.

"Tommy, thanks a million for this. I owe you, but go away now so that I can make some calls."

"I think I know how you can repay me, Gorgeous."

"Not now, Tommy. Go away."

Chapter 13

THE LAST KISS

Jill made the turn around the reception desk at The Memorial Retirement Center for the...well, she had made this turn a lot of times, she thought. She gave a wave to the clerk and made her way down the long corridor toward Mike's and Mary's rooms. This time, she was impatient to see them, because she had news she was sure they would want to hear. Laura Jackson had called her yesterday, and they had a long and informative talk, and she had agreed to come for a visit as soon as she could arrange it.

"Hi, Vivian," Jill said to the head nurse as she started past the nursing station.

"Hold up, Jill. I need to talk to you," Vivian called. Jill had a bad foreboding about what she was going to hear. She knew that Mary was slipping a little, and the last time she was in, there was an IV hanging by the bed. Jill turned around and came up to the desk.

"You need to keep this visit a bit shorter than you usually do. Mary is having some problems, and they both are upset this morning."

"Thank you for letting me know. I am finished with the interviews, I just want to say hello and give them some news."

"Mr. Condor had me call his grandchild and tell her to come over this morning. I think that he senses that the end is near for his dear wife. It's always hard when this moment comes, but Mrs. Condor is all he ever talks or thinks about. He's going to need a lot of emotional support, that's all."

"I see. Do you know when Lilith is coming?"

"Anytime, I suppose. Go on in there, and when she comes, I'll send her in also."

Jill frowned. It was going to be such a happy day and now... She found Mary's room and she was alone but awake.

"Mary! Hi, it's Jill. Do you feel like talking this morning?"

"Of course I see that it's you Jill. I'm not gone yet, you see. Come in and talk. I need the company."

"Well, I am excited to tell you something that Lilith and I have been working on for a long time, and it finally happened. We found your sister, and she plans to come for a visit! Isn't that exciting news?"

"Yes, dear, it's something I have wanted to know for a very long time, but I have also some reservations about it."

"I don't understand," Jill said.

"We have lived our lives and had to come to terms with the past. News like this brings together the facts but also introduces regret. Mostly, I am concerned about Mike and how he would take it. It would give him guilt about stealing my sister's place and distress that he had so little value to his mother that he could just be left with a stranger. You can tell me what you want, dear, but don't tell Mike yet, please."

"I understand, Mary. I found your sister's photo in an old magazine. Turns out that she was a well-known opera singer, and her name is Laura Jackson. She is an identical twin to you and looks exactly like you in her photographs. I talked with her yesterday, and she was excited to know about you and Mike. She plans to visit you as soon as she is able. She seems like such a nice person, exactly like you, in fact!"

"That's amazing! That means that we were working in New York at the same time! Did she say anything about her history? What happened to her when she was taken?"

"Well, I didn't ask that kind of detail, but she said that she was adopted and that her mother had given her up. I believe she meant that the woman who took her gave her up for adoption, certainly not your mother."

"Isn't that interesting? Yes, it will be good to see her. You know, I hate to say this, but Mike and I got what we wanted in life, and it appears she did also. I'm glad those two were switched, but I also recall that it created a gulf between my parents which caused them a lot of suffering. It reminds me of the story about the dark side of a shiny coin."

There was a knock on the door and when it opened they could see Lilith smiling broadly. "Did you tell her the news?" she asked Jill.

"Just now. I think Mary is taken back a little. She asked me not to tell Mike, by the way."

"Oh. Then I won't, Grandmother. Not until you tell me, that is."

Mary patted Lilith's hand which was on the raised bed rail. "Dear Lilith. What brings you in here on a working day?"

Lilith and Jill exchanged glances. "I just felt like coming by, dear."

"Well, it's always good to see you, child. I've not been myself lately, and I forget what day it is. Say, you too know each other don't you?"

"Yes, Grandmother, we've been working on your book, don't you remember?"

"Oh yes! How is the book coming along, girls?

"It's nearly done," Jill said. "If you are up to reading it sometime, I'd be honored."

"No, dear. That's too much for me. It would hurt too much to relive the past to which we can't ever go back. What I wouldn't give for a walk home from school bumping shoulders with Mike again." She started to tear and looked far away.

"Let's go say hello to Mike and leave her to recover for a moment, Lilith," Jill suggested and tugged her arm.

Mike was typing on his little laptop when they peeked into the room. He turned around smiling and waved them in.

"Girls! Makes me young just to look at you! Come in, come in."

"Hi, Grandfather. Are you well this fine morning?" Lilith asked.

"There is no answer suitable, my dear beautiful granddaughter. When did you say the wedding was?"

"Now, don't start that stuff, you old dog. You know that men are afraid of me. You'll just have to wait a bit longer for a wedding."

Looking serious, Mike asked "See Mary yet?"

"Yes, we just came from there and had a nice chat. She is as charming as always. Seems that you don't have to worry about her."

"I wish your view was correct, but it isn't. She is fading from us, and I am losing her minute by minute. I feel so helpless that there isn't anything I can do about it. There isn't anything I ever did or had that was as important to me as Mary. I'm glad that we told Jill our story so that someday people can read and understand the way we felt about each other."

"She's still here, Grandfather. Don't be so pessimistic."

"I know that I should be grateful that I could be with her for all those years, but it wasn't nearly enough time. If she leaves this earth first, I won't be able to stand my loneliness and my loss. If I go first, who will be there to comfort Mary? I fear this moment, children, more than I have ever feared anything."

"Your nurse, Vivian, said that you spent all night sitting beside Mary. You know that you're too old for that don't you?"

"Then you don't understand me at all, Lilith." He turned away for a moment and dabbed at his eyes. "I'm sorry to let you see me like this, but you see that I'm too selfish to part with her. She has constant pain, but she'll never tell you or me. Mary puts on a brave face but even she can stand but so much. I'm afraid that she is trying to stay alive just for me, just as I would do for her."

"Anything that either of us can do, Mike?" Jill asked.

"It's about lunchtime, isn't it? Why don't you both go down and get some coffee and lunch, and let me see if I can get some food into her. Come back after you eat and then I'll talk to you while she is sleeping."

Jill pulled the chair back with her foot as she placed the tray of food on the table. "Over here, Lilith!" she said rather loudly, and a few older patrons turned to stare. Lilith came with her tray and did the same.

"This place has a pretty fair menu, doesn't it?" Jill asked.

"For the kind of money they charge, they'd better," Lilith observed.

"I hope Mike can get some rest today. He has never looked so tired," Jill said.

"He won't leave her for a moment. I feel so sorry for both of them. I hope my aunt doesn't take too long to come, or she won't be able to meet either one of them."

"If Mary doesn't want Mike told, how are you going to handle it when she comes?" Jill asked.

"Gets me. We have to handle that at the time."

"We?"

"Yes, girl, we. You are in this up to and past your ears."

"I won't let you down. I was just kidding to brighten our mood. The morning was going to be so good telling them about Laura, and now I feel a bit crushed," Jill said.

"I have to go back up there and say goodbye for today, because I have a full afternoon. What are you going to do?" Lilith asked.

"Same. My editor has a long list of assignments that I have backlogged. I'll go up with you, and we can leave together."

When they got to Mary's room, they could hear Mike talking. He was still with her.

"Mary, I want you to let yourself go. I promise that I'll be along shortly, and we can be together forever. You just relax and be at peace now. You know that I love you as much as I did the first time I ever looked at your face. I have your hand in mine, and I won't let go."

Lilith whispered, "We better let them have this moment alone, don't you think?" and she gently pushed Jill back out of the door.

Jill and Lilith could see him leaning over the bed with his face nearly touching Mary's. From the door, Jill could see Mary's eyes fluttering, and she was talking but it was too low to hear.

"Yes, my dear. I love you also. Remember when we used to bathe together so long ago? And do you remember how we always slept with our faces together? It drove our parents mad! We'll do that again, somehow. Something so precious should never be lost. My lovely Mary, how wonderful is your touch. I've only lived to make you happy, and I hope that you feel that I did."

There was a moment of silence, and they could see Mike kiss her on the lips with a long and lingering tender kiss. He rose slightly and stroked her cheek with his hand, and Mary's eyes closed forever. Mike just stood there with her hand in his looking at the person he loved so much. From the side, they both could see the tears streaming down his face. Lilith rushed in and hugged her grandfather from behind, but Jill remained in the door as the outsider that she was.

Chapter 14

FINAL CURTAIN

Jill and Lilith sat down together on the big leather couch in the lobby of The Memorial Retirement Center and looked at each other.

"What time did you say that she was coming?" Lilith asked again.

"Don't be so nervous, Lilith. She'll be along shortly. After all she is ninety also, and it was a long trip from Beverly Hills," Jill said.

"Too bad Mary couldn't have lasted until now. I cried so much last night that my pillow was still wet this morning," Lilith remarked.

"I'm glad that both us were there for her at the end. I think I cried more for poor Mike than Mary. At least her struggle is over. When you spoke to your now new Aunt Laura about losing Mary, what did she say?"

"She was upset, of course. Like Mary and Mike, she found out after she was an adult that she was not related to people around her. It was more complicated in her case because of the adoption. Finding out that the mother who put you out for adoption wasn't even your real mother had to be a shocker. She said she is still coming to pay her respects to Mike and meet him. She said that she owes him that much," Lilith said.

"One of the nurses said that Mike has refused any food since Mary died three days ago. I think he wants to die to be with her. We'll have to hope he is in good enough shape to even know that Laura is here. He was inconsolable when Mary died, and I thought for a moment that he was going to drop over right there."

"Yes, I thought so too. He seemed to lose his mind for a moment. I've never seen him like that before. He has nothing left to live for now. Oh, look outside. I think that must be her."

It was, and Jill and Lilith got up together and held the door for Laura who was being assisted by a very handsome young man. She moved forward at a slow but steady speed and kept her arm lightly on her companion's arm, keeping her head erect.

"Hello, Aunt Laura!" I am Lilith, your grandniece, and this is the writer, Jill, that you spoke to when she found your photo in Look magazine."

Laura smiled a pleasant smile at each of them in turn, and Jill had to hold her breath because of how much she looked like Mary. It was like Mary had never left. This was Mary.

"By the way, I want to introduce my grandson, James Zether Williams, to both of you," Laura said and motioned toward the handsome man beside her.

James nodded politely but remained silent.

"How I have been looking forward to this day, girls. I wish Mary could have been here today. I never knew that she existed until that day Jill called me. Imagine, I had a twin for ninety years and never knew. I took Mike's place, and he took mine. From what I hear, we both had a good life, but I wonder what it would have been like if we were never switched. We'll never know that, will we?"

"Mike has not been told that you are coming, and he has been very depressed after Mary passed away, and we frankly don't know what to expect when you meet," Lilith said.

"Don't worry, dear. If I look like my sister, we will instantly feel comfortable with each other. After all, Mike would have been someone I would have loved also. It could have been either twin taken, and the outcome would have been the same."

There was a moment of awkward silence then Jill spoke, "Ms. Jackson, I have nearly completed the book we spoke of, and I would be pleased to have you read it before it is published. I am sure that it will give you a lot of insight into the lives of these two interesting people that, unfortunately, you never knew."

"Yes, Jill, but pleasure mixed with pain. We'll see, but thank you for the offer."

"If you are ready Aunt Laura, it's this way," Lilith said, and they led the way down the long corridor toward Mike's room. The four stopped briefly at the nurses station, and Vivian came out to greet them.

"You must be Laura! I am Vivian, one of Mike's nurses. I cared for your sister for quite a while, and I have to tell you that a sweeter person could never be found. It is a privilege to meet you, but I'm also sorry that you were found so late. Mike is taking her loss poorly, as we expected he would, and has denied himself any nourishment since his Mary passed away. I think it would have been too late after today."

"May I see him now?" Laura asked.

They walked the short distance to Mike's room, and Vivian opened the door. Mike was lying on his back with his arm partially covering his face. His little computer was closed, and the room was perfectly neat and orderly.

Lilith came up around to the head of the bed as Laura stood at the foot patiently watching. "Grandfather, I have someone who wants to talk with you. Can you hear me?"

He put his arm down, and his head turned toward Lilith. His eyes opened slightly, but he didn't respond.

"I know how weak you must be, Grandfather, but there is someone here I know that you'll want to see. She's standing right at the foot of the bed. All you have to do is look down there."

Mike slowly looked down at Laura and at first made no indication that he saw her. Then as they watched, he opened his eyes wider, and they could tell that he recognized her.

"Mary? You are here?" he said weakly. "Mary, I haven't lost you?"

Lilith started to say, "Grandfather..." but was interrupted by Laura who held up her hand.

"Yes, Mike, I'm here." She moved slowly around the bed and never took her eyes from his. Lilith stepped back and away to let her come close. Laura reached out and took Mike's hand in hers. "I had to be here for you, Mike. You were always there for me."

"Oh, Mary, to see you again. I thought we were parted, and I couldn't stand not being able to see and touch you."

"Yes, Mike. I feel the same way. I had to tell you that I love you at least one more time," Laura said.

Mike looked like he was about to sit up and then relaxed and a peaceful look came onto his face. "Thank you, Mary, for letting me share your life. I'll love you...."

EPILOGUE

Jill's phone rang, and she reluctantly picked it up. After Mike passed away, she had a hard time gearing herself back up to be productive. She missed visiting the Condors at the nursing home, and she missed the conversations with Lilith. She got a nice note from Laura thanking her for allowing her to share those last moments with Mike, but the note made Jill's mood even lower.

"Hi, this is Jill."

"Hi, Jill. Vivian here. We found a note attached to the inside of Mike Condor's computer addressed to you, and his granddaughter said to tell you about it."

"That's news to me. What is the note in regards to?"

"Seems that Mr. Condor wanted you to have his computer. We think that he wrote something on it for you. Want to stop by and pick it up sometime?"

"Yes, I sure will. Can you leave it at the desk, and I'll stop by tonight. Thanks so much for the call."

That was a pick-me-up call for sure, Jill thought. She wondered what Mike could have written her that he didn't say during all those hours she spent with him. Well, she would just have to wait until she opened this surprise.

After she got back to her apartment, she made a cup of tea and opened the little laptop. After a few minutes the screen came on, and the note from Mike came on the screen.

Ode to Mary

It would be my joy to live my life again
If Mary were there to hold my hand
And guide me here and there and sustain
My love of her till forever as the sands
Of time run past as endless waves of rain
Bid her farewell? I cannot bear to command
My lovetorn heart to do so I must abstain
And hope to meet my love once more in the grand
Fields of heaven

THE END

A WORD TO MY READERS

The worst and the best writers seek one thing above all others. A reader who not only reads their book, a work of astounding personal effort, but who shares his/her experiences with the world. We want to know what you think about our work. Truly we do. Of course, we want you to like it, and us, and will be so grateful if you take the time to give us even the smallest amount of praise. I really entreat you to do so.

If you have constructive criticism you want us to hear, please, out with it! Writing is such an isolating experience. I begin to live in my books and come to nearly feel that my characters are real. When someone criticizes one of them, I feel their pain. And some of my own.

But if you enjoyed this novel, I beg you on scuffed knee to give a positive review for me. I assure you that is the best way to see more of my work in the future.

Thanks again for reading this far.

Alexander Francis

OTHER NOVELS BY ALEXANDER FRANCIS

Are We A Band Yet?
Mick Grundy...Spy Hunt
Mick Grundy...The Russian Connection
Mick Grundy...Elapid
Beware the Exit
The Green Scarf
Revenge of Jesus
An Anthology of Childhood
Schemers and Dreamers

Please visit afnovels.com